"You and the children are having a good time."

His eyes twinkled. He was more lighthearted than Coralee had seen him since he moved back to Spring Hill. Was it the influence of the twins? Or was he as pleased to be back on good footing in their friendship as she was?

"As you can see, we're having an elegant high tea," she declared, sipping pretend liquid. To Coralee's surprise, Jake lowered himself right down next to Louisa on the tablecloth they had spread over the floorboards.

"Could you spare a cup of tea for a guest?" He spoke to Louisa in complete earnestness, watching while the little girl pretended to pour from a teakettle into a cup.

"Yes. For you." Her little face was serious, the tip of her tiny tongue peeking out as she focused on handing him the cup with great care.

He brought it to his lips and slurped loudly. "Ah, that was very good. Thank you, Miss Louisa."

Both children giggled at his antics. Coralee couldn't suppress the ache that hit her.

After earning a degree in business and jumping from job to job, **Mollie Campbell** was more than a little surprised—and pleased—to find that writing was the perfect fit. A lifelong Midwestern girl, she currently lives in Indiana with her husband, two young kids and a rather energetic beagle. When she's not writing or reading, she loves watching superhero shows with her husband and collecting antiques.

Books by Mollie Campbell

Love Inspired Historical

Taking on Twins

MOLLIE CAMPBELL

Taking on Twins

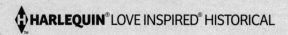
HARLEQUIN® LOVE INSPIRED® HISTORICAL

Recycling programs for this product may not exist in your area.

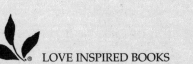

LOVE INSPIRED BOOKS

ISBN-13: 978-0-373-42529-7

Taking on Twins

www.Harlequin.com

Printed in U.S.A.

I consider that our present sufferings are not worth comparing with the glory that will be revealed in us.
—*Romans* 8:18

To Brian, who will forever be my favorite
and the perfect hero for my love story.

Chapter One

May 1859
Spring Hill, Nebraska Territory

"Not again!"

Murky green liquid fizzled in a glass beaker as Coralee Evans pushed a strand of hair out of her face and slumped back in a wooden chair. She let out a deep breath, ruffling the bits of herbs and papers that littered the table in front of her. Unfortunately, Papa's extensive notes weren't getting her anywhere today. How would she ever discover the right formula when every herb burned or turned into a bubbling mess?

"How is this one going?" Her youngest sister, Cat, peeked into the room from her post at the apothecary shop's counter. Cat's face grew skeptical when she caught sight of the mess on the worktable. "I suppose it's no better than yesterday's experiment."

Coralee pushed away from the table with more

force than necessary. "I'm going out to clear my head for a bit. You'll be all right here alone?"

"Sure. And I'll try to get rid of that mess while you're out." Cat eyed the chaotic table, her mouth turned up in a wry smirk.

Coralee arranged a silk-lined bonnet over her hair and stepped out onto the uneven boardwalk. She ambled past the row of neat wooden storefronts, trying to calm the worries that swirled relentlessly. Pausing, she examined the wares displayed in the window of another new shop, the third one that had opened that week. A sudden light touch on her elbow and a familiar masculine voice startled her out of her reverie.

"Imagine running into you on my first day home, Coralee Evans."

She turned and instantly lost herself in deep brown eyes that brought back a lifetime of memories. Her heartbeat faltered. "Jake! What a surprise to find you back in town. I haven't seen you since…" Her voice broke as she swallowed around the lump in her throat. "Since Alan's funeral."

The slight edge of coolness in his eyes softened. "Coralee, I'm so—" he began, but she broke in before he could finish, not ready to talk about Alan with him yet.

"I needed a break from some work at the shop. How about stopping over at Aunt Lily's for a bite to eat?"

Jake hesitated, eyes drifting over her. Coralee flushed under his scrutiny. What did he see after all the years apart? Finally he nodded and offered his arm. They crossed the dusty street, weaving between passing wagons and deep ruts. She pointed out some of the changes to the town since the last time Jake had been back. New buildings popped up every day in Spring Hill as immigrants poured into the Nebraska Territory. Coralee searched for small talk that would steer them far from digging up the past.

"How long have you been in town, Jake?"

"I got in two days ago. I spent yesterday settling in at the boardinghouse and visiting my folks."

"You'll be staying for a while, then?" She couldn't hide the surprise in her tone. A town the size of Spring Hill could only support one doctor.

Before he could answer, they approached the café, pausing to exchange brief greetings with a couple they passed on the sidewalk. The young man held tight to his companion's hand where it rested on his arm and the lovely lady's face flushed under his attention. Young love. A sharp pang of loss cut through Coralee's heart.

As they continued she caught a glimpse of her and Jake reflected in the pane-glass window and longing washed over her. It had been a long time since she'd walked arm in arm with a gentleman. She deliberately focused her eyes high above them, examining the familiar block letters painted on the building, proclaiming Lily's Café. She was able to breathe easier when Jake pulled his arm away so he could open the solid wood door and hold it for her to enter.

Once inside, they found the only empty table in the busy eatery. Jake scooted out a chair for Coralee and waited as she seated herself. "Everything looks just like the last time I was here, years ago."

She glanced around the narrow room, trying to see it through Jake's eyes. The tables scattered throughout were all set with white cloths and simple dishes, clearly used but clean. There was little in the way of decoration, but the dining area was warm and comfortable. What did the space look like to him now, after frequenting the finest dining establishments in St. Louis?

An awkward silence fell over them as they waited. Coralee drummed her fingers on the table as her gaze was drawn to Jake's strong face. The tanned features, straight nose and generous mouth she had known since childhood were framed by a few new creases. As he sat there across from her, something in the way he held himself was more attractive than she remembered.

But thinking about Jake's good looks would only lead to problems. Coralee snapped out of her thoughts and pulled her eyes away before Jake found her staring. She glanced around the room in an effort to look unaffected, searching for an innocuous topic to break the silence. "Oh, Jake, there's Aunt Lily, visiting with her customers. She'll be so glad to see you."

She caught Aunt Lily's eye just as the older woman noticed her companion and rushed over with a cry. "Jake Hadley, as I live and breathe! Young man, you give me a hug." She enveloped Jake in an embrace as he stood, then stepped back to look him over. "You look good, boy. Your mama said you've been working in a fancy hospital in St. Louis?"

"Yes, I spent the last three years there, after graduating from the university. I learned a lot. I doubt I'll face many of the same kinds of cases practicing out here, but it was a good place to learn the latest techniques."

Coralee caught a whiff of fresh air and soap clinging to Jake as he greeted Aunt Lily. For a moment she was so distracted by his presence that she nearly missed his words.

"Wait. You'll be practicing in town? On your own?"

Pride radiated from him as a smile broke out on his face. "I've secured an arrangement to train with Samuel Jay until he retires. Then I'll inherit the practice. It's a good opportunity. He's one of the best doctors in the Nebraska Territory and I'm pleased that he asked me to work alongside him."

A chill sliced through Coralee, erasing every trace of the warm attraction she had been feeling. "You're working with Dr. Jay?"

Jake glanced at her, obviously noticing the change in her demeanor. "He visits St. Louis several times a year to see his sister and he always stops at the hospital. I spent some time with him there. When he learned that I hoped to come home after my training, he offered me the position."

"That's just fine, young man." Aunt Lily spoke with a smile but Coralee thought it might be a bit forced. The older woman was certain to be concerned about Coralee's response to Jake's announcement. She had good reason to worry. Coralee and Dr. Jay had gone head-to-head more than once in the year since Papa had died and left her his shop. But that man had gone too far this time. He had only been in town for ten years or so, but it was a small community. He had to know how close she and Jake had been. Had he sought out Jake on purpose to hurt her?

"I'm excited to have a chance to practice medicine here. St. Louis was an interesting change of scenery, but Spring Hill has always been home. And, of course, I need to be close to my folks to help Pa out around the farm when I can. They're not getting any younger. I never thought the details would line up so I could run a practice here so soon."

"Jake, my boy, I'm so pleased for you. You aren't staying with your ma and pa?"

"Samuel felt it would be better for me to live in town to start, to be closer to the clinic until I build up a professional relationship with people in the area. After some time, I'll move out there to help my parents more."

Jake continued talking with Lily but Coralee didn't hear a word. Anger was building up and she just wanted to get away before she embarrassed herself. She cut into their conversation. "If you'll excuse me, I need to get back to the shop. It was nice to see you, Jake." She nodded in his direction but couldn't meet his eyes. "I'll see you tonight at home, Aunt Lily." She dropped a light kiss on the older woman's wrinkled cheek and left before they could stop her. She heard Aunt Lily call her name, but kept going.

If she turned around, her temper might well get the best of her.

She was so aggravated that the walk back to Holbrook's was a blur. "Coralee?" Cat looked up in surprise from a box of jars she was sorting as her sister stomped into the store and huffed behind the counter. "What on earth happened?"

"That man!" Coralee tossed her bonnet on the counter, breathless with frustration. "I don't know what Samuel Jay thinks he's doing, but I will not stand for it."

Cat gently rested her arm around Coralee's shoulders and walked with her into the small back room. "Sit down and tell me what happened."

"Jake Hadley is back in town. And he's training to take over Dr. Jay's practice." Coralee sank into her chair, trying to hold back tears. "Alan's dearest friend, recruited by the man who wants to close our shop. Dr. Jay must know our history and have some motive for hiring Jake, of all people. The man has always acted like he would go to the grave running that practice." Coralee ran a shaky hand over her face, trying to calm herself.

Cat listened to Coralee pour out her frustrations with the old doctor, but she was never one to jump to conclusions. "Jake is from Spring Hill and I'm sure he's a great doctor. He would be the most logical choice to take over the practice. Yes, you've had trouble with Dr. Jay, but that doesn't mean Jake is part of it."

Coralee snorted. "The old man didn't even wait until we properly mourned Papa. He started in right away, telling his patients that I'm untrained and incapable. He refuses to come to us for even the most basic supplies." She rose and started pacing the room, unable to sit still. "Just last week Mrs. Bernard told me he hired her oldest grandson to ride over to the steamboat dock to pick up loads of supplies for him. He'll do anything he has to in order to hurt our business, including using Jake."

"Be that as it may, we know Jake. He would never hurt anyone out of spite, especially not you."

But Cat didn't know Jake as well as her older sister. Coralee had experienced the kind of pain Jake could cause and she would not put herself in that position again. Her focus had to be on how she could keep Papa's shop open, supporting what was left of her family and giving the people of Spring Hill an alternative to Dr. Jay's exorbitant fees.

"I know how important this shop is to you, how running it helped you cope with losing Papa and Alan. We'll find a way to keep it open."

Coralee's heart softened at Cat's earnest tone. No matter what, her sisters were behind her as she fought for their future. Her path was clear: she would never have the family she had dreamed of as a girl, but God had given her the shop. She would do everything in her power to make it the success Papa would have wanted. She needed it and the town needed it.

After Coralee rushed from the café, Jake stood for a moment in shock. "What just happened?" he muttered.

"Well, dear," Lily chimed in, direct as usual, "you're working for the man who wants to ruin her livelihood. What do you expect?"

Jake examined Lily through narrowed eyes, taking in her familiar honest face and work-worn hands. "Lily, I'm not sure what that means."

"Means Dr. Jay has it out for Coralee's business, that's what, honey."

Jake's mind retraced the conversation with Coralee. "She did seem upset when I mentioned Dr. Jay. But he's an excellent doctor and a good man. Kind, caring, intelligent. Why would he try to harm Holbrook's?"

"Maybe you should ask him about all that, Jake." Lily patted his hand. "Now, do you need anything for lunch?"

"No, Lily. Thanks." Jake's mind was already turning as he waved goodbye. He walked back to the office, hands stuffed deep into the pockets of his cotton trousers. People flowed around him but he didn't even notice as he mulled over the turn of events. Samuel Jay couldn't be as bad as Coralee seemed to think. The older man had already taught him so much and Jake was looking forward to several more years of training under him.

He took a deep breath and straightened his slumped shoulders. Coralee's problems with Samuel didn't need to have anything to do with him. Although the incident had reminded him why coming back to Spring Hill was a risk. Now that he was in town to stay, he would see her far too often. But that was a chance he had to take. His parents needed him.

Her beauty had taken him by surprise, though. The hard years since he had seen her last had given her a strong, confident air that was appealing. In many ways, she was still the lovely girl he'd grown up with. She only stood as high as his shoulder with the same wavy dark hair, pale blue eyes and delicate nose. But he could read the shadow of loss lingering in her face as clear as day.

Jake approached the small clapboard building that housed Samuel's office and living quarters. Nestled near a bend in the creek, it was a peaceful spot in the midst of the busy town. Jake appreciated working in this picturesque little corner after seven years of dirt and noise in the city.

When he walked through the front door, he heard Samuel conversing with a patient in the exam room. Jake went to his desk at the back of the empty waiting area, settling in with a pile of patient files he needed to read through. But instead of the stack of paper, Jake's mind would only focus on the image of lovely blue eyes. Before they'd turned cold with anger, that is.

Jake shook his head and grabbed the first file from the stack. He couldn't get distracted by a pretty face and he couldn't let a misunderstanding about motives endanger his position in the practice. He had to get to the bottom of Lily's comments about his mentor.

Ten minutes later the exam room door opened

and a middle-aged woman with a boy of about seven or eight exited with Samuel Jay. The doctor walked them to the door, giving the mother instructions on caring for the boy's finger. Jake guessed it must be broken, judging from the splint. He took a moment to gather his thoughts as they left, then stood and stepped toward the doctor as he closed the door.

"Jake, I trust you had a nice lunch." The older man turned and placed the papers in his hand on top of the stack on Jake's desk.

"Uh, I…" Jake couldn't quite find the words to confront his employer until Coralee's angry expression flashed in his mind. This was awkward, but assuming she was right without seeking Samuel's opinion would be worse. "That is, yes, lunch was fine. But I wanted to ask you about Holbrook's Apothecary. You haven't mentioned how you work with the shop, yet."

Samuel stiffened and his tone turned cold. "Hadley, I want you to understand this. William Holbrook was capable, although not a person I cared for. But that daughter of his does not belong in the field of medicine. I refuse to allow my patients to be misled by her delusions of knowledge." The flash of anger faded as a stern look crossed the older man's face. "I hope you'll come to recognize that as the truth and that this won't be an issue in your work. Now, please continue familiarizing yourself with my patients." Samuel turned on his heel and withdrew to his office without another word.

Jake stood stock-still for a moment, not sure what

to think. He had to admit, although he knew Coralee to be skilled, she didn't have medical training beyond what her father had taught her. Samuel was a strong proponent of proper education and certification for those who held patients' lives in their hands, and Jake had to agree. Perhaps the older man wasn't as aware of Coralee's considerable experience as Jake. The hours he had spent in the shop with her and Mr. Holbrook had proved to him that she knew what she was doing.

But as much as he wanted to believe she was still the accomplished girl he had grown up with, Jake didn't know who she was anymore. Samuel had a reasonable concern and he was now Jake's mentor. Jake would not take the word of a woman he wasn't sure he could trust over that of a good and reputable man.

That Sunday, Jake joined his parents, Ezra and Beth, at Spring Hill's small church. As the service started, he glanced curiously around the building. It had been finished right after he'd left for medical school and housed both church services and the school. Ma would have loved teaching the local children in a building like this when Jake was young rather than at their kitchen table. Would his relationship with Coralee be different if they had attended a more formal school? If so much of their time hadn't been spent together at Holbrook's? He couldn't imagine what he would be doing now if he hadn't spent so many hours learning basic remedies and a love of medicine from Coralee's father.

Jake tried to focus and listen to the sermon but his mind wandered. Coralee sat with her aunt and sisters across the aisle and several rows ahead of his family. Every time he caught a glimpse of her, his attention derailed.

He knew when he'd returned to town that there would be tension between them. But he hadn't prepared himself for the onslaught of emotions every time he saw her. His heart ached with ugly emotions he thought had healed. Pain from the lingering sting of her rejection when he'd tried to lay his heart out for her. Jealousy that always flared when he remembered how she'd turned to his best friend while he'd been away at school. He was sure now that no length of time could erase that hurt from his heart.

His trip down memory lane was cut short when the congregation stood to sing a final hymn. As the ending notes faded away, the congregants all turned to greet their neighbors with happy conversation. Noticing that everyone around him was occupied, Jake slipped out the side door. He waited by his parents' wagon while they socialized, trying to look like he wasn't hiding. He couldn't bring himself to face questions from all the folks who would want to welcome him back to town when he had so many unwanted feelings distracting him.

Finally the couple finished greeting the other churchgoers and joined him. It was a fine spring day, so his mother had packed a picnic for them to share before his parents headed back out to their farm.

Jake gathered up the picnic basket and blanket before his father could try to reach for them and led the way to a quiet spot by the creek. Soon they had the blanket spread on the grass and Jake helped Pa lower himself onto it. Ma laid out the food and they all filled their plates and said a prayer.

"Son, how've you liked your first few days working with the doc?" Pa shoveled his wife's delicious cooking in his mouth as he waited for Jake's response.

"Just fine, Pa. Samuel is an excellent doctor, just as I thought in St. Louis." Jake hesitated, not sure if he should bring up Coralee and her accusations against the older doctor. But he needed some perspective on the conflict. "I ran into Coralee the other day." He tried to sound nonchalant, but judging from the look on his mother's face, he wasn't succeeding.

"Oh, Jake," Ma breathed, her voice hopeful but laced with traces of worry. "I've been praying that you two could start to get along again, now that you're home for good. How did it go?"

He shrugged off her concern. "She's convinced Samuel is doing anything he can to force her to close Holbrook's. I spoke to him and he doesn't approve of her running the shop, but I can't believe he would do anything more than state his opinion."

Ma considered his words for a moment as she chewed a bite of her lunch. "I haven't spent much time with Coralee since your pa's accident." She gestured to her husband's arm and Jake flushed with guilt. While Pa was recovering from the farm accident that cost him the use of his left hand, Jake had been away in school, unable to help at all. But now he finally had a chance to secure his practice in Spring Hill so he could be near his parents to help out. He had to make this work.

Ma's soft voice pulled him back to the conversation. "Coralee's always been kind and honest, Jake. I understand that you trust Dr. Jay and believe in him, but Coralee is a good woman, too."

"Ma, how good could the woman be when we all know I can't trust her any farther than I can throw her?"

A compassionate smile graced her face. "Jake, I know she hurt you, but there are reasons behind the things people do. You should give her a chance. Maybe time has changed both of you for the better."

Jake didn't quite know what to say in response. His relationship with Coralee had ended seven years ago. He should be past the pain by now. But he still couldn't bring himself to even try to understand Coralee's motives. There couldn't be any good reason for the way she had hurt him. Just when he had been ready to confess his love for her, she had started a fight about him going away to medical school. Without giving him a chance to explain his plan for them, she had stormed out. Less than a year later his best friend, Alan, had broken the news that he and Coralee were going to be married. He understood how

Alan had fallen for her, but he would never understand why she had betrayed him that way.

"Talk to Coralee, Jake," Pa said. "You've already talked to the doc. Now find out her side of this and get it settled. And you know I think you ought to settle the past, too. But I suppose you won't listen to your old pa any more now than you did when it happened." He grabbed another cookie and leaned back on the quilt, done saying his piece.

"Fine, Pa. I'll go see her about Samuel. But you're right. I'm not going to dig up the past. It's done and buried." Jake reached for more lemonade, determined to ignore the knowing look his parents exchanged.

He put off the visit for several days. But, finally, he knew he had to confront Coralee. He left his room at the boardinghouse early to stop by Holbrook's before starting his day at the clinic. As much as he wanted to avoid any contact with Coralee, in a small town like Spring Hill there was no way to steer clear of her forever. He wasn't ready to trust her, but he supposed hearing her side of the conflict with Samuel wouldn't cause any harm.

All too soon, he approached Holbrook's Apothecary. The old pane-glass door was now embellished with the shop's name in gilded letters. As he pushed the door open, the familiar scent of herbs and soap filled his nose. Nostalgia washed over him. He missed the hours spent discussing remedies and diseases with William Holbrook. He had always admired the older man's passion for healing.

Inside, the shelves that lined one long wall contained neat rows of the same bottles, tins and jars that he remembered. But the counter in front of the shelves now held a large copper scale and several small displays instead of Mr. Holbrook's piles of paperwork. To his surprise, the small tables on the other side all sat empty. He hardly remembered a time when there hadn't been at least one customer waiting for an order.

"Jake!"

He turned just as a dainty figure swathed in flowered muslin launched into his arms. Laughing at Cat's exuberance, he swung her around before setting her back on her feet. It was good to see that her unconventional, passionate spirit hadn't changed with the years.

"Coralee said you were back, Jake, but I wasn't sure you'd have time to stop in. All that responsibility with Dr. Jay, you know," Cat quipped with a wink. She glanced at the door behind the counter. "If you're here to see Coralee, she's working with some ingredients in the back. Peppermint, this time. It smells wonderful, unless it burns." Cat's pert nose wrinkled at the memory of the acrid smell and Jake grinned.

"It's all just part of the job, Catrina, my girl."

Cat shot him a good-natured smile and sudden seriousness settled over Jake. Life had been much simpler when they were growing up. Before Coralee had broken his heart, before he'd left Spring Hill, before Alan had died.

He shook off the gloomy thoughts of the past and

looked around. The middle Holbrook sister wasn't in the store as he expected her to be. "How's Cecilia?"

"Oh, she's fine," Cat answered, waving one hand in her usual flippant way. "You know she was covering the school when Alan was sick and couldn't teach?" Jake nodded. "The school board asked her to take over the position after he…" Her voice trailed off as she glanced at the workroom door again. Her brow furrowed and she caught her bottom lip between her teeth, looking as if she was hesitant to even mention Alan's death. But she shook it off, smoothing her already perfect hair. "Anyway, Cecilia seems to love it. I think being in charge of an entire roomful of children sounds dreadful." She shuddered dramatically, making Jake chuckle.

"I'm glad she's doing well, even if her career makes you ill," he teased.

Cat's light laugh dispelled the somber mood. She pointed toward the office door. "You'd better go see her, Jake. She was hopping mad the other day after she talked to you."

"What's going on with Dr. Jay, Cat?" He had to know what his lifelong friends saw in his mentor.

Her hands clenched at the mention of the doctor's name. "Oh, the man is a bother. He doesn't like Coralee running Papa's shop and he tells his patients not to come here. She's working so hard to keep things going, but business is too slow these days." She gestured to the empty tables. "I think Dr. Jay will come up with a way to get at her no matter what she does."

Jake studied the closed workroom door thoughtfully. He trusted Cat, but he also trusted Samuel. "Cat, it's been good to see you again. I'm going in. Come and check on me if you hear her throwing things." He winked and squeezed her hand as he headed behind the counter. He paused with his knuckles raised to knock, took a deep breath and prepared to face Coralee.

Inside the workroom Coralee stood at one end of the large wooden table. Wiping her hands on the canvas apron covering her navy blue dress, she pushed back the strands of hair that always seemed to come loose. Jars of herbs, half-full beakers, a small metal scale and Papa's marble mortar and pestle sat before her, evidence of an early morning full of work. She hoped she was close to figuring out which elements would create the right amount of pain relief with the fewest side effects. But this process wasn't as easy as extracting the usual herbs like dogwood, ginger root, lavender or spearmint. Mixing elements to form a new compound had been Papa's idea. After too many failures, Coralee was beginning to think a single herb had to be the answer.

A firm knock sounded on the door several times before she noticed. She shuffled her notes into a haphazard pile and covered the remnants of burned peppermint and yarrow with a cloth. When it came to making Papa's shop a success again, she couldn't be too careful. "Come in," she called, trying to smooth her hair again.

When the door opened to reveal Jake, her breath

caught for a moment. His chocolate-brown eyes made all thoughts of chemistry and herbs disappear. She couldn't help admiring the width of his shoulders, broad chest and strong arms as he stood outlined in the doorway. Coralee flushed, realizing the direction of her thoughts. She had given up the right to notice Jake's looks a long time ago.

"Good morning." His deep voice was a bit cool. Not surprising, after her shameful behavior at the café the week before. In spite of her embarrassment, her traitorous heart started to beat faster as he stepped into the room. Closer to her.

Coralee forced herself to sound aloof to cover her unwanted reaction. "Good morning. I hope you haven't come to spy on my work for Dr. Jay. I'm certain he would love to get his hands on anything he could use to undermine my business more."

Jake stiffened at Coralee's sharp words. "I *came* to speak to you about the problem you seem to have with Samuel." His eyes flashed and Coralee realized baiting him might not have been the best response. "I don't want working in the same town to be awkward, but you aren't making it easy to get along. Samuel believes that medical professionals should be educated and governed. He doesn't know anything about your experience, just that you aren't certified." Jake gave her a hard look to go along with the forceful words. "He might be a bit old-fashioned concerning his feelings about women in the field, but that's all it is, Coralee. It's not personal."

"I shouldn't be surprised that you would take his

side. Do you have a problem with my level of experience, as well?" She turned sharply on her heel and marched to a glass-fronted cabinet full of clean jars and beakers. Her reactions weren't smoothing things over at all, but she couldn't seem to get her emotions in check. Alan, Jake, the failed experiments, Dr. Jay, declining business at the shop… It all swirled in her mind, making her tense and snappish.

With her back still turned, she heard Jake retreat to the doorway. "I'm sorry you think that of me." His voice sounded tight and maybe a little wounded. "I'd hoped we could work together, in spite of our past. But I can see that you haven't become any more reasonable than you were the night I told you about St. Louis."

To her dismay, tears filled her eyes. She stood facing the cabinet, pretending to search for something. If she didn't reply for long enough, maybe he would just leave.

It must have worked. A moment later she heard the door slam behind him.

For the next several days Coralee threw herself into her experiments. She spent hours bent over her table pressing tablets and brewing teas. Many of the tinctures she had mixed weeks before were ready for a few of her patients to test. In spite of some mild success, nothing was effective enough to market to the public. As much as she wanted to make a brilliant discovery, she was about to hit a dead end. With each compound she marked off Papa's list, Coralee grew more and more worried.

In the evenings she tried to relax in the living quarters behind Lily's Café with Cat, Cecilia and Aunt Lily. Their conversation flowed around her, but her mind whirled with thoughts of herbs and Jake. Why did she behave so dreadfully every time she saw him?

"Coralee?" Cecilia's sweet, concerned voice broke her out of her dark thoughts. "What's going on? You're so quiet and distracted these days."

She looked around the table at what remained of her family. The shop's success or failure affected them, too, so she might as well include them in the problems. "As Cat knows, our customer base is dwindling. My experiments on Papa's research for the new medicine aren't going well. I don't know what to do to save the shop."

"We still have customers coming in, Coralee. Enough to keep the shop running. We can pay the bills and we have some money in the bank." Cat sounded unaffected, as always. But her confidence didn't weaken the constant pressure in Coralee's chest.

Cecilia reached over to rub Coralee's shoulder as she chimed in with her usual optimism. "Papa would understand if things don't work out. He loved the shop, but he wanted us to be happy more than anything."

"Maybe you're right. But Papa trusted me to run the shop the way he would. I know I can do this. I have to do this."

Aunt Lily clucked her tongue. "Now, girl, you

worry too much about that old shop of your pa's. Your life can be much more than just running that place, my dear." Coralee started to argue, but Lily shushed her and went on. "I think I see what the problem is here. It seems you don't think you're meant for anything more than that shop. But I'm here to tell you that's altogether wrong, child. God has great things for you, happy things. Maybe this is just one small part of your story, not the whole thing."

Cat and Cecilia nodded along with Lily's words, but Coralee couldn't accept that. God had placed her in the position of running Papa's shop, carrying on his legacy. She had accepted that His will for her didn't include her own family, so the shop had to be her sole purpose now. It had to be enough.

Coralee went to bed early, just to have some time away from her family's prying eyes. But no matter how much she tossed and turned, she couldn't sleep. Jake's presence in town had stirred up feelings she had hoped were long buried, disappointments she had tried so hard to force away in the years since Alan's death.

Frustrated by the emotions rising in her, Coralee left her room. She tiptoed through the house, hoping she wouldn't wake anyone. It only took a few minutes over the stove before she settled in a chair at the kitchen table with a china cup full of steaming tea. She had just started trying to formulate some kind of words of prayer when a voice startled her.

"Mind if I join you?" Aunt Lily stood in the doorway, a thin blanket wrapped around her shoulders.

Without waiting for an answer, the older woman crossed the room to the teakettle, fixed herself a cup and settled at the opposite end of the table.

Coralee examined her dear aunt, the woman who had been such a mainstay in her life. Sitting there in her nightdress with a loose braid pulled over her shoulder, Lily Holbrook looked older than Coralee had noticed before. Maybe even a little frail. All the more reason she had to get the shop back on track. Cat depended on it for her livelihood and soon enough Aunt Lily would, too. She was a strong woman, but she couldn't run the café forever.

"Well, my dear, something must be bothering you. After the week you've had, you ought to be sleeping like a baby."

Coralee considered brushing her aunt's concern aside. She wanted to. But she was humble enough to admit when she needed wisdom. "It's been years since I've spent so much time around Jake. I'm…having a hard time understanding my own feelings about him right now." The words came out more faltering than she'd intended, but they were out, all the same.

Understanding filled Aunt Lily's face. "You have so much history with him, dear girl. Not all good, though, I'd guess. I never did understand why he took off and you started spending your time with Alan."

Coralee twisted a lock of long hair between her fingers. "The last night we talked before he left… Aunt Lily, he never even told me he was applying to medical school. Never bothered to ask my opinion. I thought…" Her voice broke, raw emotion rising to the surface. "I thought he was going to tell me he loved me that night. I was so sure he felt the same way I did."

"But, instead, he told you he was leaving."

Coralee stared into her tea, focusing on the tiny bits of herbs settling in the bottom so she wouldn't lose her composure. "He was so excited. Of course, I knew he'd planned to become a doctor. But he had already applied and been accepted in St. Louis, without ever considering what would happen to me."

Lily sipped her tea thoughtfully. "You were both young and impulsive, dearest. Are you sure he meant to leave you out of it? Could it be that he didn't realize how his actions would seem to you?"

"If he was in love with me—planned to spend his life with me—how could he make such an important decision and not *want* to include me? His medical training took him away for seven years, Aunt Lily. If he had professed his love, that choice would have affected my life, too. It wasn't a priority for him to include me."

The older woman shrugged, unconvinced. "I've known Jake Hadley just as long as you have. He's always been an honest, kind man. I can't imagine that he meant to hurt you."

"Well, he did hurt me." Coralee was getting a bit tired of the way Aunt Lily kept defending Jake. Shouldn't she be taking her niece's side? "If he loved me, why did he just leave? Yes, we had a misunderstanding. But after that night, he didn't try to clear things up with me, didn't even say goodbye. He just left." Tears were threatening to overflow. Coralee tried to blink them away but they spilled down her cheeks anyway. "He abandoned me. Just like Papa. Just like Alan. They all left." She rested her head on her arms as a sob escaped.

She felt Lily's arms come around her and turned into the older woman's shoulder. Since Mama had died when Coralee was four, Aunt Lily had been a mother figure in all the girls' lives. Now her comforting embrace broke open the floodgates. Coralee let all her frustration with Jake and the situation at the shop flow out with her sobs.

Eventually the tears slowed and Aunt Lily pulled away to look into her eyes. "Dear girl, I'm so sorry. You've had your share of loss already at such a young age. Now, it may be hard to swallow, but losing people is part of life for all of us. Don't sell Jake short because of past mistakes or the chance of losing him in the future. All you have is today. Try to be open to what the good Lord is telling you."

Aunt Lily patted Coralee's back gently as she headed for the door. "I'm going to try to get some sleep. I'll offer up a few extra prayers for you and Jake."

The late-night talk didn't calm any of the worries in Coralee's mind. The next day she was more determined than ever to make the shop profitable again. A few hours into the work, she was stopping every few minutes to stretch her aching back and rest her strained eyes. She wanted to push through Papa's list as fast as she could, but she kept mixing up the measurements and grabbing the wrong herbs. Her conclusions would never be accurate with mistakes in the process. A break was in order.

She stepped out of the workroom and joined Cat at the counter. Coralee had always loved mixing remedies at the shop's counter. The recipes were so ingrained in her mind that she could relax while her hands did the repetitive work. No customers were waiting, so the sisters set to work putting together some of the basic restoratives that were always in demand.

Sometime later, the bell above the shop door jingled as an elderly woman in stained calico and a worn sunbonnet shuffled in. Coralee couldn't contain her grin. "Good afternoon, Mrs. Bernard. I'm glad to see you're able to make it to town again."

The old woman's thin lips stretched in a smile, revealing several missing teeth. "This fine weather is giving me back my strength. I told that son of mine that he was bringing me along to town and that's final. Good boy still listens to his old ma, most of the time."

Coralee felt her tension melting away as she spoke with one of her favorite customers. She enjoyed visiting with the people who frequented the shop, building trust with each of them. "He must be a smart man. All due to good parenting, I'm sure."

Mrs. Bernard's leathery skin wrinkled even more as she cackled in response.

Her joyful spirit was infectious, lifting the weight

that had been on Coralee's shoulders the last few weeks. "Now, what can I help you with today?"

"It's that cough again. Keeps me up at night, it does." Coralee could see the woman searching for words. She wouldn't meet Coralee's eyes. Was something else wrong this time?

"If there's something you need, I can help you. You just have to tell me."

Mrs. Bernard sighed. "My boys didn't find much in the mine last year. Made this a hard winter. I've held off awhile, but the cough's getting worse. Maybe you have something that costs less than the Ayer's?"

"Ah." Understanding dawned. She couldn't afford the Ayer's Cherry Pectoral that she always came to get when the cough started bothering her. "Well, I could pick out something else for you." Coralee leaned over the counter and lowered her voice. "Or, you could do me a favor and try a new mixture I've been working on. Of course, not knowing how well it will work, I couldn't charge you for it."

A flash of relief washed over the old woman. Then she straightened and pursed her lips. "Yes, I do believe that would be a fine arrangement. Thank you, Mrs. Evans." Her shaky voice was laden with genuine gratitude. This was the reason the shop had to stay open. Papa had been right: the people of Spring Hill needed a place they trusted for their medicine, a place that cared about them.

Coralee turned toward the shelf that held the Ayer's Pectoral. Her step faltered when she caught sight of Jake watching from a table, almost sending her smashing into the bottles. How long had he been there?

She grabbed several bottles, one full and one empty. With her back turned to the counter, she poured the curative, sealed the bottle and wrapped it in brown paper.

"All ready, Mrs. Bernard." She walked the old woman to the door and handed her the package, thanking her for stopping by. Then she turned to Jake. He looked tired, but there was a hint of approval in his eyes.

"I saw that." He leaned back in the chair and crossed his arms as that warm hint grew into full-fledged admiration.

She shrugged and moved behind the counter with her head high. "You saw me fill an order for Mrs. Bernard? It's for the cough that keeps bothering her. She comes in every few weeks."

He laughed, the enthusiastic sound contrasting with the weariness in his features. "You know what I mean. I saw you pour the Ayer's Pectoral into the bottle you told her was a test mixture. A *free* test mixture." She flushed under his direct gaze. "That was commendable, Coralee. It was something your father would have done."

She brushed at the tears that threatened to fall when he likened her to Papa. "Mrs. Bernard is a lovely woman. I hate to see her suffering and not do something about it. Now, what brings you in today?"

In an instant his mirth disappeared and weariness flooded his features. "I came to ask for your help.

I've been out south of town for the last few days, caring for several families. It's cholera."

A knot formed in Coralee's stomach. There hadn't been a cholera outbreak in the area for years. Would this one turn deadly, as so many others had? Though she'd never seen it herself, Papa had told her about his experiences with the sickness. She knew how it could ravage a town in no time, starting with stomach pain and nausea, progressing to fever, pale skin and lethargy. If the patient didn't show signs of recovery in the earliest stage, they most likely wouldn't pull through.

Jake ran a hand over his face before continuing. "Samuel left for St. Louis right before I received word. He'll be gone for at least six weeks, caring for his sister, so I'm handling this on my own. The youngest Smith boy found me this morning. Mr. Smith and the oldest two children are sick now. I'm out of camphor and hoped you could spare whatever you have."

"Yes, I have quite a bit. I'll get a crate." She was a bit hesitant to continue. Every time they were together, they fought. But he looked so worn out. What if things took a turn for the worse and he was out there alone? "Several families with cholera is a lot to handle on your own. I could ride out with you and help. If you want."

"No." Jake drummed his fingers on the counter, refusing to meet her gaze. "If I can just get the camphor from you, I'll be on my way."

She came around the counter to stand in front of

him. "Jake, you need help. I know what to do out there."

"I don't doubt your abilities. But I can't expose you to cholera."

She planted one hand on her hip, searching for the words that would convince him he couldn't do this alone. Coralee wanted to keep her heart as uninvolved as possible, but she couldn't leave him to handle an epidemic on his own. "But you'll expose yourself without any concern for your own health? Exhaustion will make you more susceptible, after all."

With a sigh, he raised his hands in surrender. "If you're sure you want to do this, then I guess you can come. I have to admit that I could use the help. Thank you."

Coralee flashed him a smile in the hope that he would see she was confident about helping. Then she turned her focus to the task at hand. Handing him an empty crate, she directed him to a shelf filled with jars of camphor. Then, with Cat's help, she started gathering supplies to stock her travel case.

Conflicting emotions churned inside Coralee now that she had a minute to think through what they were facing. She wanted to help. And Jake needed someone out there with him. But was she ready to take on the long, emotional hours ahead with her former love by her side?

Chapter Two

While he packed jar after jar into the crate, Jake tried not to regret agreeing to Coralee's help. His first reaction had been to stay as far away from her offer as possible. He was weary to the bone and didn't want to distract himself in such a critical time. And, despite his best efforts, Coralee was a distraction. But if he was honest, her actions with Mrs. Bernard had reminded him of why she was so good at what she did. She had a way with people that made them feel cared for and respected. And he needed the help badly.

Jake fitted a lid onto the full crate and turned to the ladies. "All packed. Are you ready, Coralee?"

"Yes, let's go." She was all business and that was fine with him. He couldn't open himself up to emotional complications with this woman. He carried her case and the crate of camphor outside to the wagon and turned to help her climb onto the hard seat. He joined her and urged the horse into motion and they headed out of town in silence.

Through his exhaustion, Jake took in the familiar landscape he had missed during the years he'd been away. St. Louis was tight with buildings and people, unlike these rolling hills covered in swaying, knee-high grass. The late-afternoon sky above was endlessly clear, a blue so bright it almost hurt his eyes. As difficult as coming back had been, this was where he wanted to spend the rest of his days.

Coralee's quiet words brought him back to the present. "How bad is this outbreak?"

He glanced over. She was staring straight ahead, more than a hint of worry written on her face. A sudden desire to fix the problem and erase that worried look took him by surprise. "I'm not sure yet. It seems confined to an area south of town. The fellow that helps out at the Wallace place came to get me first. They told me their neighbor, old Mr. Howard, was sick, as well." Jake swallowed, trying to clear away the sudden dryness that was making it hard to speak. "He passed away before I got there."

Coralee murmured, the gentle sound of sympathy making his eyes burn. He blinked hard. "I made some rounds to the neighbors after that, just to see if anyone else is ill. Mrs. Felder and the Smiths are sick. And Mr. Trask rode by the Wallace place when I was out there last night and told me the Rileys are ill, as well. I'm going out there after we see the situation at the Smiths."

Coralee's hand shot to her mouth, eyes growing

wide. "Oh, no, not the Rileys. We see them at church every Sunday without fail. Their twins…"

Jake shook his head. "When Aaron started feeling sick a few days ago, Liza got Phillip and Louisa to the Trasks. I checked on them this morning and they're fine."

Relief flooded her face. The pure beauty of her expression hit Jake like a punch to the stomach, forcing the breath right out of his lungs. For a few moments he couldn't pull his eyes away from her as she gazed at the wildflowers lining the well-worn dirt road. His hands itched to bury themselves in that mass of soft hair, to run over her smooth cheek. She must have finally felt his stare because she turned to him, a curious look on her face.

Jake twisted away and cleared his throat again, working to get a handle on his emotions and force them back into a corner of his mind. She might be beautiful, but he couldn't afford to let her close enough to hurt him again.

They traveled in silence until he turned the wagon toward a log cabin in the distance. "There's the Wallace farm. I haven't been out to check on them yet today. They…" He hesitated, not sure how much to tell her, but realized she would have to know soon enough. "They aren't going to last long, so I'm trying to make them comfortable." She nodded somberly and they both stared ahead for the rest of the drive, each lost in their own thoughts.

After he pulled the wagon up next to the cabin, Jake helped Coralee down and grabbed their cases.

He led her inside the small home, hoping their services were still needed. To his relief, Mr. and Mrs. Wallace were still breathing. But both had sunken eyes and a weak, irregular pulse.

He and Coralee worked with quiet focus. They spoke in hushed tones to encourage their patients to drink a bit of the tea Coralee prepared. They wiped the older couple's faces with damp cloths and they changed blankets. They administered calomel and rubbed the patients' stomachs with camphor to ease their discomfort. It wasn't much, but it was all they could do.

While Jake was arranging Mr. Wallace's blankets, the older man's eyes fluttered open. He took a moment to speak with his patient. "Mr. Wallace, it's Jake Hadley again. I'm here with the apothecary, Mrs. Evans. I want you to know…that is, I'm sorry, but I don't think you or your wife will recover."

To Jake's surprise, the older man's pale face broke out in a peaceful smile. "Young man, that news isn't as bad as you think," he rasped as his eyes slid shut. "My hope isn't in this life. It's in Jesus and He doesn't quit when I do." The older man fell silent and Jake stared at his sleeping patient as stillness washed over him.

Jake's spirit stirred at Mr. Wallace's confident faith. Where Jake had always struggled to live out his convictions, this man was bold even in the face of death. A longing lodged in Jake's heart. Could he learn to rest in his faith so completely that even death didn't frighten him?

It was late by the time Jake and Coralee finished caring for the Wallaces, but they headed toward the Smith farm. Driving through the falling darkness, Jake didn't realize he had been wrapped up in his thoughts for too long until Coralee broke the awkward silence. "What was it like working at such a large hospital in St. Louis?"

"It was a great experience. There was such an interesting variety of cases. At such a large institution, we saw some rare diseases that were fascinating to study. And with so many patients there was something different to study every day."

Remembering his time at the hospital, Jake felt enthusiasm welling up. It was nice to share that experience with someone who understood medicine. Even if that person was Coralee. "At the practice here, I only see a few patients at the office. I'm out making house calls most of the time for the same farm injuries or common illnesses."

Jake glanced at Coralee and saw her eyes were wide, lips slightly parted in rapt attention, encouraging him to continue. "Most of the physicians at the hospital studied the newest medical research to use in their treatment plans. That aspect fascinated me. And that's how I ended up connecting with Samuel. He always visits the hospital on his trips so he can keep up on the most recent advances."

Coralee tensed at his mention of Dr. Jay. "Jake, I understand you've spent time with the man and you trust him. But you've known me since we were children. Why can't you believe me when I tell you that Dr. Jay is doing everything in his power to close down my shop?"

Jake felt frustration growing and tried to fight against it. He needed her help. How would they be able to work together if they kept fighting every time they talked? "Are you sure you want to get into this right now? I already told you my opinion."

"Yes, I believe I know your opinion of Samuel Jay." Coralee pursed her lips, brows knitting together.

He had to get the conversation back on solid footing. He ran a hand through his hair and took a deep breath. No one else got under his skin as fast as this woman.

"Listen, Coralee, I'm sorry." He wasn't about to budge on his opinion, but he could put aside his pride to defuse the situation. He turned to look into her eyes, hoping she could see his sincerity. "I need your help right now. Maybe after we get the outbreak under control, we can sit down and talk about this."

She nodded and her eyes softened at his concession. The azure pools drew him in, flooding him with memories of the days when he had been in love with her. Carefree days when he'd thought their hearts would beat together forever. As it turned out, her heart had never beat for him in the first place.

It was nearly the middle of the night by the time they arrived at the Smiths' cabin, but light pooled on the ground under the windows from a lantern lit inside. Jake knocked on the door and Mrs. Smith came to welcome them, looking weary. They followed her into a single room, stifling, thanks to a fire crack-

ling in the large fireplace. Little Timothy Smith was
sleeping soundly on a blanket laid out in front of it.

"Thanks for coming, Doc. My oldest two, Sarah
and David, are in the loft. James is back there." She
gestured at a bed in the farthest corner, where they
could just make out the shape of her husband under
the mound of quilts.

Together, Jake and Coralee examined each patient. They found that the three sick members of the
Smith family were in the earliest stage of the illness.
Jake was confident they would recover with the right
treatment. But Mrs. Smith continued to look worried in spite of his assurance. He set her to making
a hearty broth while Coralee fixed a batch of chamomile tea. Jake encouraged each patient to drink as
much tea and broth as they could handle.

"Doc, are you sure this is good for them? My ma
always said the only way to cure the cholera is a
spoon of castor oil every hour."

Jake shook his head. "I recently trained in St.
Louis, ma'am. One of the most successful doctors
at the hospital taught that taking extra fluids could
improve the outcome of many ailments. I've seen
it work myself. I hope you'll trust me that it won't
hurt your family to try." The woman nodded and let
Jake continue, but she stood close by, looking wary.

Working together, Jake and Coralee cleaned up
and cared for each of the sick family members. Jake
managed to convince Mrs. Smith to get some sleep
while he and Coralee kept watch over her family.
Each patient needed to have tea and broth around

the clock, so he and Coralee settled into the rocking chairs near the fireplace, hoping to rest between rounds. But after several hours, they found themselves awake and reminiscing as soft light from the sunrise began to filter into the cabin.

"Remember when someone dared Cat to climb that huge tree by the creek?" Coralee's eyes sparkled as she recalled the incident. "She was so determined to get all the way to the top, she never even thought about how she'd get down." The quiet laugh that accompanied her story captivated Jake. It felt just like the hours they'd spent at Holbrook's when they were younger, laughing and teasing as they'd cleaned shelves.

"I remember the look on her face when she realized she had to come back down the way she went up." Jake grinned. "She was more determined to get down with her dignity intact than she was to climb it in the first place. And you were downright panicked when she started sliding down that lower branch to show off."

"Papa would have never let me hear the end of it if she'd hurt herself doing something that silly. And you know we would have had to tell him, since he was the only one in town then who could have stitched her up." Jake chuckled along with her. It felt good to share an easy moment together. The intensity that had colored all their interactions since he'd returned home had left him on edge.

Jake was proud of how hard Coralee had worked over the last few hours with him. She was compassionate and gentle with the patients, but efficient at the same time. Where another woman might have recoiled at the things they had seen that day, Coralee remained unaffected by the ravages of cholera. She hadn't balked at any of the unpleasant tasks they'd had to perform to care for their patients.

Listening to her gentle voice reminiscing about their shared childhood, Jake's imagination took over. He could see them like this, working side by side, sharing their days and nights, healing their community together. But memories of the pain she had caused him surfaced again. The past was always right there, reminding him that she had shattered his dreams once already. He couldn't put his heart into her hands again.

Coralee noticed the moment the shuttered look passed over Jake's face. She had been enjoying their companionable conversation more than she'd expected.

During their five years of marriage, she and Alan had been the best of friends. She had known him as long and as well as she had Jake. When Jake left so abruptly for medical school, Alan had been there. His support had helped heal her shattered heart. She still ached from losing the one person she could share the most personal parts of her life with. For a few moments, talking with Jake had felt almost as intimate as talking with Alan.

She wasn't sure what she'd said to make Jake shut her out this time, but she felt bereft the moment he did. Maybe it was time to clear the air between them. "Jake, what's wrong? Why do you always push me away? Is it the situation with Dr. Jay? Because I—"

At that moment Mrs. Smith stirred as she woke, cutting Coralee's words short. They each went to tend to their patients one more time before they moved on. Upon leaving, Jake gave Mrs. Smith instructions so she could continue caring for her children and husband. Coralee left some camphor and chamomile with her to help ease their discomfort.

They loaded up in the wagon again and started out in the pale early morning light. Jake went over his plan for their visits that day. "If you feel comfortable on your own, I think today we'll split up. Mrs. Smith said her youngest visited Mrs. Felder last night and she wants someone to check in. I'll leave you with her for a few hours while I go check on Aaron and Liza." He glanced over, one eyebrow raised in question.

Coralee nodded. "That sounds fine. How was Mrs. Felder when you were there last?"

A mischievous smile crossed Jake's face. "I think you'll see for yourself."

Try as she might, Coralee couldn't pry any more information out of him. She didn't know Mrs. Felder well, but had heard talk around town. The older woman had come west with her son just the year before, built a sturdy cabin and started farming a plot. But her son had soon heeded the call of the frontier and headed farther west, while his mother had refused to leave. Coralee could imagine what the woman must be like to stay and hold the claim all on her own. She smiled to herself. A day with Mrs. Felder might be an interesting experience.

As it turned out, she was right about that. Jake introduced Mrs. Felder to Coralee at the door of the cabin, then left to visit the Riley family. Coralee could see immediately that the woman wasn't in much danger of expiring from cholera. Mrs. Felder talked from the moment Jake left, with hardly a pause for breath. She led Coralee inside, then promptly lowered herself into a rocking chair and directed Coralee to cover her with a quilt.

"Now, if you'll just straighten my dishes over there on the shelves. Everything has gotten to be such a mess while I'm incapacitated."

Coralee examined the neat stacks of plates and bowls on the indicated shelf. Had Mrs. Felder set Jake to unnecessary chores during his visit, too? She shrugged and moved to do her patient's bidding.

"That young doctor tells me you're the apothecary. I approve of a young woman taking on a venture like that."

"Thank you, Mrs. Felder. The shop was my father's. He trained me and left the shop to me when he passed last year."

"Ah, a wise man. A woman alone needs means of supporting herself. Take me. That son of mine has a wandering spirit something fierce. But I can make my way fine without him. I work my vegetable patch and grow the finest produce you've ever seen. That and eggs from my prized chickens keep me just fine." The older woman kept up a steady stream of conversation as she handed Coralee a cloth. "For the dusting. This furniture is in an awful state." Coralee examined the fine wood pieces scattered around the cabin, trying to hide an amused grin. There wasn't a speck of dust anywhere in the room.

"Young Dr. Hadley sure is a handsome fellow. You have a beau, Miss Evans?"

Coralee flushed at the direct question. "It's Mrs. Evans. My husband passed two years ago."

"Oh, well, I'm sorry for that, my dear. My Fred's been gone five years. He was a good one and I miss him every day." She looked at Coralee with compassion. "How are you handling life by yourself?"

Coralee's eyes welled with tears at the question. But, to her surprise, the ache in her heart was much less painful than usual. She focused on the lighter feeling for a moment. "You know, for so long I thought it would be unbearable forever. But maybe it's starting to be a little less difficult."

The older woman nodded, looking quite pleased. "That's the way, Mrs. Evans. You'll always miss him, but it gets easier. Now, about the handsome young doctor…" She paused, eyebrows raised and eyes glittering with interest.

Coralee wasn't sure what to say. Yes, Jake was handsome. Spending time in such close quarters while they worked, how could she not notice his broad shoulders and arms thick with muscle? Or the short beard that made her long to trace his strong jaw to feel the texture?

She managed a strangled laugh as she tried to dismiss the older woman's obvious hinting. "Oh, yes, Dr. Hadley is a fine man. But as you know, a widow must be prudent. With my position as Spring Hill's apothecary, I can hardly go chasing after a man."

Mrs. Felder's eyes narrowed and Coralee got the impression the older woman wasn't fooled by the forced airiness. She motioned Coralee into the chair beside her. "Seems to me you might think you'll be a widow forever. At your age and as lovely as you are, that's a bit like giving up on the good Lord. You don't strike me as one to give up so easily."

Coralee swallowed hard at the blunt words. Was she giving up on what God might have for her? She decided to repay Mrs. Felder's bluntness with some honesty of her own. "I'm not sure I can risk loss like that again. Losing Alan was…it was terrible." Mrs. Felder nodded, understanding and compassion written on her wrinkled face. "How can I take that chance again? What if God takes everyone I love?"

"Oh, my dear." Mrs. Felder placed her hand on Coralee's. The gentle touch relaxed a tension she hadn't noticed growing. "We're guaranteed to lose ones we love now and then. But that doesn't mean loving them isn't worth the trouble. The people in our lives that we love are precious gifts, and the Lord says good and perfect gifts are from Him. So I can't help but believe they're worth it, even for a short time."

The words stuck in Coralee's mind. Knowing the hurt she had experienced, would she go back and choose to not love Alan? Never. Every day with him was a beautiful memory to her now. So maybe opening up to love again was worth the risk of heartache.

"Now, there's a broom in the corner. The floor is terribly dirty." Coralee stifled another laugh at the woman's obvious overstatement as she reached for the broom.

Mrs. Felder chatted about everything under the sun while Coralee cleaned anything that could be cleaned. Whether it needed cleaning or not. She finally convinced Mrs. Felder to have some lunch with her, along with chamomile tea in case there was some hint of sickness left in the woman after all.

Coralee answered a knock at the door just after they finished. A burst of warmth rushed through her when she saw Jake waiting outside. What would he think if he'd heard Mrs. Felder's teasing? But as soon as she took in the look on his face, she sobered. Something was wrong.

"It's Aaron and Liza Riley." A chill swept over her. He met her gaze, pain radiating from his eyes. "I don't expect them to last the night."

Mrs. Felder gasped, a wrinkled hand covering her mouth.

Coralee wanted to break down in tears at the thought of those sweet two-year-olds, soon to be orphans. But this was not the time to be weepy and fragile. The children needed strong adults to stand in their parents' place.

"What can we do?"

"I'm not sure we can do anything. I've given

them what I can to make them more comfortable. But while I was there, Liza spoke to me about the twins. They don't have any family to take them in since Aaron's parents died three years ago. She loves their life here. This is where they chose to start their family. Liza wants them to grow up here, not be sent back east."

Mrs. Felder clucked her tongue. "Of course they should have a family here, where their parents wanted to be. The poor darlings. Do you know of anyone looking to adopt a child?"

Jake shook his head and Coralee's heart sank. "No, and even if I did, most families couldn't take them both and I won't have them separated. I...I promised Liza I would care for them until I find the perfect family to settle them with." His voice cracked with emotion as he spoke.

Mrs. Felder nodded with determination. "Dr. Hadley, I appreciate your concern for an old woman these last few days. But I certainly wouldn't expect you or Mrs. Evans to spend time around here when other people need you more." Jake's skeptical expression almost made Coralee snort in laughter. Mrs. Felder acted as if she wasn't the one who had been adamant about needing their attention. "You two go on and find those dear children a home."

Coralee and Jake bid the older woman farewell and loaded up the wagon. Jake sat for a moment, the reins loose in his hands, eyes focused far across the grassy hills. A pang of compassion hit Coralee. He had taken on a great deal of responsibility in just a few days and he was handling it with such grace. He looked so forlorn that she couldn't help resting a comforting hand on his forearm.

He shifted to face her. "I need to check on the Wallaces again. But it might take some time to get word out about the twins and find someone willing to take them." He ran a hand through his short hair as he turned toward the open prairie again.

"We'll split up. If you take me back to town, I can go calling with Cecilia to start the search for a family. Then you can visit your patients again. And maybe get a little rest."

Jake's drooping shoulders straightened, giving him a new look of purpose. "Yes, that's a good plan. Thank you. The lack of sleep is catching up with me."

They rode in silence for most of the trip to town. He dropped Coralee off at Lily's Café and immediately headed back out of town. Coralee went in search of her sister to see if she was free to start looking for the twins' new family.

All afternoon, Coralee and Cecilia visited their neighbors in town. Their first stop was the mercantile, next door to Lily's. Mrs. Collins was tending the counter and greeted them with a cheerful smile. After a few moments of small talk, Coralee got to the point. "I suppose you've heard about the cholera outbreak south of town."

The older woman cringed. "Such a frightening thing, cholera. Is it contained? Do we need to worry here in town?"

"Oh, no, it doesn't seem to be spreading very quickly. However, several families have been hit hard. In particular, it's only a matter of time for Aaron and Liza Riley."

Mrs. Collins gasped. "Oh, just terrible. What of the children?"

"That's why we stopped in. The twins are fine, but Liza's wish is for them to find a family here in Spring Hill. We came to see if you would be able to take them, or if you know of anyone who may be looking to add to their family."

"Oh, my. Mr. Collins would never stand for another child. Our youngest just married last fall, you know. No, we couldn't. But you know all the news filters through here. If we get word of someone who might be able to provide a home for the children, I'll come right to you."

They finished their visit and moved on. Each place was the same: they would chat for a moment before Coralee explained the twins' situation. The men would shake their heads, the women murmur in distress. Then each would state with certainty that no, they couldn't take on two toddlers. Here and there, someone would remember a relative who might have an interest in one child. But as soon as Coralee insisted that it must be both children, they would recant. She made sure to remind each neighbor that if they thought of anyone, they could let her or Jake know.

Coralee and Cecilia finally headed home just in time to have supper with Cat. As soon as they ate and cleaned up the quick meal, Coralee fell into bed, exhausted and deflated from the difficult day.

Her sleep was so deep that she didn't wake until Cecilia shook her shoulder. Bright daylight filled the room, disorienting her for a moment. "How long did I sleep?"

"Oh, it's about noon." Coralee shot up. She had planned to ride out to help Jake again after getting a few hours of sleep, but now half the day was gone. "Don't worry about that." Cecilia spoke as if she'd read Coralee's thoughts. "Jake is here and wants to speak to you. I don't think he has good news." Cecilia left Coralee to dress.

She chose a red calico dress with a tiny rose pattern, then parted her hair and arranged it in a quick bun at the nape of her neck. Jake was waiting for her in the parlor, looking drained. A sinking feeling filled her at the grief written on his face. "It's the Rileys, isn't it?"

"And Mr. and Mrs. Williams," he confirmed. He dropped into a chair and rested his elbows on his knees, hands clasped and head low. For a moment Coralee wasn't sure what to do for him. But a nudge in her spirit gave her the answer.

Perching on the edge of a chair near him, she leaned close. "Lord, we grieve for the dear neighbors we lost today, but we know they're celebrating with You now. Please give Jake peace and rest so he can care for the others who are sick. And point us to the perfect home for little Phillip and Louisa. Amen."

When Coralee raised her eyes, Jake was staring

at her. The look on his face was one she hardly expected to see from him. Flushing under the admiring gaze, she tried to ignore the fluttering of her heart. It had been so long since anyone had looked at her like she was beautiful. The moment stretched between them. His expression was intense, but not in the fuming way it had been a few days ago.

"Thank you for praying for me, Coralee. I guess I need it right now." He paused, looking like he was searching for words. "I've never lost patients of my own," he finally admitted. "Of course, patients at the hospital died, but I was just a student. With Dr. Jay away, the people in this town are my responsibility, my patients. And I lost five of them. Leaving two innocent children orphaned." His eyes searched hers, begging her to understand. "Cecilia told me you didn't find anyone to take the twins yesterday. I stopped by the Trasks' to be sure they're all healthy and Mrs. Trask said they can't keep the children any longer. But my hope is that I can find a home for them soon. They deserve a big, happy family to surround them with love."

A pang of regret made Coralee let out a slow breath. After all this time she couldn't believe she still hoped he would include her, consider her a partner. But there he was, shouldering all the responsibility for the twins himself. "We'll find someone. Everyone we spoke with knows to contact us the moment they hear of a family who could take in two toddlers. Word will spread and the perfect parents will turn up anytime now."

Jake nodded and stood. "I can't stay too long. I'm going to get a few hours of rest, if I can. But I'm heading to get the twins after that."

Coralee's heart ached for the sweet children. "I could go with you. I've spoken to the twins on many occasions at church. They might be more comfortable leaving the Trasks with someone they're familiar with."

He hesitated but then nodded in agreement as they walked to the door. Pausing, he turned to her before stepping outside. Bright midday sun slanted through the open doorway, outlining his tall frame.

"Until later, then, Coralee." Intensity buzzed between them, making it hard for her to catch her breath. All she could do was nod, words sticking in her throat.

After he was gone, she sat to rest, emotions swirling inside her. The way Jake had looked at her had been so familiar. It had felt like they were close friends again. Or a courting couple. But they were neither of those things and she didn't want them to be. The risk of losing another man she cared about was too great. Her eyes drifted shut and light sleep claimed her, filled with visions of Jake taking her in his arms.

She woke an hour later with a start. Cecilia had returned from her errands and joined her in the parlor. The middle Holbrook sister finished tying off the thread on the skirt hem she was mending before turning to Coralee.

"How are you feeling?"

Coralee took inventory of herself before responding. "Still tired, but better. Not a bit sick, if you're worried about that."

"Oh, that's good. I was a bit concerned. But I also wondered how you feel after working so closely with Jake."

"Working with Jake." Coralee searched for the words to explain the last few days to her sister. "We fight a lot when we're together. But he managed to put our past aside and work with me as a professional. That was nice, to be honest."

"I don't want to pry, but I have to wonder if there are some feelings developing again between you and Jake." Cecilia spoke with gentle earnestness, as she always did.

As much as Coralee wanted to avoid the question, Cecilia's genuine concern made it impossible not to give her an honest answer.

"I don't know what he's feeling, but I can't stop thinking about him. As a man, not just a colleague or Dr. Jay's protégé. But I don't think he trusts me. And I'm not planning to fall in love again."

Cecilia's mouth curved into a slight smile, understanding filling her eyes. Coralee felt a wave of sympathy as she studied her sister. Cecilia was lovely. She was elegant and ladylike with a quiet, calm disposition. She should have had suitors lining up to call on her, but she never seemed interested in any of the local men. Now, Coralee thought that maybe Cecilia had experienced a bit of inconvenient love herself that made her keep men at arm's length.

"Coralee, I can only imagine how frightening it must be to think of falling in love again after all you've lost. But I don't want to see you alone for the rest of your life." Cecilia moved closer and took both Coralee's hands in hers. "You're not an old woman with only a few years left to live out on your own. You can still have the family you used to dream about."

Coralee tried to smile at her sister through the familiar ache that bloomed in her chest. "We all know that's just not possible, Cecilia. I suppose my childhood dreams of love may not be out of the question just because I lost Alan, but I'm not ready to take that risk again."

Cecilia's eyes narrowed as if she wanted to dig deeper into her sister's words. "Remember, God can use more than just birth to make a family."

Coralee averted her gaze. She didn't want to spend any more time talking about her crushed longing to have a baby of her own. That ship had sailed after five childless years of marriage.

To her relief, Cecilia didn't say more about it before leaving to help Aunt Lily at the café. Coralee spent the early afternoon catching up on rest and praying about her future. It had been so long since she'd spent time in prayer on a daily basis and the words seemed stilted at first. But praying with Jake earlier had reminded her that God was always there to listen to the words she couldn't say to anyone else.

When the time came to get ready to leave, she shook the wrinkles out of her dress and let her hair down. Making several thick braids, she twisted them together into a pretty chignon. She searched around in a bottom drawer for a narrow bow that matched her dress. Turning her head back and forth in front of the mirror, she checked the hairstyle and pinched her cheeks for a bit of color.

Will Jake like this shade of red on me? The thought popped into her mind unbidden. She realized she'd been studying herself in the mirror far longer than necessary. What was wrong with her? She felt like a schoolgirl, giddy about a young man coming to court her. But Jake was not courting her. This was hardly even a social event where she should be worrying about her looks. She was helping out in a time of crisis.

Settling a straw bonnet over her hair, she worked to pull herself together. She had to remain above reproach to keep the community's respect. Acting like a silly young miss would give Dr. Jay more fuel for turning the town against her. She had to get a handle on these errant thoughts before Jake arrived to pick her up.

Just like a man who's courting a woman.

Chapter Three

Jake only had time for a short rest before he drove to the café to get Coralee. They headed straight to the Trask farm, Jake's nerves building the closer they got. Outside the weatherworn home, an older girl with tightly braided hair was hanging laundry on a line stretched between two trees. Three toddlers ran around the yard under her supervision, stopping in their tracks to stare as the wagon drove by.

Mrs. Trask came out of the cabin, shielding her eyes from the bright sun with one hand as she watched Jake help Coralee down from the wagon seat. The woman looked disheveled and weary, clothed in a work dress that had seen better days. Jake tried hard to relax. He wondered if children could smell fear like the wild dogs he used to chase out of Ma's vegetable patch.

Mrs. Trask didn't bother to approach the wagon, leaning against the cabin just outside the door. "Have you come for the little ones, then?"

Jake could only offer a curt nod. Mrs. Trask pushed away from the wall. "Good. I'll get their things."

He was sure he turned pale as the woman returned to the house. "What am I going to do with two babies?" The words came out haltingly.

Coralee rested a hand on his arm and Jake was sure he saw a hint of humor in her expression. "It will all work out. I can help you with them until we find a family. Cat can handle the shop on her own for a bit longer."

They both turned as Mrs. Trask came back with a small bag. She waved a hand to her daughter, who gathered up two of the little ones in the yard and walked them over. Louisa and Phillip held on to the Trask girl's legs for dear life as Jake took in their matching chubby cheeks, round noses and rosy mouths. Two pairs of clear blue eyes stared up at him.

He didn't know if he should reach for them or wait until they came over on their own. But Coralee started gently coaxing them closer to her. His heart hammered against his ribs. She was beautiful, kneeling in front of the twins, making silly faces and talking in a calm voice.

Jake had never spent time around children. Ma had lost several babies after his birth, leaving him an only child. He had never minded it, maybe because he'd had such good friends in Alan and Coralee. But now, faced with two tiny people that were his responsibility, Jake was falling apart.

Coralee had pulled a handkerchief from her

pocket and convinced Louisa to come closer. They admired the lacy trim, then with a quick twist and several knots, Coralee formed the piece of cloth into a simple doll. Louisa giggled with delight and hugged the doll close. How did Coralee know how to do that?

Standing, she went to the wagon and rummaged in her apothecary case, returning with a small tin. She knelt by Phillip, who moved close to watch her with great interest. With a dramatic flourish, she showed the child how to pull the lid open and place several rocks inside. It was a simple toy, but the boy took it with great seriousness. He knelt in the dirt to pile more rocks in the tin and dump them over and over.

It seemed like the most natural thing in the world for Coralee to help the children relax. Jake had no idea how to do that. How was he going to care for these two when he couldn't even convince them to look him in the eye? Not knowing what else to do, Jake took the children's bag from Mrs. Trask and loaded it into the wagon. Coralee lifted each child into the back, then climbed in and sat on the floor with one twin on each side of her.

She shrugged when she noticed him watching. "I'll sit back here with them, so they won't be afraid or try to stand and fall."

Another wave of apprehension washed over Jake. It hadn't even crossed his mind that they might fall out of the wagon if he left them in the back by themselves. He had never been in a position where he knew so little about something so important. Even when he'd started medical school, he had studied beforehand to teach himself basic anatomy and procedures. He had wanted to have some knowledge going in. But now that he was responsible for the needs and safety of two little people, he had no idea what to do.

He thanked Mrs. Trask for keeping the children, then directed the wagon toward town. The entire way, Coralee kept the twins entertained by telling stories and singing little songs. This was a side of her that he had never seen. It came so easily to her, while he was struggling to find even a few words to say to the little ones.

Once in town, Jake drove the wagon to the café to drop Coralee off. He was so distracted by the weight of having the twins in his care that he almost drove straight past the building. Why on earth had Liza trusted him with her children? He parked the wagon behind the café and turned to Coralee and the twins.

"Well, here we are."

Coralee glanced up from the children. "It's suppertime and I'm sure they must be hungry. Why don't you all eat with us tonight?"

"Oh, yes. Thank you." Jake hated that he was still at a loss. Of course, they would be hungry. His medical training had taught him all about children's physiology and illnesses. But he was realizing how little that had to do with the day-to-day responsibility of raising them. He glanced at Coralee again, wondering if the desperation he felt was showing on his face.

It must have been pretty obvious because she scooted close behind the wagon seat and reached up to touch his arm. "Just come in and have supper. We'll help you with anything you need." Relief calmed a little of his fear. He wouldn't be on his own with the twins just yet.

Jake jumped down and helped Coralee out of the wagon. He hesitated before gingerly lifting Louisa into his arms. Was he holding her right? He didn't want to hurt her. With great care, he handed the little girl to Coralee. Picking up Phillip, Jake started to feel a bit of confidence. After all, he hadn't dropped Louisa.

Coralee led them inside and called for her sisters.

Cecilia peeked in from the kitchen, gasping when she saw the children. "Oh, Coralee, they're darling!"

Coralee just smiled as Cecilia turned to Louisa. "What a lovely dress. Is that your favorite color?"

Louisa's smile was cautious but she seemed to enjoy the attention. "Yes, pink."

"And it looks beautiful on you. Is that a doll you have?"

The little girl held out the handkerchief doll Coralee had made. "Coree made it."

Cecilia winked at her sister. "That Coralee is very talented, isn't she?"

Louisa nodded happily. "She's nice."

Jake's heart melted a little. These poor children needed that sort of kindness right now. No matter what his personal feelings might be where Coralee was concerned, he hoped she would be a bright spot in the twins' lives.

Through the conversation, Phillip just watched with wide eyes. When Cecilia tried to engage him, he buried his face in Jake's shoulder. A surge of protectiveness took Jake by surprise. He rubbed the boy's back and rested his cheek on the small blond head.

Cecilia couldn't seem to get enough of the twins. "Oh, they're just the most precious little things. Don't you just wish you had a dozen of them?"

As soon as the words left her mouth, the ladies all froze. Jake wondered what the sudden tension meant. Cecilia blushed. "I'm sorry, Coralee. That was insensitive."

Looking from one woman to the other, Jake had to ask. "What's wrong, Cecilia?"

Silence followed his question. Even Louisa and Phillip seemed to pick up on the change in atmosphere and stilled. Finally, Coralee threw up her hands. "Not that anyone needs to know, but Cecilia forgot for a moment that Alan and I were never able to have children. I may never have children. That's what's wrong. Now, I'm going to get the food ready."

Coralee retreated to the kitchen, her words hanging heavy in the air. Cat shrugged and went to help her sister. Cecilia bit her lip. "I'm sorry, Jake. That was awkward and it's all my fault."

He patted her shoulder. "No, you didn't bring it up on purpose. It's no wonder she was upset, though. I can't imagine…" Jake's voice trailed off as he thought of Coralee's pain. He cleared his throat around the lump that suddenly formed. "I would hate to know I could never have children of my own. It's terrible—"

The conversation was cut short when Louisa pulled at the leg of his trousers. "I hungry, Jake."

He rested one hand on top of her head. "Me, too. I'm sure the ladies will have food on the table in no time."

Mealtime brought another set of complications Jake would never have expected. Coralee and Cecilia settled each wiggling child on a chair and used strips of cloth to loosely secure them. Coralee showed Cat how to cut pieces of softer foods for the little ones to eat. Jake made mental notes of everything the women did so he could at least feed the twins by himself.

As they ate, Jake got a peek at more of the twins' personalities. The women were busy talking when a mischievous look appeared on Louisa's little face. Watching her out of the corner of his eye, Jake saw her chubby hand shoot out and grab a piece of bread Phillip was just bringing to his mouth.

"No, Lou!" The little boy howled in frustration while his sister stuffed the bread into her own mouth. Coralee turned and cooed over Phillip, oblivious to what had caused his tears. It was all Jake could do to cover his amusement. Who would have thought that such a tiny girl could already be so ornery?

"It's been several days since we had any customers." Cat and Coralee's discussion drew Jake's attention away from the children. Cat's words surprised him. He hadn't realized Holbrook's was struggling that much.

Coralee's shoulders drooped. "Hopefully, I can

make significant progress on the medication soon. Otherwise, I don't know what we're going to do."

Her comment piqued Jake's interest. "You're working on a medication? Is it something new?"

She shifted in her chair, frowning at her plate. "I wasn't planning to say anything until it's finished. But, yes, I'm working on a formula that Papa wanted to develop before he passed."

"That's great. How's it coming?" Jake had known Coralee long enough to see from the look on her face that this medicine was important to her. Heaviness settled over him. There was no reason she would need to share a project like that with him. But he still found himself wishing she had wanted to. Wishing she wanted to involve him in something so vital to her business.

Coralee pushed food around with her fork, refusing to meet his eyes. "I'm not as close to finding the key ingredient as I'd like to be." Without giving him a chance to reply, she turned to Cecilia, asking about her plans now that school was out of session until fall.

Jake's heart fell. Coralee was sending a clear message that she didn't want him involved in her work.

Suddenly, Cat sniffed and covered her nose with a handkerchief. "I believe one of the children might need attention," she declared. Jake started to chuckle at her regal announcement until it hit him that he might need to attend to them himself. And he had no clue how to change a diaper.

Much to Jake's relief, Coralee and Cecilia jumped

in again, rescuing him from embarrassing himself with his profound lack of knowledge about children. Coralee searched through the bag Mrs. Trask had sent for the children. She pulled out two large rectangles of white cotton while Cecilia dampened several rags. Together, the sisters cleaned the children and put on their fresh diapers. Jake tried not to get caught staring while still managing to catch every move they made so he could replicate it.

As Coralee and Cecilia cleaned up, Jake heard a sound at his feet. He looked down to find Louisa standing in front of him, little arms stretched toward him. "Up?"

Her voice was quiet and tentative. Jake's heart expanded in his chest as he cradled the girl in his arms. The love he already felt for these children was overwhelming, even after only a few hours with them. Coralee's revelation flashed in his mind. His first thought was how painful it must have been for her to realize that she would likely never bear a child. But as he considered how much he already cared about the twins' well-being, he started to wonder if his reaction had been impulsive. Maybe a family could grow out of people who just needed each other.

Louisa rubbed her eyes as she snuggled against his chest. "I think she's tired." Jake wasn't sure how he recognized the signs, but it was encouraging. Maybe he could learn how to care for the twins, after all.

Coralee lifted Phillip into her arms and he stuck a thumb in his mouth, staring at her with wide eyes.

"Phillip is, too. I'm sure this has been a difficult few days for them. It's time for a good night's sleep."

Jake already felt more confident at the prospect of taking them home by himself, thanks to Coralee's easy example. His room at the boarding house wasn't large, but it would be plenty big enough to make temporary beds on the floor. The proprietress, Mrs. Hardy, missed her grandchildren in Virginia. She had jumped at the chance to help with the twins if the need arose. He was sure this could work for the short time they would be in his care.

He took the bag with the twins' belongings from Cecilia and headed to the wagon. Louisa snuggled in his arms and Coralee carried Phillip. Something about walking alongside her with the children felt right. Jake shoved that notion back where it came from. The last thing he needed was to be distracted by impossible fantasies.

After setting Louisa on the wagon seat, he climbed up beside her and took Phillip from Coralee's outstretched arms. He looked down into her lovely face. "Thank you again, Coralee. Your help has been invaluable."

"I'm glad to help. Will you be all right by yourself with the twins, Jake? Two children can be a lot to handle."

He tried to draw on the small burst of confidence he felt earlier, but it had waned. "I'm sure we'll get along fine."

"What are you going to do with them while you're

working? I could help you for a little while until you get into a routine."

Jake considered her offer. A few days ago he would have refused her flat-out. He still wasn't sure his heart was ready to have her back in his life. But once they'd learned how to steer clear of their past, spending time with Coralee had been downright pleasant. The twins liked her and she was such a natural caregiver. He had been wondering what he would do with them during the day. Focusing on patients visiting the office or traveling to make house calls would be difficult with the children underfoot.

"Yes, I could use some help. Could I drop them by here on the way to the clinic in the morning?"

Coralee agreed and said goodbye to Jake and the twins. Phillip whimpered a little at leaving her, tearing at Jake's heart. These children had lost so much in a short time. As he drove to the boardinghouse, one twin snuggled close on each side, Jake wondered if it would be harder than he expected to let them go when they found a permanent home.

But several hours later, he was questioning that sentiment. It was going on midnight and the twins were squirming and giggling together on their makeshift pallet on the floor. Every few minutes one of them would get up and run a circle around the room until Jake put a stop to it and got them both tucked back in. Mere moments later, they started all over. Hadn't they been tired when he'd brought them home?

After far too much time spent chasing them

around the room, both toddlers finally curled up in their bed and fell asleep. Jake snuck in a few hours of fitful rest before Phillip woke, disoriented and crying. Jake pulled the little boy up into bed with him, hoping that would buy him another hour of sleep. His heart warmed a few minutes later when he felt Louisa climb into the bed, too. The peaceful quiet didn't last long, but those moments stuck with Jake as morning light filled the room.

It took longer than his usual routine, but Jake was pleased when he managed to get all three of them fed, cleaned up and dressed. He had never realized how many buttons were on children's clothing, much less how hard they were to manage while the little ones wiggled. But soon they were on their way, Jake holding one child in the crook of each arm, their bag slung across his back. He felt rather like a pack mule.

Jake came around the corner of the café to see Coralee standing by the back door. The twins squealed and reached for her. Caring for two tiny children was daunting, but seeing her waiting for them was a reminder that he didn't have to do it alone. Even with his whole body aching from struggling to keep the twins in his arms, her warm smile managed to take his breath away.

It was possible that he was playing with fire. The last thing Jake wanted was to let his heart get entangled with Coralee again. Relying on her was already bringing back feelings he didn't want to relive. Jake shook off the worrisome thoughts. He needed help with the twins, that was all. Accepting her offer didn't mean he would fall in love with her again.

Watching Jake walk toward her, one child clutched in each arm, Coralee wondered if offering her time was a mistake, after all. She had tossed and turned all night, guilt over the time she'd been away from the shop warring with an unwelcome desire to spend more time with Jake and the twins. And humiliation topped it all off. Cecilia's slip-up yesterday had forced her to tell Jake about her inability to have children; the last thing she'd ever wanted to discuss with him. Even now, remembering the words that had come from her lips made her flush with shame.

To be honest, Jake's response had been the worst part. She had overheard him tell Cecilia how terrible it was. His tone of voice and the way he had stumbled over his words made his opinion clear. He felt sorry for her. Her condition horrified him. It was just the response she'd imagined from a man. And it was one more reason she couldn't open her heart again.

But in spite of that certainty, in the bright morning light just a glimpse of Jake walking down the boardwalk made her heart race and palms sweat. What was it about holding the children that made him even more attractive?

He greeted her with a distracted smile, struggling to keep his hold on both children. Thankful for the distraction from her admission the night before, Coralee held her arms out for Louisa. The girl launched her little body into Coralee's hands with a giggle.

Jake visibly breathed a sigh of relief once they were all safe inside the house.

"How was your first night with the twins?"

He dropped into a chair, leaning back and letting his eyes drift shut. "They settled down, but it took a bit longer than I expected."

She had to stifle a laugh at the vision of Jake trying to wrestle both children into bed. "You seemed a bit…out of your element yesterday."

For a moment it looked as if her comment had hurt his pride. But then he relaxed and chuckled. "I'm glad you and Cecilia showed me the basics last night. Facing two children who need you for every little thing is mighty intimidating. I had no idea what to do with them."

"I'm impressed at how well you've taken to temporary parenting. They look rested and happy. They're dressed and fed. That's quite good for your first try." Even as the words left her mouth, Coralee wanted to shove them back in. Her face flushed. Had her tone sounded as flirtatious to him as it did to her?

Jake didn't seem to notice. "Well, I appreciate that you're willing to help me. Once again. It means a lot that I don't have to do this by myself."

Coralee turned to busy herself breaking up a squabble between the twins. She was likely to say something else foolish if she responded to his gratitude.

She felt his eyes on her as she tried to calm the children, making her self-conscious. Was she doing something wrong?

Finally he rose and stepped toward the door. "It looks like you'll be fine, then. I'm going to check in at the office before I head out to see how our cholera patients are recovering."

"If it's around mealtime when you return, why don't you plan to join us?" What was getting into her? Coralee hadn't intended for an invitation to slip out, but he looked pleasantly surprised as he agreed. Then he kissed each child on the head and left. She took a deep breath. At least now she didn't have to worry about accidentally flirting with Jake.

Coralee took the twins outside to play along the creek where it ran behind the café. It was soon clear that Phillip was adventurous enough to do anything Louisa suggested. And she suggested too many things.

First, the little girl pointed her brother to a large rock. "You climb dat?"

Phillip ran right to it and tried to climb up, little legs swinging in the air when he couldn't get a foothold. Coralee couldn't help laughing as she gave him a push up. Later, Coralee turned around to find Louisa encouraging her brother to eat a leaf she'd found. She barely grabbed it from his hand in time. That girl was one to keep an eye on.

After their morning in the fresh air, they joined Cecilia for lunch at the café. The children had worked up an appetite and ate with intense focus while the sisters talked. The cute little ones drew the attention of every woman in the place, many of whom stopped to coo over the twins. Coralee tried to ask if any of them could provide Louisa and Phillip with a permanent home, but to no avail. She couldn't understand why it was so hard to find them a family. They were darling, well-behaved children. Easy to love. If she were in a position to have a family, Coralee would have adopted them in a heartbeat.

When they returned to the living quarters, Coralee laid the children down for naps and left them in Cecilia's care while she checked in at Holbrook's. She had to get some work done on the medicine to start making up for lost time. Business at the shop wasn't going to improve without her there, putting in time to find a solution.

Coralee sat in her workroom for three-quarters of an hour before pushing away from the table in frustration. All she had done was stare at Papa's list of ingredients and think about the sweet babies sleeping back at home. She wasn't going to accomplish anything today. That much was clear. She put away Papa's notes and headed home, stomach in knots.

Louisa was just waking when Coralee returned and peeked into the bedroom. She picked the girl up, holding the warm, tiny body close. Little fingers curled into the hair at the nape of her neck and Louisa's soft voice reached her ears. "You find me, Coree."

Familiar longing washed over her. She had spent so much time wishing and waiting for children during her marriage. Children that never came. It had taken a long time to get past the disappointment of realizing she would never be a mother.

Coralee tried to savor the sweetness of the little girl cuddled in her arms rather than brood over things that could never be. Right here in front of her were two darling children that needed people to love them. Even if she couldn't be their mother, she could love them while they were there.

Toward evening, Coralee and the twins were sitting in the middle of the parlor floor enjoying an indoor picnic when Jake peeked into the room. Coralee flushed, horrified that he'd caught her in such an undignified position. But Jake's bemused grin somehow made her feel less self-conscious. In all the years they had known each other, he had seen her doing sillier things than this.

"It seems like you and the children are having a good time." His eyes twinkled. He was more light-hearted than Coralee had seen him since he'd moved back to Spring Hill. Was it the youthful influence of the twins? Or was he as pleased to be back on good footing in their friendship as she was?

"As you can see, we're having an elegant high tea," she declared, sipping pretend liquid from an empty cup while making a silly face at Phillip. The little boy dissolved into laughter, crumbs from a thick slice of bread dotting the front of his shirt. And everything else. To Coralee's surprise, Jake lowered himself right down next to Louisa on the tablecloth they had spread over the floorboards.

"Could you spare a cup of tea for a guest?" He spoke to Louisa in complete earnestness, watching while the little girl pretended to pour from a teakettle into a cup.

"Yes, for you." Her little face was serious, the tip of her tiny tongue peeking out as she focused on handing him the cup with great care.

He brought it to his lips and slurped loudly. "Ah, that was very good. Thank you, Miss Louisa."

Both children giggled at his antics. Coralee couldn't suppress the ache that hit her. A strong, intelligent man like Jake acting silly on the floor to amuse two little children was a powerful sight. She turned away, hoping Jake didn't have any idea what direction her thoughts were taking. She was thankful for the distraction when the twins tired of tea and clambered to their feet. They headed to a corner where she had spread a sheet over several chairs to make a tent for them to play in.

"How did everything go with the children today?" He sat with both arms wrapped around one knee, eyes on the little ones even as he spoke to her.

"It was wonderful. They played all morning and took a nap." She smiled at the sweet voices drifting out from the corner. "Jake, they're so well behaved. Aaron and Liza were doing a wonderful job raising them."

His chin lifted in pride, as if she had just given him the compliment. "I'm glad to hear they weren't too difficult. Were you able to get to the shop at all?"

Her heart sank. It was the first day she'd been in the shop for some time and she hadn't made any progress. "I stopped by while the children were sleeping. Cat has been running things well without me, so not much needed my attention."

He nodded and rose from the floor. "I suppose I should get them home and let you enjoy your evening, then." He reached out a hand to help Coralee stand. She tried not to focus on the sensation of his rough hand holding hers.

"I meant it this morning when I invited you to join us for supper. Please, we would be glad to have all three of you."

"That's very kind, but I don't want to impose. You've just spent all day with the twins. You must be ready for some peace and quiet. And we had supper here last night."

Coralee shook her head. "It's no trouble. We always have plenty to eat. I'll go tell Cecilia." She headed to the kitchen before he could answer, hoping to keep him from refusing. She'd spent the whole day with Louisa and Phillip, but she still found herself longing to keep them close a while longer. She refused to examine the possibility that she might want Jake around longer, too.

While she helped Cat and Cecilia finish the dinner preparations, Coralee heard the twins getting louder with Jake as they played in the parlor. When it was time to sit down, she and Jake each wrangled a child, doing everything in their power to keep them in their chairs. What had gotten into the sweet, silly twins she had played with all day?

She lost track of how many times they placed Phillip back in his seat before Cecilia remembered the strips of fabric they had used the night before. But even then, he refused to sit quietly. "Coree. I want play."

"Phillip, we're eating. Don't you want to eat? You must be hungry after your busy day."

"No!"

Jake took a turn at convincing him. "You have to eat something. Coralee and Cecilia are sharing this nice supper with us. It will hurt their feelings if you don't eat."

Phillip slumped in his chair, arms crossed over his chest.

Coralee glanced at Jake across the table. "It's fine with us if he doesn't want to eat."

Shaking his head, Jake looked pointedly at the little boy. "No, I think he needs to. It isn't polite to refuse what people offer to share."

"But he's lost so much. Maybe he just doesn't feel like eating."

Jake's eyes speared her and, for a moment, Coralee braced for an argument. But Jake visibly swallowed his words and turned to cut up Louisa's food, dropping the subject altogether.

Before Coralee could say more, the sound of the front door slamming echoed through the room. Cat stomped in, dropping into a chair at the table with a heavy sigh. Coralee exchanged a look with Cecilia. A lifetime of living with Cat had taught them to approach her head-on when she started acting pouty like this.

"What's going on, Cat? Is something wrong at the shop?"

Cat speared her with a glare. "No, nothing's wrong at the shop. Because nothing happens at the shop. Ever."

Coralee drew back at her sister's vehement response. She hadn't expected Cat to be angry with her. "You were fine this afternoon. You said you didn't mind watching the shop for me." She reached over to stop Phillip from smashing each pea on his plate one at a time.

"I don't mind helping out, Coralee. But I'm there by myself all the time now. Holbrook's is your dream, not mine. When there are customers coming and going, I like the work. But I didn't see a soul today except you. And you holed up in the workroom the entire time."

Cat's words cut straight through her heart. She had to find a way to take care of her family. But instead, she had been spending all her time helping everyone but her sisters. How would the shop ever recover if she didn't focus her attention on it?

Jake and Cecilia watched the scene, heads swiveling back and forth between the two sisters. Coralee's hand shot out and caught Louisa's falling fork before it clattered to the floor, even as she met her sister's sullen gaze head-on. "Cat, I'm sorry. You're right. I haven't been at the shop as much as I should be."

"It's not just that, Coralee. I know you're not having much success with Papa's research. Maybe that's a good reason not to pin all our hopes on it."

Coralee bristled. "Of course Papa's research is the key. He wouldn't have wanted me to work on it if it wasn't important."

"I'm not saying it isn't important, Coralee." Cat rolled her eyes. "I'm saying there must be other things we can do to get customers in the shop right now, while you work on it."

"Papa's medication will bring all the customers we need." Coralee knew she was being more stubborn than necessary. But she needed Cat to understand how vital the medication was to the shop. She turned to wipe butter off Phillip's hands with a damp cloth just as he reached up to smear it in his hair.

Cat arched one eyebrow, voice turning frosty. "And just how much progress did you make on it this afternoon?"

Louisa grabbed at Coralee's sleeve, leaving a trail of beef juice that soaked into the fabric as she tried to wipe it off. "Cat, I'm working on the formula as much as I can. There's…a lot going on." She had to force the words out around the lump in her throat. She was failing her family, no matter how hard she tried.

Cat's tense posture softened. "I'm sorry, Coralee. I know how hard you're working. I don't want to put extra pressure on you." Leaving her plate barely touched, Cat rose and whisked Phillip into her arms. "Let me clean up this rascal for you."

Cecilia's smile was sympathetic as she grabbed several plates and followed Cat to the kitchen.

Coralee felt Jake's eyes on her but she busied herself with wiping Louisa's hands and face. How had she let Cat bait her into an argument like that in front of a guest? This was a family affair and no matter what their relationship had been in the past, Jake was not family.

As she helped Louisa climb out of her chair, Coralee glanced up. He sat at the end of the table, arms crossed over his chest, head tilted to one side. Waiting for her to acknowledge him. He wasn't going to let her get away with pretending he didn't hear the argument. Family business or not, his posture made it clear he had every intention of including himself in what was going on at Holbrook's.

"Is business really that slow, Coralee?"

Jake watched her shoulders droop as she let out a pent-up breath. Then she fixed him with a pointed look. "Yes, it is that slow. It's hard to keep customers coming in to buy medicine when the only doctor in town advises them not to."

His stomach clenched. Was Dr. Jay more responsible for the problems at Holbrook's than Jake wanted to admit? "What about this medication of your father's? It's clear you don't want to tell me about it, but if you'll trust me, maybe I can help."

She picked at nonexistent crumbs on the table-cloth, a grimace of indecision tightening her lips. "It's a medication for pain." Jake's heart flipped when she began her explanation. He leaned in closer, willing her to go on.

"Papa hated to see his patients suffering from terrible side effects when they just needed relief from minor pain. He had gathered a list of potential ingredients to test and I've been working my way through those for a few months. But I'm not sure what the next step is when I run out of options."

"I could come by the shop and look over what you have. I learned about a few new developments during my time at the hospital. Maybe we can come up with a few more things for you to try?" He could see her hesitating. Happy laughter floated in from the kitchen, where Coralee's sisters and the children were washing the dishes. "Why don't we take a few minutes and go now? I'm willing to bet Cecilia would jump at the chance to play with the twins a little longer."

"I don't know, Jake."

He tried to look charming and innocuous. Her project had piqued his professional curiosity. Although he had spent much of his free time growing up helping Mr. Holbrook in the apothecary shop, he had never seen the process of discovering a new medication in person. The idea was fascinating. "You said you haven't accomplished much recently with everything that's happened. Maybe a few hours of work combined with someone else's perspective will get the project moving again?"

That hit the mark. Her face was so easy to read that he saw the moment she decided to let him help. He mustered his most disarming smile as she sighed. "You win, Jake. Let's go."

Coralee explained parts of the process as they

walked to the shop. "Papa started with his reference books and remedies he already had on the shelf, looking for ingredients he knew had an effect on pain. He got as far as compiling a list before..." She paused and swallowed hard. Jake's heart ached, knowing that she had gone through such pain. But in the blink of an eye, she shook off the sadness and continued. "I've worked through much of the list already, without anything to show for it."

"How are you testing the ingredients?"

"For each one, I make up a batch of any forms I think might work. I have a few patients with chronic pain who still come to the shop. They've been kind enough to help me try the medicines as I go. Usually, I try a very low dose to begin with, then a higher one later if there aren't any side effects."

"But you haven't had any success at all?"

She flinched at the direct question. "There have been two formulas that helped the pain for one or two of my patients. But they also made them feel terribly sick for days. That's not what Papa wanted for his medicine."

They fell into silence, both considering the problem. The streets of Spring Hill were quiet as they walked through the gathering dark. Now and then they passed a couple enjoying a stroll. Escorting Coralee on such a lovely evening reminded Jake too much of the days when they were courting. If that wasn't bad enough, entering Holbrook's alone with her after-hours felt intimate, in a way. He fought to keep his personal feelings in check. This was a professional experience. A friend helping a friend, at most.

But that was hard to remember as he bent over Mr. Holbrook's notes with Coralee. A soft, flowery scent reached his nose every time she shifted to point out an entry on the list. He reached for a page at the same time she did and their hands brushed, sending shivers up his arm. As soon as they finished going through the papers, he moved to the other side of the table, needing space between them.

"So that's how far I've gotten." She was focused on the pages, shuffling through them over and over as if something she had missed would jump out at her.

"You've covered most substances I would have suggested. I'm sure one of these will turn out to be just the right ingredient."

Coralee nodded, but she was still fixated on her father's notes, reminding Jake that it had only been a year since she lost him. He moved to rest a hand on her shoulder, giving in to an urge to comfort her. But even before her eyes shot up to meet his, she shrugged off his touch. He stepped back, running a hand through his hair, feigning indifference.

"Jake."

He met her eyes, seeing confusion swirling in the blue depths. He broke in before she could continue, not sure he could stand to hear what she might say next. "I'm sorry. That was too familiar. I don't want to ruin the truce we've had the last few days. I value your willingness to offer your help with the twins. And I want to help you in return."

She stared out the window into the dusk, so still that he wondered if her thoughts had turned to the loss of her father again. Or Alan. The familiar pang of jealousy swept through Jake, just as it did every time he thought of her marriage to his best friend. Finally she turned back with a curt nod. "I think I've spent as much time here as I can handle today."

"Sure. We'd better get back and see if the twins have your sisters tied up in a corner while they ransack the house." His heart swelled when Coralee laughed, the light sound chasing away the hurt that had threatened to settle between them again.

Jake helped her clean up the materials and they left the shop, walking slowly back to the café. This time, they walked in silence. Jake was torn. Deep in the corners of his heart, he still felt lingering hurt from her rejection all those years ago. He still longed to understand why she had turned so quickly to Alan. But at the same time, he was afraid to ask. If he did, he might find out that everything he'd thought she had felt at the time had been in his imagination. He had been so sure, but maybe she had cared more for Alan than for Jake all along.

As they approached her home, Jake wanted to linger, feeling a twinge of regret that the evening was over. Regardless of the pain of their past, he couldn't help wanting to be near Coralee, to help her. But he forced himself to bid the ladies good-night and gather the pink-cheeked, droopy-eyed twins to return to the boardinghouse.

He settled the children in bed, but they didn't stay there. He heard Louisa's sniffles first. Then Phillip whimpered for his mama. Jake's heart ached. He had wondered if the children would ask about their parents eventually. Pushing back the covers, he climbed out of bed and settled himself between the twins on the floor. Phillip started to sob. "I miss Mama."

Jake held him close. "I know, Phillip. I'm so sorry."

Louisa snuggled close on his other side. "When Mama coming back?"

His eyes slid shut as a wave of sadness washed over him. "She can't come back, sweetie. I get to take care of you for a little while, but soon you'll have a family to stay with forever. You'll love them, I know it."

The tears continued for several long moments. Jake didn't know what to do besides hold the little ones tight and murmur what he hoped were comforting words. Finally the sobs quieted and both children fell asleep, heads resting on his chest.

Even after such a long, tiring day, he tossed and turned, unable to get comfortable on the floor with little bodies draped over him. Worries plagued him, first about the twins, then about Coralee. He hadn't known business was that slow at Holbrook's. Coralee had told him that Dr. Jay was impacting her customers. Jake had assumed it was just a few easily swayed patients overreacting to the doctor's negativity. But seeing how upset the usually unflappable Cat had been at dinner, he suspected things were worse than Coralee had let on.

Jake rolled to his other side as carefully as possible, trying to find a comfortable spot without waking the twins. Instinctively he wanted to fix the problem for Coralee. He was caught between her and Dr. Jay, feeling loyal to each of them in different ways. Maybe that made him the perfect person to defuse the situation. A surge of determination helped Jake's mind settle. He had a plan. Finally he relaxed into sleep alongside the twins.

Morning dawned bright and cheery, matching Jake's mood. He was ready to solve some problems. Even the twins' orneriness didn't diminish his optimism.

All through breakfast, Phillip insisted on smacking his spoon on the table, sending bits of food flying everywhere—and garnering disapproving looks from the other patrons. Louisa appeared to be the picture of good behavior. Until Jake helped her out of her chair after the meal and found every bite he'd thought she'd eaten stashed in the folds of her dress. Picking up the bits of food from the floor under the table made them late once again.

But Jake was steadfast. He had realized last night that his approach to Coralee was all wrong. He had been defensive, deflecting her criticism of Samuel every time the doctor's name came up. Jake decided that rather than just hoping to avoid the topic, he could work on winning her trust. If he took the time to get involved in her work and what was happen-

ing in the shop, maybe he could gain her confidence
again. Then he could show her the situation from his
perspective and she would see that Samuel wasn't as
bad as she thought.

Chapter Four

Getting dressed the next morning, Coralee felt a renewed drive to work on Papa's formula. Cat's frustration with their lack of customers had reminded Coralee how important her project was. Just as she finished twisting the last strand of her hair into a low chignon, she heard Jake and the twins in the parlor with Cecilia. Before she even stepped all the way into the room, Coralee could see his eyes gleaming. She stifled a laugh. He couldn't seem to stay still, almost bouncing in place.

"You look like a child waiting to open a gift. What's so exciting?"

His grin broadened. "I hoped you would let me work with you at the shop some today. Another pair of hands. The work you showed me last night was fascinating."

"Oh." She tried to think, but her mind felt fuzzy. Did she want Jake by her side at the shop while she worked on Papa's project? He stood watching her, near to bursting with enthusiasm. It was hard to resist. She found herself thinking it might be nice to share the work with someone. Her sisters and aunt were supportive, but they didn't have the least bit of interest in medicine. Even Cat didn't care to discuss remedies, in spite of all the time she spent at the shop.

Lightness swept through her. It might be helpful to have Jake around. She gestured for him to come along and took Louisa's hand as the four of them headed to the door. They walked down the boardwalk, Louisa toddling next to Coralee. The little girl was happy to be where there were people, head swiveling to watch everyone they passed. Phillip, on the other hand, tried to run for the rocks that lined the edge of the busy street. Jake held him tight. "Phillip, you must hold my hand."

Phillip stopped pulling at his hand, but only for a moment. A dog outside the livery stable caught the boy's attention and he tried to take off again. "Dog, Jake. Want to see dog. Pease?"

"No, Phillip, we can't go see that dog. We don't know if it's a nice dog. Please stay with me." After much wrestling, Jake managed to get Phillip in his arms so they could walk past the dog without the boy running off after it.

The exchange wasn't extraordinary, but Coralee was engrossed in the scene. Watching Jake fathering the twins so naturally was bittersweet. She was thrilled that Jake was gaining confidence with the children in leaps and bounds. Their parents would

have wanted them to be with someone who cared
for them and who was trying so hard to be a good
guardian. They would have loved the way Jake cared
for the twins.

But at the same time, Coralee's heart ached that
she would never see children of her own with a father
who cherished them like Jake cherished the twins.
It was a relief to finally enter Holbrook's. The twins
ran to greet Cat with loud excitement. Working on
the medication would be a good distraction from all
the feelings the twins' presence dredged up.

At the shop, Cat feigned reluctance as she agreed
to keep an eye on the twins while Coralee and Jake
worked. But Coralee knew better. Her sister was
bored to tears without customers in the shop. She
felt better about asking when she saw Cat's affec-
tionate response as the twins clambered all over her.
Maybe she enjoyed the children more than she let on.

Coralee stepped into the workroom, swallowing
hard when Jake followed her in. The room seemed
to shrink with his presence. She grabbed some of her
tools. The best course of action was to get involved
in the work as soon as possible so her mind didn't
wander. "You saw last night where I left off with
Papa's research before the cholera outbreak. I think
right now we can begin a new ingredient."

Jake moved closer. She felt his eyes on her as
she started grinding some dried onion with Papa's
marble mortar and pestle. "We'll start by using the
onion powder to make a liniment and some to dis-
solve in water. I've heard of women who use the juice

of cooked onions for several remedies, so we'll move on to that next."

"Onion? That's just an old folk remedy. I saw it on your list, but I didn't think you'd really consider using it." She turned to look at him, noting a slight frown on his face. Didn't he think she knew the difference between a reasonable option and an old wives' tale?

She pursed her lips. "Yes, Jake. I know the origin of using onion medicinally. And I am still going to test it. I could never be certain of my results if I skipped any items." She didn't tell him how hard she'd had to fight Papa to get the remedy on his list. She had good reason to include it, but Papa had been sure herbal remedies wouldn't produce the results he was looking for. She didn't want to have the same argument with Jake now.

He raised his palms and took a step back. "I didn't mean to imply you're making a mistake. I'm used to a more modern approach. I'll help with any mixture you want to try. You're the boss." The eager light shone in his eyes again. He was actually enjoying this process. And he was willing to work on what she wanted, without criticism. That was a change from the man she remembered.

Standing next to Jake in the shop brought to mind moments that were branded in her memory from the years he had helped her and Papa. There were the moments that had made her fall in love with him, of course. But also the moments she had relived time and again since he'd left for medical school, unable to believe she hadn't noticed them when they happened.

Looking back, she was able to see all the times he had insisted they do things his way. The times he'd seemed to listen to what she had to say, then turned around and did what he'd wanted in the first place. If she hadn't been so blinded by her youthful feelings, maybe she would have seen it earlier. Maybe she would have realized he was more worried about what he wanted from their relationship than about her feelings.

But now here he was, encouraging her to follow her process even though he doubted the ingredient. Calm washed over her, a stark change from the anxiety that had settled in the pit of her stomach the last few days. Jake helping with her research might not be such a burden, after all. Maybe he had changed more than she realized.

They worked side by side for several hours that morning, grinding, measuring and mixing. After lunch at the café, Jake returned to the clinic and Coralee took the twins back home for naps.

The rest of the week followed a similar pattern. Jake would bring Louisa and Phillip to Coralee every morning. He spent time at the clinic or traveling out of town to visit patients when needed, but for several days, he worked with Coralee at Holbrook's.

With the help of her sisters, Coralee was able to keep the twins for Jake while also putting time into her research. By the next week, she was testing the last item on Papa's list. With no success. The two patients who had tried the last few formulas for her both reported no improvement in their level of pain. Nothing worked well enough to advertise and draw new customers into the shop. And Coralee refused to make false claims with a medication that didn't work. Heart heavy, she cleaned up the last experiment and filed Papa's notes away in the cabinet.

She left the workroom and joined Cat in wiping down the dozens of glass bottles that lined the shelves in the shop. The daily task was usually rather therapeutic. But today the repetitive task wasn't helping Coralee relax. The bell over the door jingled, the merry sound setting her nerves further on edge. She turned to see Jake removing his hat as the door swung closed behind him.

"Good afternoon, ladies. No testing on this lovely day, Coralee?"

His cheerful voice made Coralee's sour mood worse. "No, Jake. I've worked through Papa's entire list. And before you ask, no, nothing worked. My patients were both in yesterday to tell me those last few remedies didn't help one bit."

He sobered at her words. "I'm sorry. I know how much you wanted—needed—something to come from the research." He paused, long fingers turning the brim of his hat. "Since you hit a wall with your experiment, maybe you could focus on other ways to get customers back in the shop."

Coralee turned away, grabbing a bottle from the shelf in front of her and wiping it for all she was worth. Tears stung her eyes. She had failed. Papa had entrusted her with his shop and his project and she hadn't been successful with either one. If she couldn't manage the promising idea Papa had started for her, how would she come up with anything new to improve their business?

But Cat was quick to agree with Jake's comment. "We could have such fun with the shop, Coralee. Special sales, interesting advertisements. We could run a contest." Her youngest sister was almost ready to jump up and down, her eyes sparkling. Of course. Anything that seemed like fun and games would get Cat's attention in a heartbeat.

Coralee faced her sister, back straight and chin high. "I won't have this shop become a circus, Cat."

Cat stepped back, excitement draining from her face. Guilt chased away the frustration that had been building in Coralee. Once again, her feelings about the shop had caused her to lash out and hurt someone she loved. Taking a deep breath, she rested a hand on Cat's shoulder. "I'm sorry. That was harsh and you didn't deserve it."

She glanced at Jake, not sure if she wanted to continue with him there. But he had been so supportive while they'd tested her last few formulas. She wanted to trust him. "This project was important to Papa and I feel as if I've failed him." The tears were welling up again, but this time she couldn't stop them. "Dr. Jay will get what he wanted all this time, after all."

She stiffened when Jake's arms came around her, pulling her close. For a moment she didn't know what to do. But it felt so natural to be this close to him that she couldn't help but relax into his embrace. As the tears slowed, she became aware of the scent and warmth of his skin. She hadn't realized until this moment how much she missed Alan's touch.

As lovely as it felt, Coralee knew she didn't have any right to enjoy Jake's embrace. She pulled away, wiping at her eyes. She couldn't meet Cat's gaze, but felt her sister watching with interest. Cat would certainly have something to say about that hug when Jake was gone.

"I guess we have to do something to get customers in again, even if it isn't selling Papa's medication." She forced herself to look at Jake and Cat in turn, hoping she wouldn't see pity in their eyes. "Let's come up with some ideas."

Jake spoke up right away as if he had already thought through the problem. Almost as if he had expected her experiments to fail. She shook off the thought, determined to give trusting Jake a try. "I saw some interesting promotions run by various stores in St. Louis. I was thinking a few of those ideas might do well in this situation."

The three of them brainstormed for another half hour before Coralee realized the time. "We'd better get home to relieve Cecilia of the twins." As she and Jake walked back, her head swirled with the ideas they had talked about. A small seed of excitement was taking root for the first time in months. Maybe Papa's project wasn't the only way to revitalize Holbrook's, after all.

* * *

On Saturday, Jake woke looking forward to spending the day with Louisa and Phillip. Those two had burrowed into his heart faster than he could have imagined possible. Several nights before, he had found himself awake in the early hours when both children crawled into bed with him. Their little bodies snuggled close, so trusting and innocent, had cemented what he was starting to admit to himself: he loved them. Letting them go when they found a family would be one of the hardest things he had ever done.

Jake drove the twins to his parents' farm for a few hours that morning. As soon as he stopped the wagon, Phillip tried to jump off the seat, anxious to run, as always. Jake grabbed the boy, swinging him wildly down from the wagon before letting him go. The resulting giggle warmed his heart. Louisa sat on the seat, waiting like a tiny lady for Jake to help her out of the wagon. He planted a soft kiss in her hair as he lowered her to the ground.

"Jake, my dear. Nothing could make a mother prouder than seeing her son caring so well for these sweet, orphaned children."

He turned to face Ma, her words making him feel self-conscious. "They make it pretty easy. I'm the one who still isn't sure what he's doing." He greeted her with a hug and offered his arm to escort her back to the house. They joined Pa on the porch, where he was enjoying the shade in a handmade rocking chair.

"Tell us about your week, son." Even as he spoke,

Pa's eyes followed Louisa and Phillip around the yard, a smile playing on his lips.

"The twins seem to be adjusting well to our schedule. They've had moments of missing their parents, which is heartbreaking. But those moments are getting less frequent and they're happy most of the time. Coralee, Cat and Cecilia have been invaluable."

"I heard this week that you're spending time at Holbrook's as well as the clinic." Ma's expression was carefully neutral. Jake sighed, not at all surprised that the chain of gossip in their small town had already reached his mother's ears. She was a wonderful woman, but the grapevine of information ran straight through her.

"I'm helping Coralee with some new promotions at the shop. I assure you, there's nothing else going on."

"Oh, I am glad to hear that you're working with Coralee. You were so angry with her before. I hope that's changed?"

He considered that for a moment, realizing he hadn't thought about her betrayal in some time. But there was still a pang of hurt when Ma brought it up. "I'm not angry, exactly. She's…different than when we were growing up. More selfless and thoughtful. I've seen how generous she is with patients, but she also treats them with great dignity and respect. And she loves Louisa and Phillip."

Pictures of her with the twins filled his mind, making him smile. "She's completely natural with them." He turned to his mother. "But pain like she caused doesn't just disappear. I can handle spending time with her because no matter how hard I try, I still care about what happens to her and her family. But I can't let her back in my heart."

Ma tilted her head toward him, a sad smile softening her face. "Then I'll keep up my prayers that you'll be able to forgive her someday. It's the only thing that will heal both of you." She patted his hand as she rose. "Now, I'm going to take the children to visit my chickens."

Jake and his father sat listening as the voices of Ma and the twins floated on the breeze. Pa shifted in his chair, rubbing his chin with one hand. "Son, I think you need to consider your part in what happened before you decide you get to keep holding a grudge. Coralee deserves an apology as much as you do."

He stared at Pa for a moment, dumbfounded. What did he need to apologize for?

Pa shook his head and sighed. "Jake, do you remember what you told me about that night?"

Jake tried to think back. "I told you I was going to propose to her, but before I got the chance, she got mad and stormed out."

"When you got home that night, you said the first thing you did was tell her about medical school. Look at it from her perspective. You spent all that time with her, acted like you cared for her, but then announced you were leaving. Before you told her about your feelings or asked her to marry you. Did she even know you'd applied to that school in St. Louis?"

Realization dawned and his heart dropped. "Oh, no. She had no idea I planned to go to St. Louis. Until I told her I was leaving just a few weeks later." His head thumped the chair as he slumped back. "Pa, you're right. The things she must have thought of me."

His father chuckled. "Son, I hoped you would realize this yourself a long time ago. But we all make mistakes where women are concerned. Just be glad you get a chance to make it right now."

"I don't know how I can. So much time has passed." And there were so many hurts piled up for both of them.

But Pa shook his head and clucked his tongue. "It's never too late to apologize, Jake. Don't keep putting it off."

Jake tried to enjoy the rest of the time with his parents. But in the back of his mind, he couldn't reconcile his pain with Pa's insistence that he needed to apologize to Coralee. She had hurt him just as much, if not more, than anything he had done to her. Sure, he had approached telling her about school the wrong way. But did that justify her response? From what he could see, she had run straight to Alan without a second thought.

On the other hand, Pa seemed to think Jake needed to take responsibility. Maybe if he tried to explain his side of that night to Coralee, it would help him get past the pain she had caused. He decided it was worth a try. The worst that could happen would be that they would fight again, and there was nothing unusual in that.

He got his chance after church the next day. After the service, he left the twins with his parents and went in search of Coralee. His first glimpse of her across the churchyard made his heart race. She was beautiful in a simple, striped dress, with a woven bonnet that framed her face. But a burning sensation filled his chest when he saw that she was laughing and talking with a tall, slender man. She leaned toward the fellow, resting her hand on his arm in a way that struck Jake as far too familiar. Surely she would have told him if she was courting someone. Or one of her sisters would have mentioned it.

Jake approached the pair, noting the abrupt halt in their conversation when he stepped into earshot.

"Good afternoon, Coralee." He nodded at each of them, determined to stay civil. But he placed himself as close to Coralee as propriety allowed while holding out a hand to her companion. "I'm Jake Hadley."

The other man took his hand with a firm grip. "Charlie Albridge. I run the bank over on First Street."

Jake tipped his head in greeting then turned away from the banker, speaking in a low voice for Coralee's ears alone. "There are some things I'd like to discuss, if you can spare some time."

She glanced between the two men before responding. "I'm sorry, Jake. I have an appointment with Charlie over lunch. Maybe we can talk later this week when you bring the twins in."

Something hard and tight lodged in Jake's stomach as he watched Coralee take Charlie's arm and walk away.

Jake had no right to her attention. He wasn't even sure he wanted it. But that didn't mean he was going to be happy about some other man spending time with her.

On Monday morning Coralee spent a few hours nailing up signs for the new promotions they had planned for the shop. She tried to stay hopeful, but by afternoon, worry had set in again. The signs advertising special sales on their products did nothing to get people into the shop that day. She knew she needed to give it a few days or even weeks to see the effectiveness. But she had wanted to see customers rush back into Holbrook's. The people of Spring Hill used to love the shop. She wished that could be enough to bring them back.

She and Cat attempted to stay busy on Tuesday by preparing some basic remedies and organizing the shelves. Coralee tried to hold tight to the small sliver of hope that remained in her. She insisted they prepare in case there was a rush of customers in the next few days.

Cat took the day off on Wednesday. It had been two days and they hadn't seen any extra customers. Cat promised to check in later in the day, in case the shop got busy, but Coralee just shook her head. There was no point in hoping.

When Jake and the twins walked into the shop

that morning, Coralee was at one of the small tables across from the counter, trying to keep herself together. She managed a tight smile when the twins yelled their exuberant greetings. Phillip launched himself into her arms and she cradled him close, burying her face in his soft hair. The boy rested his chubby hands on either side of her face. "Coree sad?"

Her heart nearly burst at his sweetness. She forced a more cheerful demeanor for his sake. "Not now that you're here." He smiled and snuggled close again.

"The signs look great, Coralee. Have you had many customers?" Jake's fingers drummed on the counter. He almost looked as enthusiastic as Phillip. She hated to disappoint him. He and Cat had been so sure their promotions would work.

She let Phillip down to join Louisa behind the counter and shook her head. "I've noticed people looking at the signs, but no one has come in." She turned to face him head-on. "I know it's because of Dr. Jay, Jake. Maybe you still don't want to believe it, but he's made his patients distrust me."

He sighed. "Are we going to get into this again? Samuel is a good man. He wouldn't spread untruths to make his patients stop coming here."

"Then why aren't they? You admitted he doesn't want me running the shop. How is it so hard for you to believe that he would go a step further and try to stop me?" She crossed her arms and leaned one hip against the counter, waiting for his excuse.

His lips pressed into a firm line. "What I understand is that you keep blaming him for something I've seen no evidence of."

"Just because you haven't seen him telling people not to come here doesn't mean he hasn't. He's been away most of the time since you got here. You don't know what he would or wouldn't do."

Jake turned away for a moment then looked back at her, face softening. "I don't think we're going to come to an agreement on this by arguing. And I don't want to argue anymore." He stepped closer, leaning against the counter, just inches away from her. "Is that really what you're most upset about, anyway?"

She felt like she was melting under those deep brown eyes, sinking into feelings she didn't want to have for Jake.

Coralee turned away, focusing on the twins' laughter as it floated from the workroom where they were stacking empty tins like blocks. "I suppose you're right. No matter what Dr. Jay has said to his patients, I'm the one responsible for the shop's success or failure." She faced him again, longing for someone to understand the swirling emotions that kept threatening to overwhelm her. "I know Papa's medicine is the answer. There's something he missed that would solve the problem, an ingredient he didn't think about. But I don't know where to start to find it."

Her eyes locked on Jake's when his hand came up to lightly touch her cheek. "I know his work is important to you. I'm sorry if I haven't supported your efforts enough." His words, combined with an intimate smile, took her breath away. The bell over the shop door jingled and they jumped back from each other, the fragile moment shattered.

Jake coughed weakly when they turned and found his mother watching them with a knowing smile. Amusement flashed in her eyes as Beth hugged her son in greeting. "I wasn't sure if you'd be here today, Jake. I saw the lovely signs and decided to stop in and see how things are going." She turned to Coralee and pulled her into a hug, as well.

Louisa and Phillip must have recognized her voice. They raced from the workroom, almost knocking Beth over as they threw themselves at her. Laughing, she knelt and spoke to them with mock sternness. "Have you both been my good little darlings today?"

The twins nodded, bouncing on their toes with restrained excitement. Clearly they knew what was coming next. "Excellent. That means you deserve this." Beth pulled two peppermint sticks from behind her back. Shouting with joy, Louisa and Phillip took the treats and ran off to enjoy them.

"Jake, those children are just delightful." Beth's proud grin looked just like any grandparent's Coralee had ever seen. How would Jake's family react when the children went to a permanent home? She pulled her attention back to the conversation just in time to hear Jake bring up Papa's formula.

"Ma, Coralee and I were just discussing an issue with a medicine she's working on. Your mother had quite a few good pain remedies, is that right?"

"Oh, yes, Mama was quite good with herbs. Her mother was Pawnee, you know. She used several things for pain. Ginger, lavender, peppermint. Her favorite was a tea made from willow bark."

Beth kept talking about her mother, but Coralee couldn't follow the words. Willow bark. Of course. It was in many of the curatives on her shelves, but not in Papa's notes. Maybe he hadn't gotten to finish his list, after all. Her mind whirled with possibilities.

After a few more minutes of small talk, Beth said her goodbyes. Coralee just waved, distracted. Should she grind the bark and press the powder into tablets? Or would it be best as a tea? She looked up when Jake cleared his throat to find him watching her with eyebrows raised.

"I was going to leave the twins with you for a few hours, but if you want to work, I can stay and help."

Coralee hesitated. It had been wonderful having someone work with her on the last few ingredients. Jake was always interested in her process and results. But this project was so important to her. Did she want to share her moment of discovery with him?

Of its own accord, her head started nodding and she found that she did want him there. She couldn't imagine finishing the project without him after all his help. His wide grin in response was worth the risk. Knowing he wanted to do this with her made it even more exhilarating. Shaking off the unprofessional thoughts that tried to rise, Coralee squared her shoulders and headed to the workroom, Jake trailing behind.

"I don't have any willow bark in the shop right now. Do you mind taking a walk out to the creek with me to gather some?" She flushed at how hard her heart was pounding while she waited for his answer. What did it matter if he didn't want to go?

But he nodded and called the children over. "Sounds like a fun trip. Let's go."

Coralee went to the cabinet at the back of the workroom and placed a large, sheathed knife and several cloths in a basket. She put the closed sign in the window and locked up the shop as they herded the children out.

Warm midday sun beat down as they walked to the creek that snaked past the edge of Spring Hill. The tall grass crunched under their feet. It had been too long since they'd had a good rain.

Coralee picked Louisa up and pulled her bonnet forward to shade her little face better. "Louisa, can you point to your eyes?"

Louisa's little face scrunched up as she put a finger next to each of her eyes.

"Very good. How about your nose?"

This time, Louisa pointed to her nose right away. "Nose!"

"How smart you are. Where are your ears?"

With a happy laugh, the little girl grabbed both ears.

Feeling lighter than she had in weeks, Coralee chuckled along with her, pleased with how much the little girl knew.

When they reached the edge of the creek, Coralee set Louisa on her feet and pointed at a familiar wispy, low-hanging tree. "I'll just cut a section and be right back."

But Jake took hold of the knife before she could. "No, I can get it so you don't risk getting that pretty dress wet."

Her heart danced behind her ribs. He thought her dress was pretty? She tugged at the skirt. It was just a plain, cotton work dress. "Do you know how to cut it?"

He grinned. "I couldn't forget after your father made me practice every time he needed bark."

A smile played on her lips as she watched Jake jog down the bank and jump onto a fallen log to get close to the willow tree. He scored a rectangle of bark with the knife then carefully peeled it off. She hadn't expected him to perform the task with such ease after years without practice.

Papa had taught Coralee not to take too much bark at a time from one tree. So they stopped at two more willows nearby. The last one shaded a lovely shallow bend in the creek. Jake turned to her with an enticing look that made butterflies break out in her stomach. "How about stopping for a quick wade before we get to work?"

She hesitated, glancing around. They were away from any buildings, but still within view of the town. Her professional reputation was already in question with most of the town, thanks to Dr. Jay. A fun dip in the cool water sounded wonderful. But Coralee couldn't take the chance that someone would see the proprietress of Holbrook's Apothecary gallivanting in the creek. And with a man, no less. She shook her head firmly. "That sounds nice, but I'd like to get started on that bark."

Regret pricked at her when his face fell. But he just nodded and swung Louisa up into his arms. "Then we'll head back to the shop. Let's race, Phillip." He took off at a slow pace, letting the little boy keep up with him while he bounced Louisa, making her laugh.

When they arrived at the shop, Coralee went right to work shredding one of the sections of bark. Jake set up her equipment, knowing exactly what she would need. At some point, Cecilia arrived and took the twins to have a nap, but Coralee hardly noticed. By the end of the afternoon, she and Jake had several forms of curatives made from the willow bark. And Coralee was exhausted but satisfied. Finally she knew they were on the right track.

Chapter Five

Jake had loved watching Coralee in her element while they'd worked on the willow bark. Her father had usually stuck to remedies with a well-known recipe. He had never been one for experimenting. That Mr. Holbrook had even come up with the idea to create a new medication had surprised Jake.

But Coralee's personality was perfect for the process of discovery. He could see how much she loved the trial and error, making careful notes and checking items off her lists. When they were growing up, Jake had never seen the side of her that thrived on solving problems. He found it fascinating to watch.

As fun as it was to see her at work, he knew the next day he had to spend a little more time at the clinic. He still loved seeing patients, but it was getting harder and harder for him to sit in the office alone when he didn't have anyone to call on.

In St. Louis, work at the hospital and his classes had kept him busy nearly every minute. Any time he could carve out to sit by himself was a relief. But since he'd started helping Coralee at the shop, the hours he needed to spend at the clinic catching up on paperwork were too quiet. His mind kept wandering to Coralee and the twins. He wondered what they were doing at that moment, wishing he could stack up the patient files and go to the shop instead.

Around noon the door opened and a well-dressed man entered. He didn't speak to Jake at first, examining the room with interest as he removed his hat. Jake stood from his desk to greet the stranger. "Welcome. I'm Dr. Hadley. What can I do for you today?"

The man shook his hand with a firm grip and nodded his greeting. "I'm Charles Johnson. The American Pharmaceutical Association sent me from Philadelphia to speak with a Dr. Samuel Jay?" One eyebrow rose in question as he glanced around the empty clinic.

"Dr. Jay is currently out of town. I'm his associate. Perhaps I can help?" Jake had to admit, curiosity was getting the best of him. What would a representative from the assembly of pharmacists and apothecaries need with Samuel?

"Well, I suppose since you're a physician, as well, you could be of some help. It's been brought to our attention that a facility operating here in Spring Hill may have some questionable practices."

Understanding hit Jake with all the force of a railway car. This man was in town to investigate Holbrook's. And Coralee. "I can assure you, Mr.

Johnson, the only apothecary shop in this town is Holbrook's and they are above reproach."

Mr. Johnson's eyes narrowed. "I believe that will be for me to decide. It appears I can already guess at your views of the facility, so I'll just ask you to point me in the direction of the shop."

Even though he was several inches shorter, Mr. Johnson managed to look down his nose at Jake while he waited for a response. Jake couldn't let this pompous little man project his bias on an unsuspecting Coralee.

"I wouldn't be a good citizen if I let a visitor to our fine town get lost. I'll walk you over." He didn't let the man protest as he ushered him to the door and locked up. He did his best to keep up a running commentary as they walked, giving Mr. Johnson all the details he could think of about the town. He wasn't going to let the fellow talk his way into going to Holbrook's alone.

Jake held the door for Mr. Johnson at the shop, noticing that Coralee was in the back. He made sure to call for her before the other man could dismiss him. "Coralee? There's a special visitor from Philadelphia here to meet you."

Coralee came out of the workroom, wiping her hands on her apron. The smell of steeping tea wafted out of the room with her. Jake stepped closer to her as he made the introductions. "Mr. Johnson, this is Coralee…Evans, proprietress of Holbrook's Apothecary. Mrs. Evans, this is Charles Johnson." Even in the midst of trying to protect her, Jake choked as he said Coralee's married name. Would the pain of her betrayal ever truly heal?

Thankfully, no one noticed Jake's hesitation. A welcoming smile lit Coralee's face as she extended a hand to shake Mr. Johnson's. "It's quite a trip from Philadelphia, Mr. Johnson. What brings you clear out to little Spring Hill?"

"I've come at the request of the American Pharmaceutical Association to examine this facility and its operators. It's our responsibility to ensure that the quality of operations is up to certain standards. We have received a complaint that leads us to believe your work here is not."

Coralee went pale. "From whom? Who is that unhappy with the shop?"

"I'm sorry, I can't reveal the source of a complaint. But we take each and every one of them quite seriously."

Jake saw her relax her clenched hands and straighten her shoulders. She was fighting hard to keep herself together in front of this stranger. Jake felt a burst of pride. That was the girl he remembered.

"Mr. Johnson, I am confident you'll find only the highest quality of work here at Holbrook's. But, of course, we'll cooperate with anything you need."

Mr. Johnson set his bag on one of the tables. "Then I'll just set up my materials over here and we'll get started examining your selection of curatives." He leaned closer, lips pursed as he looked Coralee over from head to toe. "I haven't inspected a facility run by a woman before, but be advised that I will not go easy on you because of it."

Coralee raised her chin and marched to a shelf with Mr. Johnson following. Jake stood back, forcing his breath to come evenly. Something about this man got under his skin. It was clear that he wouldn't be spending much time at the clinic until this Mr. Johnson was out of their hair. He didn't trust the man to treat Coralee fairly.

All afternoon, Jake watched Coralee go through every bottle and tin with Mr. Johnson. The man questioned her time and again on the ingredients in each remedy, the common uses, even the shelf life. And with every correct answer, Jake wanted to smirk. Coralee was just as knowledgeable as any man who had been trained back east.

Late in the day, the shop bell jingled. Jake looked up to see a middle-aged woman, breathless and tear-streaked, heading for the table where he sat. "Doc, my husband fell out at the farm. He's bleeding and can't get up. His partner's out there with him, but he needs you real bad. Can you come?"

Jake's chest tightened at the thought of leaving Coralee alone with Mr. Johnson. But he had a job to do, a responsibility to the people of Spring Hill. "Of course, ma'am. I'll be right with you."

He walked over and pulled Coralee aside, speaking in a low voice. "I have to go, but I'm going to stop by your place on the way out and have Cat come over." He searched her eyes for any hint of discomfort. "You can handle things here until she arrives?"

She nodded and threw a glance at Mr. Johnson over her shoulder. "He's not dangerous, Jake. I can certainly tolerate an irritating person for a few hours if it means keeping the shop's name respectable."

He couldn't help a smile. That was the Coralee he had known for years. Strong, confident, self-assured. She would indeed manage the situation just fine. He tipped his hat to her and Mr. Johnson and left to care for his newest patient.

Coralee was growing increasingly frustrated with Mr. Johnson. She was on the verge of testing her new medicine and wanted to focus on it. But this man waltzed into her shop uninvited, accusing her of negligent practices, and proceeded to treat her like a criminal. They had spent all afternoon and into the evening going through every one of her remedies. It was clear that he was waiting for her to slip up. But Papa had taught her well and she fielded his interrogation with no problems.

When Cat arrived not long after Jake left, Coralee could see she shared the same dislike of the situation. Cat had never been able to hide her feelings well. Coralee was very glad that Mr. Johnson's back was turned to her sister most of the time. His lacking sense of humor would only lead to problems if he saw Cat's long-suffering eye-rolls or condescending smirks.

Nonetheless, Coralee was thankful Jake had sent Cat over when he'd had to leave. Mr. Johnson had seemed to dislike her from the moment he'd walked in. Oh, he was courteous enough. She didn't think he would do anything untoward. But knowing that this complete stranger wanted her to fail was disconcerting. And it reminded her all too much of Dr. Jay's unreasonable dislike. She had a suspicion that the anonymous source that led Mr. Johnson to travel here had been none other than the old doctor.

Finally, Mr. Johnson glanced at his pocket watch and flipped his notebook shut. "I believe we should call it a night, Mrs. Evans." She nearly sighed in relief but didn't want to give him any reason to doubt she was capable of handling the shop. "I'll come by tomorrow and we can discuss the next step." She nodded and saw him out. As soon as he was past the large glass window, she collapsed at the table with Cat and dropped her head into her hands.

"Coralee, that was impressive. The man is a dunce, but you handled him well. Better than I ever could have."

They both chuckled. If Cat was in charge, she might have thrown the man out on his ear before he'd taken two steps into the shop. But too much was at stake for Coralee to send him packing. He couldn't force them to close the shop, but, combined with Dr. Jay's efforts against her, word of another negative opinion would discredit her entirely. No amount of work on Papa's project would make the town trust her again if an official Association representative declared that she was negligent. No, it was better to put up with him until he was satisfied and left them alone.

But after a night of little sleep and a great deal of worry, Coralee wasn't sure she was ready to face another day of Mr. Johnson's questioning. She felt tense and crabby by the time she arrived at the shop that morning. But when she caught sight of a familiar tall figure leaning against the corner of the building, it all melted away. A smile lifted the corners of her lips.

"Good morning, Jake. I didn't expect to see you waiting here at this early hour."

He grinned as he turned to face her and her breath caught. "I wanted to see how the rest of your day went with Mr. Johnson."

She stopped in front of him, maybe closer than necessary, but she couldn't seem to help herself. "It was the same as when you were here. He didn't let up until late and he's coming back today."

Jake's jaw clenched. Did he disapprove of her cooperating with Mr. Johnson?

"Then I'll stay." She started to protest. She had monopolized so much of his time already. His patients needed him. And she didn't want all the town gossip to start revolving around the widow apothecary and the eligible doctor.

But Jake cupped her elbow with one hand and guided her toward the shop door. "I can stay. People know how to find me if they need me. Just like when I'm helping out at my parents' farm."

She was thankful to have Jake's silent support when Mr. Johnson walked in a half hour later. The man looked utterly dour. "I hope you had a nice evening, Mr. Johnson." She tried to be as civil as possible, given that she wished he was anywhere but in her shop. "Our town is usually quite peaceful and quaint."

He just harrumphed and dropped his bag on a table with a thump. As Mr. Johnson rummaged around in the bag, Jake quirked an eyebrow at Coralee. She did her best to stifle a giggle before Mr. Johnson turned and saw her laughing at him.

"Now, Mrs. Evans. Let's sit and chat." She joined Mr. Johnson at the small table, heart racing. Was he about to tell her he would try to get her run out of business?

But to her surprise, he leaned back in the chair, fingers steepled over his vest, looking relaxed. "I believe I need to offer you an apology. I came here certain that I would have to report this facility to the Association with evidence that it is not being run properly." Coralee's heart sank. He felt bad, but he was still going to give an unfavorable report of the shop.

"But I've been surprised. You have an unexpected depth of knowledge that some of the men in our Association don't even possess."

Pride welled in her. If only Papa could have heard those words.

Mr. Johnson continued with a smile that looked out of place on his usually grim face. "I would like to recommend that you pursue admission into the Association." He adjusted his jacket sleeves, waiting for her answer. But Coralee was speechless.

"Won't the leadership balk at the idea of a woman applying for admittance?"

He tipped his head to one side with a slight shrug. "It's possible. But the bylaws in no way prohibit female entrants. And if you score as well on the entrance examination as I expect, the leadership will have no choice but to admit you." A hint of sly amusement crossed his face. Coralee was shocked to realize that Mr. Johnson was a rebel deep inside.

Her eyes strayed to Jake, sitting at the table behind Mr. Johnson, watching the entire scene. He met her gaze with wide eyes and a shrug. She knew what he was thinking: was this what she wanted?

"I'll think on it, Mr. Johnson." She shook his hand as they stood.

"Yes, fine." He pulled a sheaf of papers from his bag and handed them to her. "Here you'll find all the necessary paperwork. If you decide to proceed, a proctor will come to administer the examination after we receive your application. There's a guide to the examination here, as well. I hope it will go well for you, Mrs. Evans." He smiled at Coralee, nodded at Jake and took his leave.

Once he was gone, Jake faced Coralee. His grin turned into laughter, a deep, resonant sound that made warmth spread through her. She couldn't help joining in. "Can you believe that?" She gasped the words between relieved giggles. "That unpleasant man turned out to be our accomplice."

Jake's gaze turned intense as their laughter faded. "I'm proud of how you handled the whole situation. I know I wouldn't have been as kind to someone who walked in trying to question my work."

She blushed. "It wasn't as easy as you seem to think. But I couldn't let my temper cause him to harm the shop." She remembered the papers in her hand and started shuffling through them. "Look at all this, Jake. The application alone is three pages long. All this is the guide for the examination." She held up a thick portion of the stack. "What if I don't know as much as Mr. Johnson thought?"

Jake grabbed the guide from her hands and flipped through it. "There's a lot to cover here, but you'll do just fine. I can help you. Between us, we'll find all the information you need to impress every member of that Association."

Coralee's excitement faded as reality set in. "Jake, I have to keep working on Papa's formula. I almost have it ready to test, but if it's successful I'll have to package and market it. And I promised Cat I would be at the shop more so she doesn't have to be here alone so much until business picks up."

He took her by the shoulders, dark eyes searching hers. "You're really going to pass up this opportunity?"

She met his intense gaze head-on, hoping he would try to understand her position. "There's too much at stake for me to split my focus between the medication and that examination."

Jake ran a hand through his hair. "But entrance into the Association would only benefit the shop. Can't you see that?"

Bristling at his tone, Coralee straightened her shoulders. "Of course I can. But that isn't the point. Jake, you always do this. The shop is my responsibility and I get to make this decision. Now instead of supporting my opinion, you're demanding that I have to do it your way. Well, I've had enough of that. I'm not taking the examination."

Seconds ticked past while their eyes remained locked. She could read the thoughts flashing across Jake's face. He almost argued with her again, but then his lips tightened into a thin line as he gave in. Shifting his eyes away, he turned toward the door. "I need to do some work at the clinic. I'll come by and pick up the twins tonight." He let himself out the door before she could react.

Heart heavy, Coralee spent the rest of the day putting the final touches on the test batches of her medication. She hated that they were back to fighting. Working on the medication with him had been a nice change from the usual tension. But she couldn't let him walk all over her just to keep the peace.

After a few more hours at the shop, she returned home to find Cat, Cecilia and the twins entertaining Charlie Albridge in the parlor. She removed her bonnet and hung it on a hook inside the door as she greeted the banker.

"Charlie, how nice to see you tonight." A wave of melancholic amusement washed over her. It was obvious to her that Spring Hill's banker had set his cap for Cat. He showed up at the oddest times with the excuse that he had business with Coralee. Then he ended up spending his visit glued to Cat's side. It was sweet, but also left Coralee fighting against the longing for a relationship she couldn't have.

To her surprise, Charlie handed Coralee a slim envelope as she took a seat near him and Cat. "Coralee, I wanted to speak with you about our last conversation. I drew up a summary of the loan terms I can offer you."

She pulled the sheet of paper out and read through the numbers, heart aching. The last thing she wanted to do was to owe the bank money when the shop wasn't bringing in much profit. But if the willow bark formula didn't work—and soon—she couldn't see any other solution to keeping the shop open.

She finished reading the paper and cleared her throat to get Charlie's attention. He had turned back to wooing Cat the moment Coralee had looked away. "Thank you for writing this up. Can I take some time to think about it? I'm very hopeful that our new medication will solve our financial problem."

"Of course. Just don't take too long. I can't guarantee those terms forever." A knock at the door kept him from saying more. Coralee's heart jumped into her throat. That had to be Jake, ready to get the twins. She answered the door and led him to the parlor. They had hardly taken one step into the room when Louisa and Phillip dropped their toys and ran to hug his legs, squealing in delight.

Coralee's heart felt ready to burst from her chest as she watched the scene unfold. Jake greeted each child with a hug then knelt in front of them. "Now, I want to hear about your day. What did you play?"

Louisa leaned in close to him, holding up the handkerchief doll Coralee had made for her. "I played dolly. Cece made a bow."

"And she looks beautiful. Phillip, what did you play?"

"Rocks."

"Did you dig in rocks? Or climb on rocks?"

"Licked them."

Jake laughed as he stood. "Well, that's a different way to play with them than I expected."

Phillip tugged on Jake's trouser leg. Jake picked the boy up. "Yes, Phillip?"

"I miss you."

Closing his eyes, Jake rested his forehead against Phillip's. "I missed you, too, pal."

It might have been the sweetest moment Coralee had ever witnessed. And it made her heart ache. Jake was turning out to be an amazing stand-in parent. Something deep within her longed to open up to him, to get close to him again. But as she watched him caring for the twins, she couldn't forget his response to her announcement about her inability to have a child. He wanted a family and she couldn't give him one. And just that day, his response to her decision about the examination had proved that he still wanted her to do things his way, no matter what she wanted. The answer was clear. Letting Jake into her heart would only lead to more pain.

* * *

All the joy that filled Jake when the twins ran to greet him melted away when he stepped farther into the house and saw Charlie Albridge sitting in Coralee's parlor. He found himself taking a side step closer to her as the twins ran off to play.

"Charlie. What brings you out to visit the Holbrook household this evening?"

"Oh, I had a bit of business with the ladies tonight. But they've invited me to stay and visit a bit now that professional matters are out of the way." Albridge smiled suavely at the women before turning narrowed eyes on Jake. "I'm sure you'll be happy to get on your way with the children after a long day."

Jake planted himself firmly in a chair without breaking eye contact with the other man. "I generally spend a few minutes visiting with the ladies, myself." Pleasure shot through his heart when Coralee took the seat nearest him. Maybe, in spite of their argument earlier, she still preferred his company to the banker's.

Cat turned to them, mischief sparkling in her eyes, cheeks rosy-pink. "Jake, we were just telling Charlie about some of the silly things we used to do as kids around here. He only moved to Spring Hill a few months ago so he hasn't heard the best stories yet."

Jake smiled at her infectious delight. "Did you tell him about your run-in with the river monster, Cat?"

Cat pursed her lips, but Jake knew her well

enough to see the slight twinkle still in her eyes. "Jake Hadley, don't you tell that story."

"Now, Cat, it's a classic cautionary tale. Mr. Albridge deserves to know about the dangers that exist in the area."

Cat laughed. "Fine, but Coralee has to tell it. It was her fault, after all."

They all turned to Coralee, who offered a bemused smile. "If you want me to, Cat, I'll tell it." Cat nodded and Coralee launched into the story.

"One year, on April Fool's Day, I was at the shop with Papa. An old man was telling him a tall tale about these gigantic fish they'd found in the Mississippi when he was a boy. Of course, it was all drivel, but Cat upset me the week before and I thought I had stumbled on a great way to get back at her."

Coralee's face glowed as she grew more comfortable with the telling. "That afternoon, I went to the creek, stuffed some burlap sacks with grass and a few rocks and threw them in. Then I ran home yelling for Cat to come see the river monster that had appeared in the creek. She ran back with me and I pointed out those lumpy sacks under the water."

She fought back laughter as she finished the story. "She was so excited to capture a real-life monster that she jumped right in the creek and dove down to those sacks. She came up dragging one and didn't realize what it was until she was clear up on the creek bank."

They all turned to Cat to see her response, laughing harder when she stuck out her tongue at Coralee.

The oldest sister just arched an eyebrow and continued. "She was spitting mad when she realized it was a prank. But I don't think she ever came up with one quite as good to get back at me."

Cat agreed and laughed, the rest of them joining in. Jake couldn't take his eyes off Coralee. He had loved her sense of humor when they were younger. Seeing her laughing and teasing again now brought memories flooding in. He forced back the longing that threatened to emerge. He couldn't ruin their tentative friendship by dwelling on what might have been.

As the laughter faded, Coralee turned to Cecilia. "How is the planning coming along for the Independence Day celebration?"

Cecilia rolled her eyes. "The women on that committee can't agree on a single thing. As the schoolteacher, they expect me to help. Or, more accurately, to do all the dirty work. But in spite of their bickering, they're managing to make things happen. It's going to be a lovely celebration, once it all comes together." Jake saw her eyes dart to the banker as she continued shyly. "Will you be able to attend this year, Charlie?"

"Yes, I'm planning to enjoy the festivities." He puffed out his chest and grabbed each lapel on his jacket with a tight fist. "After all, an upstanding banker must be a dedicated participant in his community." The women laughed, but Jake didn't find the man at all funny.

Happy chatter continued as the sisters discussed

the events planned for the holiday. Jake glanced at the twins and saw they were starting to tire as they played. He called them over, heart full to bursting when they both came and snuggled into his sides. He didn't want to leave, but they needed to get to bed. "Sorry to break up the fun, but I have two little people who need rest." He rose and gathered Louisa and Phillip in his arms, where they each curled against him and rested their heads on his shoulders.

He was pleased that they went right to sleep when he settled them in their little bed on the floor. But as he sat at the small desk in his room in an attempt to catch up on some reading, he found it was impossible to relax. The words he and Coralee had exchanged earlier in the day spun in his mind. It wasn't a conversation he wanted to relive.

Every moment he hadn't had his nose buried in paperwork at the clinic that afternoon, he had battled guilt. Coralee's comments had struck a nerve. It was hard to imagine, but in all the years they had known each other, he couldn't think of one time where they had disagreed and he had chosen to support what she wanted. How could he have ever thought she would accept a proposal from him after he had acted like such a fool for years?

Pa's words from the week before came back to mind. His father had seen that Jake had a tendency to barrel right over Coralee. And he had been right in saying that was what had made her so upset the night Jake had planned to propose to her. From her perspective, Jake had only been concerned with what he wanted, as always.

Jake put down his book, abandoning the pretense of reading. He wished he could go back in time and react better to finding Charlie Albridge visiting at Coralee's house that evening. Every time he saw the banker, jealousy took hold in Jake's heart. It seemed like he was always watching Coralee walk away toward another man. Just like she had run straight to Alan when things had gotten rough between them. That lingering thought lodged deep in Jake's heart, growing and gnawing at him for the rest of the week.

Chapter Six

Coralee leaned back in her chair, hoping the rock in the pit of her stomach would disappear. It felt like the shop workroom was closing in on her. Piles of labels and flyers for Papa's remedy littered the table in front of her, but she couldn't get into a rhythm of working on the materials.

She needed to get the new medication ready to launch at the Independence Day celebration. The booth they planned to set up would be Spring Hill's first introduction to it and she wanted everything to be perfect. The feedback she had gotten from her patients who'd tested the willow bark formula had been overwhelming. The remedy had helped. It had taken their pain away completely. And none of them had gotten sick or experienced hallucinations or any other terrible side effects. After all the hard work, worry and time, she had finally been successful in fulfilling Papa's dream.

But now they had to succeed in selling the remedy

and getting their customers back into Holbrook's. She stood and walked to the workroom window to look out at the beautiful summer morning. Her neighbors walked up and down the street, going about their daily business. They were already leery of Holbrook's thanks to Dr. Jay's claims that she wasn't qualified to run the shop. With that already in the backs of their minds, would they have any interest in the new medicine? What would happen if the town still chose to side with the old doctor?

She paced to the cabinets in the back of the room, focusing on the echoing steps of her heeled boots. Back to the window, where several children were running down the street, yelling as they chased each other. Back to the cabinets. She paused then grabbed a cloth and wiped at some fingerprints on the glass in the cabinet doors.

Jake's voice filled her head as she cleaned the glass. He would say that she was letting her fear get the better of her. And he would be right. But the shop meant so much. To her. To Papa. To her family. Even to her friendship with Jake. What if she failed the place that had been her life since she was a child?

Coralee straightened and put down the cloth. Her past and future, her family's security, Papa's legacy. It all depended on the shop remaining open. She would throw herself into selling the new medicine. When it took off—and it had to take off—things would improve.

Unable to stay still any longer, Coralee grabbed a stack of flyers. She passed Cat on the way to the shop door. "I'm going to go hang up these signs we made for the new medicine. I shouldn't be gone long. But I may bring the twins back so Cecilia can have the day to herself."

Cat just waved, busy packaging a batch of the medicine Coralee had finished earlier.

Leaving the shop, Coralee headed to the first spot where she planned to nail up handbills. Cat had designed the advertisements with a lovely, artistic flair. In a flawless hand, she had described the benefits of their new product. A showy line at the bottom announced that they would have a booth at the Independence Day celebration. The pages were quite eye-catching and Coralee was certain people were already taking an interest in them as she finished nailing up the last few.

Walking in the door at home, Coralee followed the sound of little voices into the kitchen. Louisa and Phillip were helping Cecilia dry dishes, their tiny hands wiping cloths ineffectually over each plate from breakfast. Coralee watched them from the doorway, emotions stirring. The darling children had lost so much, but still managed to be bright spots in her day. Every time she held or talked with them, another piece of her heart became theirs.

She pushed away from the door frame as she announced her presence. "Hello, Louisa and Phillip. Cecilia."

The twins turned, eyes lighting up when they saw her. "There Coree!" Chubby, wet hands reached for her. With a happy chuckle, she enveloped each child in a hug.

"How would you two like to go to the shop with me today?"

"Yes! Yes!" They danced around her, chanting loudly. She met Cecilia's eyes, waved goodbye over the noise and then led the twins outside. Taking one twin's hand in each of her own, they walked to Holbrook's. On the way, Phillip pointed at a large dog resting in the back of a wagon. "Look, dog. Woof!"

She laughed. "Very good, there's a big, brown dog."

Louisa pointed at a young mother carrying a newborn. "A baby, Coree."

"Oh, yes. What a sweet little baby." The little girl was delighted with the infant and Coralee realized what a loving big sister Louisa would be, if her permanent family happened to have more children. The idea brought a pang of loss. She would miss the twins terribly when she no longer had a reason to see them every day.

Shaking off the melancholy thoughts, Coralee focused on the children's joyous energy. She could have walked with them all day, rediscovering the fun in the most mundane sights through their eyes. When they arrived at the shop, she and the twins sat at the small tables across from the counter and drew pictures. Phillip scribbled his pencil in wild slashes across the paper, then tired of the activity and went to play with a large crate Cat had unloaded that morning. Louisa sat much longer, trying hard to control the pencil and color in the shapes Coralee drew for her.

They hadn't been back for long before the shop bell jingled and a woman Coralee didn't know entered. She wore a fashionable, sheer, silk dress with flounces everywhere. From the way she observed the shop with great curiosity, Coralee guessed she hadn't been in before.

Cat greeted the customer with her best friendly smile. "Welcome to Holbrook's. What can I help you with today?"

The woman pulled away from her perusal of the variety of bottles on the back shelves. "My father saw a notice about a headache remedy and sent me to ask about it. He suffers terribly most days, but since he had a bout of hallucinations a few months ago, he refuses to take the usual remedies."

Coralee joined them at the counter, pulse racing as she listened to the woman's story. This was just what Papa had wanted for his medicine.

Cat gestured to Coralee. "This is my sister, Mrs. Evans. She owns the shop and created the formula you're asking about."

"How lovely to meet you, Mrs. Evans. I'm Alyssa Price." Miss Price dropped into a quick curtsy. Cat smirked at the formality and Coralee shot her a wide-eyed glare. She would never forgive Cat if she offended their first new customer. "I do hope you can help my father. He's suffered so since refusing any other curative."

"I think my formula is perfect for your father. We

developed it with just such a situation in mind." Coralee grabbed a bottle of the willow bark tablets she had pressed and measured out enough to fill a small tin. "Have your father take these once a day when he needs relief. When he's out, come back and we'll decide if he needs to take them more or less often."

"Thank you so much, Mrs. Evans. My father will be so pleased to have some relief." Miss Price paid Cat for her purchase and left the shop with a swish of her lovely flowered skirt.

The sisters met each other's eyes. Coralee was breathless. Cat suddenly let out an unladylike whoop that made the twins come running to see what was happening. She grabbed Phillip and danced wildly around the shop with him. Coralee was laughing at her sister's antics and didn't hear the shop door open again.

"What are we celebrating, ladies?" Jake's deep voice made her heart leap. Heat rushed to her cheeks as she spun to face him. Of course, he would walk in right when she was acting ridiculous.

Reaching up to smooth her hair into place, Coralee tried to regain her proper composure. "We're celebrating our first sale of Papa's formula."

Warmth flooded Jake's chest at Coralee's announcement. No matter how irrational his feelings had been since their last talk, pride was quick to overtake him. Her hard work was paying off. He grabbed her hands, their softness making him want to hold on forever. "Congratulations, Coralee. I knew you could do it all along."

She met his eyes briefly then looked away. "I wouldn't have found the right ingredient without your help."

He let all he was feeling show in his eyes as he squeezed her hands. In spite of their tense relationship, he was quite proud of her. "The pleasure was all mine."

She caught her bottom lip between her teeth and looked away again. The gesture made his heart race. He let go of her hands and stepped back, needing a little space. He turned to Cat. "I saw your signs on the way here. Your artwork is beautiful, Cat. I'm proud of both of you."

Phillip reached out his arms for Jake, who took the boy from Cat. "Well, hello, my fine man. How was your day?"

The little boy looked earnestly into his eyes. "Good."

"I'm glad to hear it." He smiled down at Louisa when she leaned on his leg. "And how was your day, Miss Louisa?"

Without a word, the girl pulled a scrap of brown paper from behind her back and held it up to him. Taking it, he examined her scribbles. "What a nice drawing. Can you tell me about it?"

"Little baby. When we walked."

"You saw a baby and then drew a picture of it? How clever." She grinned, her entire face lighting up.

Jake looked back up at the ladies. "I guess we'd better be on our way."

Coralee wouldn't meet his eyes, causing a stab of pain in Jake's gut. Was she still upset about their disagreement? He wouldn't blame her. She turned away and straightened a display of bottles on the counter.

Maybe if Jake hadn't spent the whole week worrying about Charlie Albridge's relationship with Coralee, he wouldn't have noticed her behavior. But as he watched, she tugged at her sleeves then smoothed her hair, still refusing to look him in the eye. She looked nervous, uncertain. Almost…guilty. His heart ached. Could she be hiding something? At the very least, it was clear that she didn't want to talk to him. "Well, I suppose we'll see you at the Independence Day celebration. Have a good day, ladies." He tipped his hat to Cat and ushered the twins out the door.

The next two days dragged by. Jake couldn't stop thinking about what Coralee might be hiding from him. He tried to be reasonable and remind himself that she was still upset about their last encounter. But the more he thought about it, the more he was convinced that it had to do with Charlie. Surely she wasn't still holding a grudge about their fight, so it had to be something else. Someone else. The man had showed up with her more than Jake thought was necessary. And it didn't seem to be for business, as he'd claimed. By the time Independence Day rolled around, Jake was coiled tight, likely to burst at any moment.

But he had promised to help at the booth Coralee

and her sisters were setting up to sell their new medicine at the town celebration. He only hoped Coralee would spend her time out canvassing for customers rather than at the booth.

The air crackled with excitement as Jake walked to the lot beside the church where the town was staging all the events for the day. Phillip walked next to him, holding his hand and taking in all the activity with dancing eyes. Jake carried Louisa, who fussed at the loud explosions of anvils and guns erupting every few minutes. He held her close at first but by the time they reached the church, she was watching with as much fascination as her brother. Jake never ceased to marvel at the bravery the twins possessed, even at their young age.

All around the church building, people gathered to take in the sights at the booths set up by various businesses. Many stopped to admire the stage that had been built and decorated just for the occasion. A group of local musicians situated on the platform tried their best to play a stirring march over the sound of all the explosions. Red and blue streamers were everywhere, white flowers tucked in among the ribbons. Jake was impressed at all Cecilia and her committee had been able to accomplish in a few days' time.

When they approached the spot where Coralee had set up her table, he was both relieved and disappointed to see that she wasn't there. Cat greeted him with a quick hug and Cecilia waved from the wagon behind them where she was stringing up a canvas sign with the shop's name in large letters. "Excellent work on the sign, Cat. It looks wonderful. People will see it from a mile away."

She shrugged her slim shoulders. "Coralee wanted it big." They both laughed. Jake jumped in to help the sisters set up their displays while the children played in the back of the wagon. People had come from miles out in the countryside surrounding Spring Hill to celebrate the day. Many paused at the booth, so Jake, Cat and Cecilia spent the next two hours answering questions and making sales as the crowds grew. It was almost time for the orations to begin when Cecilia sidled up to Jake, frowning and chewing at her lower lip.

"Jake, have you seen Coralee yet?"

He shook his head. "I figured she was out putting up signs or directing people over here. Is something wrong?"

She fidgeted with the ribbon on her bonnet. "She went out to gather more willow bark from further down the creek. She wanted to have plenty to restock her medicine after today. She was supposed to be back before the program started."

He straightened, scanning the crowd for a glimpse of Coralee even as he spoke. "She went out by herself? With this many strangers around town? That's not a good idea."

"Oh, no, Charlie Albridge went with her. But they still should have been back by now."

Jake's vision blurred and heat scalded his belly. She was out there alone with Albridge. He jumped into action. "Keep an eye on the twins for me. I'll find them."

He ran to the stable behind the clinic and saddled his horse in a hurry. His heart pounded from more than just exertion as he rode out of town. If that man laid a finger on Coralee, he wouldn't be returning to town to join in the celebration.

Dark clouds were rolling in as Jake urged the horse along beside the winding creek. Great, now the banker may have gotten Coralee stuck out in a storm on top of whatever was keeping them.

The storm was moving fast. Jake spurred the horse on, hoping the old girl wouldn't give out before he found them. But soon enough he saw a buggy parked near the creek. He rode up and swung down almost before the horse had stopped. The buggy was empty, but he heard voices. The sounds led him to a copse of willow trees where Coralee and Charlie were cutting sections of bark while they talked. The trees were so full that the ominous clouds were hardly visible from underneath them.

Jake tried to breathe calmly as he approached. But they looked so familiar there, hidden away together in the intimate location. Even as he advanced, Coralee laughed at something Charlie said. Jake's jaw clenched.

"Coralee." The pair spun to face him, Coralee resting a hand on her chest as if he'd startled her. Good. It was better that he interrupted the tryst than anyone else. "Your sisters sent me to find you. The program has already started and they were worried."

"Oh, Jake. We lost track of time. We'll just finish cutting these sections of bark and return to town."

He planted his feet and crossed his arms, not planning to move a muscle until they completed the task. "There's a storm coming. You'd better hurry." He turned to Charlie. "I know you're new to the area, but storms can sneak up fast out here. Next time, try to keep an eye out."

Charlie eyed Jake up and down, sliding his hands into his pockets. The deliberate, casual gesture made Jake's fists clench. Seconds ticked by as they sized each other up. Finally, Charlie turned away and returned to the work. They finished without comment as Jake watched.

Once the bark was packed into baskets, the three of them left the cover of the trees. The wind was picking up and darkness falling fast. Jake's stomach pitched as he took in the green-tinged sky. That was never a good sign.

"Let's go, you two. We need to get to shelter." He helped load the heavy baskets into Charlie's buggy before mounting Dr. Jay's horse. They set off toward town, but Jake's eyes didn't stray from the heavy clouds overhead. The air felt thick and he had the sinking feeling they weren't going to make it back before the storm hit.

The wind whipped at Coralee's hair, pulling loose strands that she had to keep brushing out of her face. After living most of her life on the prairie, she couldn't believe she had paid so little attention to the weather and missed the brewing storm. She knew better than to risk getting stuck out in a tornado.

More than anything, the way Jake kept his eyes on the sky and the fast pace he set made her stomach clench. The green tinge on the horizon grew and Jake's gaze collided with hers. The words were unspoken between them, but they both knew. They had to find shelter now. Jake pointed across the prairie where they could just make out the corner of a small building surrounded by trees.

"Charlie, we have to take cover. Get over to that stand of trees." When they reached the cover of the overhanging branches, Jake had already dismounted and tied the horse's reins around a tree trunk. He did the same with Charlie's horse while they climbed out. Just as the clouds opened and rain started pouring down, all three of them made a dash for the building. Coralee reached for the door, relieved to find it was open.

The cabin was small, but seemed sturdy and there wasn't any rain leaking in. Cobwebs hung everywhere and dust coated the sparse furniture. There was no doubt it was abandoned.

Coralee crossed the room to watch out a window as the storm moved through. Charlie dropped into a chair at the table and leaned back, crossing a leg over the opposite knee. Jake secured the door and paced from one window to the other. His constant motion made her tense.

The rain came down in bursts, pushed along by the wind as it picked up. Coralee scanned the horizon for a funnel-shaped cloud, thankful when she couldn't glimpse one. Satisfied that they were safe and only needed to wait out the driving rain, she joined Charlie at the table.

The banker chuckled as he examined his blunt fingernails with a casual air. "That was a bit of a dramatic episode just to get out of the rain, eh?"

Before Coralee could respond, Jake jumped in. "Albridge, I can't believe you'd be so oblivious. In a heartbeat, a funnel could have touched down and killed us all out there. Here's a little friendly local advice—don't mess with prairie storms."

Charlie's easy posture went rigid. "Now, that's uncalled for, Hadley. The lady needed to gather bark, so I went along to see to her well-being. That storm came out of nowhere. I didn't plan to be out in it."

Coralee looked back and forth between the two men. What had gotten into them?

Jake stalked to the table and rested both hands on the scarred top, leaning over it into Charlie's face. "The fact remains, you two were expected back hours ago. Her sisters were sick with worry. That's hardly responsible of you."

The banker rose to his feet, coiled intensity written in every movement. "Are you accusing me of something?"

The situation was becoming silly. Coralee heaved a sigh. "That's enough out of you two. Honestly, you're behaving like children."

Jake turned to her, arms crossed over his broad chest. "And you're behaving like a naive schoolgirl. I guess I shouldn't expect any less from a woman who runs straight into another man's arms when things don't go her way."

The air whooshed out of Coralee's lungs. Her eyes burned. She didn't know where that horrible accusation had come from, but she had a feeling it referred to more than just today's outing with Charlie.

"Jake." She couldn't seem to get any more words past the lump in her throat. She turned away as Charlie rested a comforting hand on her shoulder.

"Hadley, that could be the most ungentlemanly response I've ever seen. And you had the gall to call me oblivious."

Jake paled as he met Coralee's eyes then turned on his heel and left the cabin, disappearing into the calming rain. Coralee straightened her shoulders and took a deep breath, blinking away the moisture that had started to gather in her eyes. She wasn't sure what had upset Jake so much, but she was finished with trying to figure him out.

She turned to Charlie, plastering a tight smile on her face. "Thank you for defending me. I'm sorry Jake was so harsh with you."

The banker shrugged. "Eh, he's got a chip on his shoulder about something, but I don't think it's really about me. I hate that he accused you of being anything less than a virtuous lady, though. That crossed the line. I'll deal with him for it, if you want me to."

Coralee lowered herself into a chair, weariness washing over her. "Of course not, Charlie. We have a history of not trusting each other, that's all."

"Is that what caused the outburst, something in your past?"

She hesitated to tell Charlie about her previous relationship with Jake. The banker was a nice man, but she didn't know him that well. There had been plenty of gossip about her and Jake in the wake of his departure. She didn't want to start it all over again by speaking imprudently.

Charlie noticed her hesitation and looked down, tracing scratches in the top of the worn table. "I understand if you don't want to confide in me. Just thought you might like a neutral party to listen."

He had a point. She let out a slow breath, deciding it was worth the risk to talk with someone who didn't have a stake in the matter. "At one time, before I married Alan, there were some feelings between me and Jake. It…well, I think you can see that nothing came of it. But now that he's back in town and we're spending time together, those old feelings keep trying to come back and I can't shake them."

"Ah, I see." Charlie leaned back in the chair, all seriousness. "I tend to believe there's a reason when feelings are that persistent. Jake isn't perfect, sure. But he's a good man. Maybe you should see where the feelings take you."

Before she could formulate a response, Charlie stood and peeked out the window. "Looks like the rain has let up and Jake's waiting for us. Are you ready?"

Coralee nodded and they left the shelter of the cabin. The stifling air had cooled a bit as the storm moved through, leaving everything sparkling with droplets and smelling of damp earth. They rode back to town without speaking, Jake leading the way with his back ramrod-straight atop his horse.

When they reached the outskirts of town, Jake peeled off and headed down Third Street. She supposed he was taking the horse back to the stable, but he didn't even spare them a glance as he rode away. Charlie looked at her with questions in his eyes, but she just shrugged. She had no excuses or explanations left for Jake's behavior.

Charlie maneuvered the buggy as close as he could to the church, parking among the other wagons and buggies that had gathered for the festivities. People were starting to emerge from nearby buildings where they had taken shelter from the storm, checking with neighbors and friends to be sure everyone was safe. Coralee thanked Charlie again for his help before hurrying to the spot where she had left her sisters.

Her knees went weak when she saw Cat and Cecilia picking up the area around their wagon with the twins' help. Cecilia turned and caught sight of her. "Oh, there she is." Both of her sisters and the twins rushed to hug her. "Coralee Evans, we were so worried about you." Cecilia's words came out in her teacher voice, making Coralee want to giggle, silly with relief.

"I'm so sorry. Charlie and I didn't notice the storm coming in. When Jake found us, we all had to take shelter in an abandoned cabin to wait out the storm. But we're all fine."

Cecilia hugged her again then pulled back to look around. "Where's Jake? A family rode into town just before you saying they thought a tornado touched down outside town. Did he leave to check on his parents?"

Coralee searched the crowd for Jake's tall frame. She had expected him to meet them here, no matter what had happened out on the prairie. But he was nowhere in sight. "Will you watch the twins while I try to find him? I'm sure he'll want to ride out and see if everything is safe at their farm."

At Cecilia's nod, Coralee took off at a brisk pace. Ezra and Beth meant the world to Jake. If they were injured or something was wrong at the farm, she knew he would be devastated that he hadn't been there to help them.

She found Jake at the clinic. As she pushed the door open, he turned from the book on his desk, wincing when he saw her in the doorway. Her chest tightened at his pained look. They had gotten along so well while they'd worked on Papa's formula. Coralee knew she couldn't risk giving her heart away again, but she had started to hope they could be friends. Now Jake's lack of trust in her was building a wall right up between them again. His behavior that morning had added one more row of bricks keeping them from a civil relationship.

Coralee stood just inside the door, fidgeting with the folds of her skirt. "I'm sorry to interrupt. I know you don't want to see me right now. But have you seen your parents? Cecilia said there are rumors of a tornado touching down outside town."

Jake's face went pale and he lurched to his feet. Hesitating, he met her eyes. "What about the twins?"

"They're with Cecilia and Cat. We'll watch them until you return."

His only response was a nod as he hurried past her and ran to the hitching post where his horse waited. Coralee watched him ride away, silent prayers for all three members of the Hadley family weighing on her heart.

Jake's stomach churned as he surveyed the damage to the landscape on the ride to the farm. His parents had planned to come to the celebration that day but, in all the excitement, he hadn't even bothered to look for them. And now they could be injured. Or worse. He urged the horse to go faster.

If something had happened to them, it would be his fault. As their only child, taking care of Ma and Pa was his responsibility. And what had he been doing instead? Chasing Coralee around on a jealous whim.

Faced with possible tragedy, he couldn't keep lying to himself. He had been motivated more by jealousy than anything else. Charlie had been out there with Coralee and Jake didn't like it one bit. He hadn't even noticed the storm brewing when he'd saddled up the horse to find the pair earlier. He had been too upset that she was alone at the creek with an eligible bachelor. And then he'd gone and yelled at them both for ignoring the weather, the same as he had.

It felt like an invisible clamp was squeezing Jake's chest as he rode onto Hadley land. He could see where a funnel cloud had made contact, tearing a winding path of destruction toward the northeast. Bits of trees and other wreckage trailed across the land as if a giant hand had scattered them from the sky. Every few feet chunks of grass had been ripped up and tossed aside. One tree near the creek was stripped bare while the one next to it had been snapped off at the top but no other branches had been damaged.

At the crest of the last low rise, Jake slowed the horse. His eyes swept the farm, stomach in knots until he saw that the farmhouse and barn were still standing and undamaged. But he couldn't relax completely until he saw both of his parents unharmed. He spurred the horse on again, watching for any signs of Ma or Pa as he approached.

At the house, he took the porch stairs in one leap and charged through the kitchen, calling for his mother. He found her in the parlor, frowning at him. "Jake Hadley, what on earth do you think you're doing? After all the excitement of that storm, your pa just settled down for a rest." She shook a finger in his face. "Don't you go waking him up."

Jake looked her over from head to toe. Every gray hair was in place in her usual simple bun. No cuts or scratches on her weathered face. No rips in the cloth of her plain brown dress. He was so relieved he wrapped his arms around her and squeezed tight. She chuckled, patting his back. "I'm glad to see you, too, dear." She leaned away and examined him. "Now let me see you. Are you all right?"

"Yes, Ma. I was just outside of town when the storm rolled through, but I found shelter. Didn't see a tornado touch down where I was, but it looks like it was worse out here."

She nodded as she returned to the dusting he'd interrupted. "We were out by the barn. Your pa made me run for shelter, but he didn't make it before the funnel hit." A chill washed over Jake. She'd said Pa was resting. Was he hurt? "We're awful thankful none of the buildings were damaged."

"The buildings? Ma, what about Pa? Is he hurt?"

His mother didn't even turn from the shelf she was dusting. "Oh, no, dear. He tripped when he was following me to the barn and didn't have time to make it inside. So he tucked in next to the wall and was perfectly safe. The tornado wasn't even that close to us. We saw it over the rise before it went the other way."

Jake dropped into his favorite chair, his body slack with relief after the urgency of the last few hours. He let his head thump back against the wooden chair and closed his eyes. Now that he knew his parents were safe, the mixed emotions of the day started to crowd in, overwhelming him.

"What had you outside of town this morning? I hope it wasn't an injury on such a festive day."

He watched Ma as she worked, amazed at how

tireless she was. "No, nothing like that." He didn't want to explain the situation to his mother. She was so perceptive that she would know in an instant what had motivated his actions. But he didn't want to lie to her and she had turned from her dusting, waiting expectantly for him to continue.

"It was Coralee. She rode out early with Charlie Albridge, the banker, to gather bark for her medication. Cecilia was worried when they didn't return on time. I went out to find them and we had to take shelter before making it back to town."

Understanding dawned on her face, just as he expected. He held up a hand before she could speak. "You don't have to say it, Ma. I'm kicking myself for letting jealousy get the better of me. I was out there chasing that fool woman instead of here protecting you." He hung his head as the guilt pricked at him again.

Ma stopped her work and planted herself on the edge of a chair, close to Jake. "You don't have to feel guilty about not being here. I know you want to help us, but even with your pa's arm, we can handle the farm. We've been through tornados before and I'd guess we'll go through them again. You being here wouldn't have changed anything if the storm had been worse."

Jake bristled. Of course it would have been different if he'd been there. Pa wouldn't have been out there working. Jake would have made certain both his parents were safe inside even if he'd had to pick Pa up and carry him.

"No, I handled the whole day badly." He picked at a loose thread on the hem of his jacket. Now Ma would see how weak he had become. Anytime Coralee Evans was involved, Jake lost any semblance of good judgment.

But to his surprise, Ma clucked her tongue at him. "No, you didn't, Jake. You helped Cecilia when she was worried about her sister. And you protected Coralee by assuring her good reputation is intact and helping her weather the storm in safety." His mother patted his hand with her wrinkled one. "That's the kind of man I raised you to be." She rose and planted a kiss on his forehead, just like when he was a little boy. "You've made me proud today, Jake."

Was it possible he had acted nobly, in spite of the jealousy that had driven him? Even if he had hated that Charlie was the one out there with Coralee, deep down, he had also been worried about her reputation and her safety. Maybe he had made the right choices, after all.

Ma returned to her cleaning, but after a moment she starting talking again. "Did I ever tell you what your pa and I saw when you were courting Coralee before you left for school?" Jake shook his head, curious where she was headed with the conversation.

"We talked all the time about how the two of you reminded us of ourselves in our courting days."

Jake started to chuckle at that. They hadn't been anything like his steady, peaceful parents.

Ma shook her head, stopping his laughter. "No, I mean it, Jake. When I met him, your pa was not the thoughtful man he is today. And I was rather good at getting us into spats with my quick temper."

"You? Ma, I've never seen you lose your temper."

She shrugged. "That's because your father was a good influence on me. After a while, he started confronting me when I got upset over silly things. He refused to sit back and let me ruin our relationship by overreacting. I had to learn to handle my temper because he wouldn't stand for anything else."

Jake stared at his mother. He would never have suspected that Ma hadn't always been the calm, easy-going woman he knew.

"And it wasn't just me. I like to think I had an impact on him, as well. I couldn't stand it when he would barrel right over me, not thinking about how I would feel. I pointed it out enough times that he must have gotten the idea. He grew to be very conscientious of what people around him felt and needed."

She stopped cleaning and rested a hand on Jake's shoulder. "I see the same traits in you and Coralee. And I see the same potential for you to help each other grow into better people. It may feel rough at first. But, eventually, you'll look back and be able to see the good that's come from those hard times. Sometimes, God puts people in your path just to push you to be better." With a quick flick of her hands, Ma folded the dust cloth. "Now, I'm off to start preparations for supper. You just take a few quiet moments then check on your pa when you're ready."

Jake took her up on that and sat still in the chair after she left, mulling over her words. He had been wondering why God would keep putting him near Coralee so often, after the hurt they'd caused each other in the past. Maybe Ma was right. Maybe part of God's plan for him included using Coralee to push him into changing.

Chapter Seven

Independence Day ended with a ball, hosted by Charlie. The twins and other women chattered with excitement all afternoon. But Coralee's emotions were as volatile as the explosives people were setting off throughout the town. Jake hadn't returned from the farm, so Coralee offered to watch the children at the party while her sisters danced. Deep down, it was a relief to have a reason to keep to herself during the event.

She hoped Jake's late return didn't mean tragedy had struck the Hadleys. On their walk to Charlie's home, she continued to pray for all three of them. Her thoughts wandered to the moment by the creek that morning when she'd turned to see Jake standing behind her and Charlie. Even hours later, she flushed with guilt. She should never have let Charlie tag along. But he had been adamant that she couldn't go alone. Coralee had a sneaking suspicion that he had been trying to impress Cat by acting gallant.

Her shoulders slumped when her mind replayed the crushed look on Jake's face under the willow trees. His attitude while they'd waited out the storm had been hurtful. But after her emotions had time to settle, she realized what the whole episode must have looked like to him.

She only hoped he would be calm enough to listen to and accept her explanation when he came to get the children. As much as his lack of trust hurt her, she would rather try to get along than continue to fight with him.

They arrived at Charlie's home to find people streaming all around, decked out in their best evening clothes. The house itself was one of the finest in Spring Hill, second only to the mayor's home. From what she had heard, Charlie had done quite well for himself banking in Mississippi before deciding to seek out adventure by coming west. It certainly would have cost a tidy sum to have enough wood shipped out for the two-story home. Not to mention the number of lovely windows and fancy touches. But of all the places in town, those rich details made it the perfect location for a ball.

Coralee tugged at the lace trim that decorated the peach silk gown she had borrowed from Cat. It had been years since she'd had a reason to dress up and none of her mourning dresses were appropriate, so her sisters had worked together to dress her for the evening. She felt out of place in the lovely gown, leading the twins into Charlie's backyard where friends and neighbors were gathering. In the midst

of the festive atmosphere, Coralee found she wasn't
much in the mood to celebrate.

Charlie greeted guests with a smile, pointing out
the tables against the house that were laden with food
and drinks. Several musicians were set up nearby
and couples were already whirling around a large
grassy area that served as a dance floor. Assorted
chairs ringed the yard, providing places to stop and
rest throughout the night.

Immediately, Cat was whisked away to dance by
a local young man. Coralee couldn't help glancing
at Charlie, not surprised when his lips thinned into
a tight line, eyes following the couple. Cecilia and
Aunt Lily made a round of the yard, greeting everyone by name. Determined to stay off the dance floor,
Coralee found a spot near the food tables where the
twins could play and run.

She watched the frolicking couples while straightening the skirts of the borrowed dress. Alan had been
an excellent dancer. The memory of his arms around
her, spinning to the music and laughing together,
surfaced. For a moment she didn't see the dancers
or the decorations. Just Alan's eyes, sparkling with
joy. But then the sky-blue eyes changed into choco-
late brown, deep and serious. Jake's face filled her
mind. The music and swirling activity seemed to
fade away as she envisioned Jake taking her hand,
wrapping one arm around her back and leading her
in a dance.

The daydream came to an abrupt halt when a
young couple, busy laughing and staring into each

other's eyes, bumped her on the way to find a drink. She nodded at their distracted apologies and tried to step farther away from the chaotic dance floor.

But she backed right into someone else, making her cheeks flame. She couldn't seem to stay out of the way tonight. She whirled around to make an apology and came face-to-face with Jake. If it was possible, dressed in a formal jacket with a dark waistcoat and tie, Jake looked even more handsome than usual. The flush deepened and she wished a cooling breeze would stir the hot evening air. She tried to step back and stumbled on her dress hem. His hands gripped her upper arms to steady her, a teasing smile lighting his face.

"Whoa, there, I don't want to have to fix up any more injuries tonight than necessary. I expect I'll be busy in the next few hours, anyway. Celebrations tend to lead to bad decisions."

Coralee tried to force a light laugh but it came out sounding strangled. "Yes, I suppose you'll have your hands full as the festivities linger on." She recovered enough from her awkwardness to remember why he had arrived late. Pausing, she searched his face for clues about his parents' well-being. No sadness hid in his dark eyes, no downward turn of his lips. "How did you find things at the farm?"

He ran a hand through his hair, already tousled. "The twister was close. Pa didn't make it to shelter, so I took the time to check him over. He's fine. But I hate that I wasn't there to make sure they were both safe."

His dedication to caring for his parents was admirable, but she could see guilt hiding in his expression. "Jake, you can't blame yourself for something that didn't even happen."

"I'm the only one they have, Coralee. What happens to them is my responsibility."

She straightened, planting her hands on her hips. "Just how old do you think your parents are?" He drew back at her tone. She tried to soften her approach, laying a hand on his sleeve. "Maybe someday they'll need you to care for them. But right now, they're still healthy and capable. They just need a little help around the farm, not a parent."

His rubbed the back of his neck with a tanned hand as she continued, trying to be gentle. "You were away for some time, but I was here and saw your parents often. They're getting along fine. Your pa isn't too proud to ask for help and your ma is the strongest woman I've ever known. Jake, they're thrilled to have you here, but you aren't responsible for them just yet."

Creases appeared on his forehead as his brows pulled together. "All those years in St. Louis, all I could think about was getting back here to help them. I thought they would be struggling without me. But maybe you're right. They've been happy to have me around but, usually, Pa has most of the chores covered when I get there."

She smiled. "See? They're so proud of your medical career. I know they would be terribly upset if you put trying to care for them over helping those who need you."

Jake stuffed his hands in the pockets of his trousers, rocking back on his heels. "I guess we need to talk about the other incident today."

Thickness in her throat made it hard to swallow. But she forced herself to meet his eyes straight-on. "That was just a misunderstanding, Jake."

"No, I owe you an apology. My comments were out of line. I'm sorry, Coralee."

Her heart softened at his words. Maybe he wanted to try being friends, too. "I know you were looking out for my reputation and acting at Cecilia's request. I assure you, Charlie insisted on accompanying me, but there's nothing between us."

His arms crossed over his chest. "He's not courting you? He seems fond of showing up where you are."

She nudged him teasingly in the arm. "You may not have noticed, but he's been trying to impress Cat for months."

The good-natured feeling drained right out of her when he looked away. "It doesn't matter, anyway. Whether he's interested in you or not, I don't have any right to question who you spend your time with."

Heaviness washed over Coralee. He didn't believe her. She turned away to keep him from seeing the disappointment she felt. How did hope keep sneaking in that he would trust her? She should know better by now.

Louisa and Phillip came running, barreling straight into Jake's and Coralee's legs. The tension disappeared and all four of them laughed as Coralee smoothed Louisa's hair and Jake swung Phillip up high into the air. He lowered the little boy and knelt in front of the children. "Are you having fun at the party?"

Phillip nodded. Louisa bounced on her toes, excitement pouring out of her as she pointed at the dance floor. "Pretty dresses. Dancing." She finished the statement with a twirl of her own.

"That was beautiful, Miss Louisa. Do you like the dancing?"

She answered without taking her eyes off the moving couples. "They spin. And holding hands."

"Would you like to dance with me?"

With wide eyes and a huge grin, she nodded. Jake took her hands and led her in a swaying dance, adding a spin now and then to make her laugh.

Standing with her hand on Phillip's head, Coralee's heart ached with how lovingly Jake interacted with the twins. Too full of emotion, she let her gaze drift around the yard, watching the guests dancing and socializing. Her traitorous heart refused to listen to her head and remember that the last thing she wanted was to get into a position to be hurt again.

Close by, a throat cleared. She turned to find the dance had ended and the twins had run off again. The musicians were starting up a new tune. And Jake was standing next to her with one hand outstretched. "Would you like to dance with me?"

Jake's stomach clenched as he waited. Coralee was staring at his fingers with wide eyes and he could see her biting the inside of her cheek. He had no idea what had made him offer to dance with her. When it came to this woman, he couldn't get his good sense and his actions on the same page. But there he stood, hand held out to her. After what seemed like forever, she finally placed her hand in his.

Leading her into the midst of the dancers, Jake felt as if every eye in the place was on them. She was by far the most beautiful woman at the ball. The color of her dress was perfect against her skin. And that delicate lace around the neck and hem echoed the loveliness of her features. Even tucked away against the house, she attracted attention. He had been surprised that she wasn't surrounded by men asking for a dance. But here she was, at his side.

There had been many occasions to practice his dancing while Jake was in St. Louis, but none had been as pleasant as this. The fiddler and banjo player kept up a constant harmony in the background. Everything smelled of summer heat and gunpowder. And a whiff of Coralee's floral scent reached his nose as they moved with the other couples.

There was little time to speak as they passed through partners, enjoying the quick movement of the dance. But every time Jake caught sight of Coralee, flushed and smiling, his breath caught. And when the steps brought them back together, he lost himself in her glowing blue eyes.

After the dance, Coralee stepped close and rose up on her toes to speak into his ear. "I'd rather not join another dance. Should we go check on the twins?"

His heart dropped even as he nodded and escorted her from among the dancing guests. He had enjoyed the dance with her more than he'd thought possible and had hoped she had, too. Still holding her arm, he led her around the perimeter of the party area, keeping an eye out for Louisa and Phillip. At least she didn't pull away from him as soon as they were off the dance floor.

"So now that the holiday is nearly past and your medicine seems likely to be a success, maybe you should reconsider taking the Association examination." As he spoke, Jake turned from scanning the yard for the twins to see Coralee's face harden. What had made him bring that up again?

"I already told you, I want to focus all my energy on the shop and Papa's medication. Why are you so convinced I have to do it your way?"

As Coralee spoke, Ma's words popped into Jake's head, the story about Pa and how he used to roll right over her. Jake didn't want to follow in those footsteps. He fought his initial reaction to argue with her. The shop was hers to run the way she saw fit. "I'm not trying to make you do what I want. But in St. Louis, I learned a great deal from meeting with colleagues. I wanted that for you, the camaraderie of connecting with others in your field."

Coralee folded her arms across her chest. "That's the case for you. It wouldn't be the same for me, way out here. Since I finally figured out the medicine, I want to give that a chance to increase our business. I still think that's the best thing for the shop."

He took a half step closer to her, well aware that they were in full view of most of the town but unable to help himself. With every fiber of his being, he wanted to encourage her rather than force his opinion on her. "I'm sorry if I made you feel that I wouldn't approve if you don't take the examination. The choice is yours and I'll support whatever you want."

His words didn't seem to have the desired effect.

Her lips pressed into a tight line as she drew her shoulders back. "What I want is whatever will make the shop successful again. We've gotten along just fine without the Association for all these years. If I can get customers coming back to us, we'll be fine."

Jake sucked in a breath. He wasn't faring well at encouraging her. Even what he thought were the right words seemed to upset her. Not about to take the risk of making her angrier with him, Jake pointed behind her. "There are the twins. Let's go see what they're getting into."

They found the children rolling in the grass, covering their best clothes in dirt and green stains. Their hands and faces were coated with a layer of sticky crumbs. Jake almost started to scold them but then caught a peek at Coralee's face.

All traces of her frustration with him were gone. One hand had come up to cover her lips. Her cheeks were pink and her shoulders twitched with barely controlled amusement. Taking another look at the twins, Jake couldn't help it. A loud laugh burst out of him. The amount of filth they had managed to cover themselves with in such a short time was absurd.

Trying to get control of his amusement and appear stern, Jake faced the children. "What have you gotten into?"

Louisa managed an expression of remorse. But Phillip stood before him proudly. "We rolled. And eat cake."

Coralee knelt in front of the boy with a handkerchief, gently wiping the linen square over his face. "Let's get you two cleaned up a little."

Jake joined her and they brushed off the children as well as they could. Then the four of them took a turn around the yard in an effort to keep Louisa and Phillip out of trouble. Jake greeted other guests as necessary, but he preferred to stand back and watch Coralee. She shone in this atmosphere, with people she cared about all around. She asked after health and family members. She remembered small details about everyone she spoke to. Each person was comfortable in her presence. And Jake loved watching it all play out.

"Why, Dr. Hadley, Mrs. Evans." Jake turned to see Mrs. Felder approaching. He hadn't seen her since the last time he'd checked on the recovered cholera patients a few weeks ago. She looked as spritely as ever. "I'm so glad to see you both here. And the darling children. My, aren't they just fine."

Coralee greeted the woman with a brief embrace. "Mrs. Felder, you're looking well."

"I feel fit as a fiddle. I hope that shop of yours

is thriving. I heard an interesting bit of information that a man from back east visited for several days."

A rueful smile fell over Coralee's face. "Yes, that's true. He was with a professional association and stopped to make sure our shop is up to standards. I believe he was pleased with us."

Mrs. Felder lit up, standing a bit taller. "Oh, my dear, that's wonderful. Of course, no one who knows you would doubt that at all."

"They certainly wouldn't, Mrs. Felder." Jake shot Coralee a look that he prayed she would understand, filled with his full support and respect. Then he turned back to the older woman. "How are your neighbors recovering? I haven't made it out that way to check on our cholera patients for some time."

"As far as I know, they're all back in fine health. Thanks to you and Mrs. Evans here. I think I can speak for all of us when I say thank you for all your efforts during the outbreak."

Jake patted the woman's shoulder, pleased with her report. "I'm just thankful we were able to catch some of the cases in time."

"Jake. Jake!" Phillip drew his attention away from the conversation. The little boy pointed at the food tables. "Treat?"

"Phillip, judging from the mess on your face earlier, you've had plenty of treats. No more tonight."

A pout formed on the child's face. Jake scooped him up before he could start to make a scene. He stepped away from the ladies, Louisa following close beside him. "How about this? We'll see if we can take a couple of cookies with us and you can each have one tomorrow."

A thoughtful look came over Phillip's face. Then a grin broke out. "Yes, cookie. 'Morrow."

Jake set the boy back on the ground, ruffling his blond hair. "That's a good boy. Now, let's go have some more fun. We'll be heading home soon."

As Jake walked away with Phillip, Mrs. Felder turned to Coralee. "Mrs. Evans, I must admit, I've heard another interesting rumor about your shop."

"Oh?" Coralee's heart sank, even as she tried to act nonchalant. Had word gotten out that the shop was on the verge of failure?

"Word has it that a certain doctor has been spending a great deal of time at Holbrook's. And working rather closely with you."

A flush started creeping up her neck. "Jake was just helping me with the formula for our new medication. And, of course, my sisters and I have been helping watch the twins some so he can work. There's nothing going on that's worth spreading gossip."

Mrs. Felder had the gall to chuckle and pat Coralee's arm. "Now, dear, don't get upset over it. Some women have nothing better to do than worry about what everyone else is or isn't doing. I wanted to find out for myself if there's anything romantic happening between you and our handsome doctor."

Trying to maintain her dignity, Coralee stared out across the spinning couples on the dance floor. Of all the emotions she had felt that day, the one she least wanted at the moment was the longing that washed over her at the older woman's words. "I can assure you, Mrs. Felder, there is nothing romantic going on between Jake and me."

"Well, I suppose that's settled. Although, I had hoped that you two might be striking up a relationship. It's clear that you care for each other in some way. But sometimes, these things just aren't meant to be."

A woman nearby called to Mrs. Felder, insistently waving her over. Coralee blew out a breath as the older woman said a quick goodbye and headed on her way across the yard. Jake returned with the twins flanking him and they went back to greeting all their friends and neighbors. But the whole time, Coralee couldn't get Mrs. Felder's words out of her mind.

The idea of people talking about her and Jake, linking them together as if a relationship was inevitable, made her want to run and hide. She couldn't let herself be hurt again. And anything more than a friendship with Jake would put her right in that position. It wasn't even about his lack of trust in her, or his tendency to push his own opinion on her. More terrifying than that was the significant chance that he would be taken from her. Just like Alan and Papa. A chill washed over her, leaving her enjoyment of the party dampened.

Once they had made a complete circuit of the party, Jake led her and the twins back to their starting point near Charlie's house. The dancing was still in full swing, but Coralee didn't feel the need to join in. At one time in her life, she had lived for dancing. But in the light of where life had taken her, the frivolity wasn't for her anymore. The dance she had shared with Jake had been enough for this night.

Several chairs nearby happened to be empty, so she sat with the twins while Jake got them all something to drink. It was getting rather late and Louisa and Phillip were finally running out of energy. Louisa leaned over to rest against Coralee's side while they watched the dancers spinning and stepping. And when Jake returned and took a seat next to Coralee, Phillip immediately climbed out of his chair and up into Jake's lap, snuggling close.

Shivers raced up Coralee's arm when Jake's shoulder brushed against hers, warm and solid. That Mrs. Felder. Her words had put thoughts in Coralee's mind that she didn't want to keep having. She turned to find his eyes on her as he broke the silence between them. "You know, Mrs. Felder wasn't wrong about what she said."

Coralee's heart raced. Had he heard the older woman's assertion about her and Jake caring for each other? That telltale flush washed across her cheeks again. "I, uh, what did she say?"

He chuckled, low and warm, intensifying her shivers. "That no one who knows you would doubt that you run Holbrook's with the utmost care. I know your medication will make a difference in the amount of business at the shop. Just look at the response this morning. Your success will be good for the entire community."

Her eyes shifted back to the dance area, where a new tune had just started. She let out a slow breath of relief. He hadn't heard Mrs. Felder's last words, after all. "I've been afraid for so long. I was so sure Papa's formula was the key, but I could only see all the ways that I might fail."

He shifted Phillip to free one hand, reaching out to grasp hers. "There was a time a few weeks ago, after the cholera outbreak, when you dropped everything to pray with me. I'd like to do that now for you."

Still holding her hand, Jake bent his head and prayed for her. "Father God, there's a lot riding on this medication for Coralee and her family. I ask You to take away her fear and help her find the confidence to do what she needs to for the shop and for herself. Please bless her business. Amen."

When he finished, they sat in silence, watching the dancers, her hand still in his. Coralee let the peace of the moment wash over her, a stark difference from the worry that had colored most of her days in the last few months. All too soon, Jake withdrew his hand and stood, Phillip asleep in his arms. "I think it's far past bedtime for a couple of children."

She stood with him, lifting Louisa. "I'll help you carry them out. I'm about ready to head home, myself."

Jake led the way, stopping here and there to say goodbye to guests they passed. Finally they made it to his wagon and rested the sleeping twins in the back. Jake then insisted on giving her a ride home.

In an effort to let the twins sleep, they whispered a quick good-night and Coralee slipped into the empty house.

Sleep claimed her in little time that night, worn out from the emotional ups and downs of the day.

But in the morning, she didn't feel as refreshed as she would have expected. The evening had ended with such a beautiful, close moment between her and Jake. That moment, paired with Mrs. Felder's insinuation that there could be emotions growing in them both, stirred questions in Coralee's heart. Did Jake feel more for her than she'd thought? Was that why he had responded with such intensity to finding her alone with Charlie?

Coralee was picking at her breakfast when Aunt Lily emerged from her room. Lowering herself stiffly into a chair opposite Coralee, the older woman took a sip of her steaming tea. "Good morning, my dear. You look as tired as I feel today."

Nodding in response, Coralee poked her fork into the egg on her plate, mashing it to bits. When Aunt Lily didn't start her usual string of conversation, Coralee looked up to find the older woman watching her with eyebrows raised. "You seem a bit distracted. If you don't mind me asking, what has you so deep in thought?"

Shoulders slumping, Coralee gave up all pretense of eating and dropped the fork on her plate. "Aunt Lily, to be honest, I'm starting to think that I'll always be stuck living in fear. I can't seem to let go of it."

Leaning back in her chair, Aunt Lily tilted her head. "I thought everything went quite well with the new remedy yesterday. What are you afraid of?"

Coralee's gaze dropped to the table, taking in the familiar cloth covering the worn wood. How many conversations had she had here with Aunt Lily over the years? Big, small and everything in between. Her aunt had walked Coralee and her sisters through life right in this spot. "The booth was a hit yesterday, for sure. People were thrilled with the medication. Cat and Cecilia are certain business will pick right back up as a result."

Frustration built in Coralee. It was hard to put into words what was weighing on her heart. "Last night, Jake kept talking about how much this will benefit the town. About how much people need Papa's formula. But I can't help thinking that Dr. Jay will just find another way to discredit us when he returns to town. He'll be back any day now and he won't be happy to see his patients ignoring his advice. It would be devastating if we finally found what Papa had been searching for, just to see the shop fail, anyway."

"I understand your fear, my girl. You've taken so much responsibility on yourself. And you have a valid point. That old grump won't take it well when he sees how you've succeeded in spite of his efforts."

Aunt Lily stood and moved to place her hands on Coralee's shoulders, holding her gaze with caring eyes. "All you can do is what God has placed before you. Dearest, the fear will be there whether the remedy does well or not. There's always something on the horizon to be afraid of if you let it linger in your heart. You just have to be stronger than that emotion. And I know you are."

Coralee tried to smile at her aunt. "Thank you for believing in me. I don't know if I'm as strong as you think I am. But I'll work on it. I can't keep living with this fear consuming me."

With a pat on Coralee's hand, Aunt Lily moved away and cleared her breakfast from the table. "That's the spirit, girl. Now, I'm off to a busy day at the café. I can't wait for this evening when I get to hear all about the crowds of customers that will fill the shop today."

Jake was pleased to get a better night's sleep than any he'd had since bringing the twins home. For the first time, they didn't cry over missing their parents, but slept the whole night in peace. And it didn't hurt that the conversation with Coralee had calmed his spirit. He could almost see how spending time with her made him better, just like Ma had insisted.

In the morning he worked on paperwork at the clinic, catching up after a busy week of home visits. It was close to noon when the clinic door burst open, letting in a gust of hot air. Samuel stalked in as Jake jumped, startled by the sudden interruption. Papers from his patient files skittered across the floor.

"Surprised to see me, Hadley?" The older man's eyes flashed and his face was crimson. Jake stared at his mentor, sweat beading his forehead. What had made Samuel so angry? He could only have just arrived back in town.

"I am, sir. That is, I'm not surprised you're back. I expected you at any time. I was just startled by your sudden entrance."

Samuel snorted and poked at Jake's chest with one bony finger. "That's what happens when you try to hide things. You get skittish."

Jake frowned as he tried to work through the doctor's words. "What are you saying, sir?"

"I know what you've been doing while I was away. Don't think I didn't have someone keeping an eye on you all this time."

"I don't know what you're getting at. There was an outbreak of cholera right after you left and we lost a few patients. Other than that, everything has gone smoothly." Jake's pulse beat hard in his veins. Samuel was accusing him of something, but he had no idea what.

"You have deliberately flaunted my wishes about that Evans woman, Hadley." Samuel spat the words in Jake's face. "I told you, she's a fraud and I don't want anything to do with her. That includes anything that happens regarding my practice. I know you were working with her while I was gone."

Jake struggled to find words to respond. He hadn't been prepared for the kind of hostility that was emanating from the older doctor. "Samuel, I didn't mean to go against your wishes. Yes, you said you didn't approve of her. But I needed extra hands during the outbreak and she's the only one in town with any kind of experience."

Samuel dropped into Jake's chair, leaning back and crossing his legs at the ankles. "But it was more than that, wasn't it? I'm aware that you've been helping her work up some new potion to sell. Why would you think I would approve of you helping her on that fool's errand?"

"To be honest, I was sure if you returned and saw how well her medication works, you would change your mind about her. Maybe even support her business. If you would give her a chance, I think you'd find that she's quite capable. Her father was excellent at his work and taught her well."

Samuel speared Jake with angry eyes. "Hadley, that shows your lack of respect for me more than anything else you've done. To think that you can sway me to your side after my many years of experience." The doctor barked a harsh laugh. "Does this position truly mean so little to you?"

The air whooshed out of Jake's lungs. Right here, he was going to lose his chance at the practice. But he needed this and his parents needed him close. The opportunity was too important to risk angering Samuel further. "I'm so sorry, sir. I can't tell you how much this means to me. Please believe that I didn't mean to disappoint you. I hoped you would be pleased with how I ran the practice while you were away."

Samuel crossed one arm over his chest and rested his chin on his knuckles. He paused as if considering

Jake's fate. "I had high expectations for you, young man. I wouldn't have left if I didn't think I could trust you. But I will not have my clinic associated with that woman." He pushed to his feet with some effort and banged his fist on the desk. "I won't sit by and let her harm people in this community under my watch."

"What would you have me do, Samuel? She's my friend and excellent at her work. I know she won't harm anyone."

"I would have you listen to the voice of experience and reason. Nothing good will come of Mrs. Evans running that shop. I will not be party to her mistakes. If you want to help her, I can't stop you. But you'll have to make a choice—the woman or an established medical practice in Spring Hill. You can't have both." Samuel turned and marched into his office, slamming the door hard behind him.

Jake sank into his chair, staring at the papers on his desk without seeing a thing. How could he choose between hurting Coralee and leaving his parents without help? Even after last night's conversation with Coralee had calmed his worry for them a little, he still knew they would only need him more as time went on. He leaned forward, resting his elbows on his knees and clasping his hands together. If there was ever a moment to practice his fledgling faith, it would be now.

"God, I believe You've put me back in Spring Hill, back near Coralee, for a reason. I want to see her succeed. But I also know my parents need me. I believe Samuel was serious about his threat to take away my place in the practice. But I don't know how I can intentionally hurt Coralee. We've come so far since I've returned home, healed so much of the hurt from the past. Please show me what to do."

He sat for a moment after finishing the whispered prayer, half expecting a voice from Heaven to give him an answer. He was a little disappointed when only silence filled the clinic. Determined to get through the day's work so he couldn't be accused of neglecting his responsibilities, he returned to his files and updated them in silence until evening fell.

Jake didn't see Samuel again that day and didn't stop to say good-night when he left the clinic. He would have to catch the doctor up on all their patients soon. But until he had a chance to think through his mentor's ultimatum, he wanted to steer clear of the man.

Cecilia was alone with the twins when he stopped by the ladies' house, much to Jake's relief. He also wasn't ready to come face-to-face with Coralee right then. Once he thanked Cecilia for her help and guided Louisa and Phillip outside, he stopped and knelt to talk at their level. "How would you like to go play by the creek for a while?" As he'd expected, they cheered and ran ahead toward the water.

Louisa and Phillip entertained themselves by throwing rocks and small sticks into the creek, squealing with each splash. Jake sat on the grass near the bank, leaning against a large rock and thinking about the conversation with Samuel. Nothing about the situation was easy. Someone was going to get hurt. Either he would hurt Coralee or he would hurt his parents. And no matter which choice he made, part of him would hurt, too.

He heard the tall grass behind him rustling and turned to see Lily heading toward them. She smiled indulgently at the children as she approached. "Hello there, darlings. Oh, Phillip, what is it you have there?"

Lily bent to examine the wet, wriggly creature the boy held out. "It a frog."

"So it is. Louisa, do you like the frog, too?" The woman let out a hearty laugh when Louisa shook her head forcefully. Then she turned to Jake. "Those are some fine children. You're doing an excellent job with them."

He stood to greet her with a hug. "Can't say that I disagree, Lily, but I'm afraid I don't have much to do with it. How are you?"

"Oh, fine, my boy. Just fine. Tell me, have you had any word on a permanent home for the little dears?"

Jake's heart clenched. He tried not to think about the eventual time when the twins would leave his care. "No, we've put the word out as much as we can. Now I guess we have to wait and see if God prompts a family to step forward."

"Then I'll continue praying for them to find the perfect family." Glancing around, Lily drew in a deep lungful of warm summer air. "Looks like you've found a nice thinking spot."

The knowing look she sent his way made him grimace. He wasn't going to be alone with his thoughts much, after all. "What makes you think that?"

She winked with a chuckle. "Just a hunch. Which you confirmed."

Jake gestured at the rock and scooted over as Lily perched on it. "You're right. I came out here to think through some things." He stared out across the prairie stretching for miles on the other side of the water. "I thought my relationship with Coralee was in a hard place when I left for school. But I think all that's happened the last few weeks has turned out to be even more complicated."

"Ah, yes. Affairs of the heart tend to be complicated." She raised a hand to halt his protests. "Don't try to tell me your heart isn't involved, Jake Hadley. I know you as well as your own mama, boy. What's made it so thorny this time?"

"It seems that as soon as we work through one issue, something worse pops up the next day. Samuel came home today. He's rather upset that I've been working so closely with Coralee while he was away."

"That quarrelsome man always has a problem with something. This town will be better off when he retires. But don't you go worrying about him. He may huff and puff about it, but there's not much he can do now that she's got her medicine. Folks will be flocking back to the shop."

Jake mumbled agreement but he knew better. There was plenty of reason for him to worry. Samuel held the key to his future in Spring Hill. After the way the older doctor had exploded today, Jake was convinced his mentor would make good on his threats if Jake made the wrong choice.

Lily hoisted herself off the rock and joined the children at the edge of the water, leaning down to point out some fish. Louisa squealed and jumped back as one splashed away, making Phillip laugh. The children's antics were adorable, as always. But this time, it wasn't enough to distract Jake from the ultimatum hanging over his head.

He was watching Lily impress the twins by skipping rocks across the creek when the realization hit him. He hadn't even considered where the twins figured into the whole mess. What would happen to Louisa and Phillip if he lost his position with Samuel and had to leave Spring Hill? He couldn't take them away, not when he had promised their mother to do everything in his power to find them a home here. He still hadn't been successful in finding a family for them. And, to be honest, he wasn't sure he wanted to keep trying. It was getting easier to envision a future with the children by his side.

He didn't feel good about it, but in that moment it seemed Jake had made his choice. Coralee's medicine had been a huge hit at their booth on Independence Day. Customers would soon be filling the store again, so she didn't need his help anymore. So he would stay away from her, enough to appease Samuel, at least. He could have his mother help out with the twins. Yes, that was the answer. He was better established at the clinic now, so being farther out of town would be less of an issue. They would move out to the farm so Ma could watch the children when he couldn't. He would be right there to take care of the farm for his parents and Samuel would be pacified. It would all work out beautifully.

Except for Coralee. He forced the unbidden thought down deep. Even though they had formed a sort of truce, Jake had no reason to think she would be upset if he stepped out of her life. Maybe she would even be better off. He seemed to hurt her at every turn.

With a renewed sense of purpose, Jake went to retrieve the children so they could get to bed. He pushed the unease in his heart as far back as possible. Samuel had not left him with any good options in this scenario, but Jake would make the best choice he could for all the people who depended on him.

Chapter Eight

The days following Independence Day passed in a blur for Coralee. The shop was busy much of the time, enough so that she and Cat both needed to be there during business hours. Coralee spent her evenings and even some early mornings replenishing supplies and stocking the shelves. There was much work to be done, but the fact that it was due to an increase in customers made it energizing for her. Papa's shop was fulfilling its purpose again.

The new medicine had drawn people's attention back to Holbrook's. And it seemed to be a help in regaining their trust. Their former customers were coming back in for other remedies, as well.

When they had been planning promotions for the shop, one of Cat's ideas was to offer perfumes, lotions and even cosmetics. Jake had told them about large shops in St. Louis that sold such products alongside their remedies with great success. They had ordered the supplies before Independence Day and the items had just arrived. Coralee almost hadn't put them out, but she was glad they'd taken the chance. The ladies' products were selling just about as well as the medicine. Cat had loved setting up attractive displays for the products she had selected and Coralee was happy to see her sister enjoy her work at the shop again.

Coralee felt as if she was floating around the shop most days. She could hardly believe that after all the time and worry, Papa's medicine was actually working. Holbrook's would be a success once more. She wouldn't need to resort to extreme promotions or Charlie's bank loan.

But even with her long, busy days at the shop, Coralee couldn't help but notice that Jake hadn't been around. In expectation of an increase in business, Jake had sent word that he would have his mother keep the twins until they knew how busy Coralee and her sisters would be. The plan had made sense, but it hurt to admit how much she missed them after just a few days apart. And how disappointed she was that Jake hadn't bothered to see how things were going at the shop after the debut of their medication. As the end of the week approached, her heart jumped every time the shop door opened and she half expected Jake to be standing in the doorway.

By Saturday afternoon Coralee was good and ready for Sunday and some time to rest. Near closing, Mrs. Collins from the mercantile stepped through the door and waved at Coralee. "Hello, dear. My, it has been a while since I've stopped in. The shop looks very nice." The older woman leaned against the counter, looking like she was settling in for a long chat. Coralee stifled a sigh. She had so many things that needed to be done.

"It's nice to see you, Mrs. Collins. Can I get something for you today?"

"Oh, yes, dear. I came for some of that lilac hand lotion I heard about." Coralee grabbed a bottle of the lotion from Cat's display and started wrapping it in brown paper. "I'm so glad to see your father's shop doing well again. But I'm a bit surprised those poor orphans aren't here. Or maybe you aren't watching them anymore, since that nice young doctor moved out of town this week."

Coralee's heart dropped to the floor. She rested a hand on the counter to steady herself. "Dr. Hadley moved? I hadn't heard."

"Oh, yes." Mrs. Collins's eyes sparkled at the chance to spread a little gossip. "He took those children and went to live with his parents. As if Beth Hadley needs more to handle." The older woman's look turned sly. "I'm well aware of the time you spent with Dr. Hadley. I was sure you already knew about his change in location."

"I simply haven't spoken to the doctor for a few days, Mrs. Collins. It's been a busy week here at the shop for Cat and me. I've been rather focused on my work and unable to help with the twins."

"Oh, yes, of course. I suppose your work would come before the little orphans." Somehow the explanation seemed to pacify the woman's gossiping urge. Although that last comment of hers hit a nerve. Coralee cared for the twins more than this meddling woman could understand.

Mrs. Collins prattled on about things happening around town, but Coralee didn't hear much of it. Her mind went back to Jake. Had he really moved and not bothered to tell her? And was she actually surprised? She had been expecting him to hurt her again. But now that she was face-to-face with the pain, she realized her heart had been much more involved than she'd imagined. The sting of tears burned her eyes, but Coralee fought against it. She had to hold herself together until the town's biggest busybody left. The last thing she needed was for gossip to fly around that the widow apothecary had unrequited feelings for the doctor.

After far too long, Mrs. Collins ran out of rumors to spread and left with her lotion. Coralee bid her a distracted farewell then fled to her workroom, wanting to be sure she was alone in case Cat came in from the garden. As soon as she closed the door, the breath caught in her throat as tears overflowed. She had been so sure that she and Jake were becoming friends again. She thought there was a way to protect her heart while also having Jake in her life. But now he was keeping secrets again, shutting her out. She had convinced herself he had changed, but it seemed that wasn't the case. A dull ache formed in her chest. Even though she had expected something like this to happen all along, the reality still hurt.

Coralee was thankful the tears cleared up before

any other customers came in. In their wake, restless energy filled her. She was horrified that the entire town seemed to be aware of all that was going wrong in her personal life. Needing to keep busy, she used the next few quiet hours to catch up on cleaning and re-stocking the shop. And to think through what was happening with Jake. No matter how she looked at the situation, it always came back to Jake not trusting her enough to include her in his life.

After closing up the shop and sending Cat home, Coralee sat alone at her worktable. Bits and pieces of prayers flitted through her mind, but she couldn't seem to form a coherent sentence. Part of a Bible verse flashed in her memory, something Aunt Lily liked to quote. It reminded her that even if she didn't know what to pray for, God would understand what her heart needed.

Feeling less stunned as the news sank in, she decided she was ready to face her family without bursting into tears of embarrassment. Coralee gathered her things and locked up the shop.

A few people were out enjoying the warm evening, but this side of town was quiet after the businesses closed. As she turned from the shop to head home, she caught a glimpse of two strangers leaning against the barbershop across the street. They weren't the kind of men who usually spent time on this street, with its nicer businesses. Even from several buildings away, she could see they were rather grimy, wearing worn clothes and tattered hats. One was gaunt; the other looked to overindulge in strong drink too often. Their presence made her uncomfortable.

Coralee tried not to look at them, but she felt their eyes on her as she headed the other way and crossed the street. Spring Hill usually felt safe, but right then she had never been happier that their home behind the café was so close to Holbrook's. She even took a shortcut over to First Street, choosing a well-traveled alley between a millinery shop and the land office.

Her breath whooshed out in relief when she finally stepped through the door at home. She would have to warn her sisters and Aunt Lily to be careful if they were out alone. There was no telling the intentions of those two loitering about town.

But thoughts of the strange men fled when she walked into the parlor to find papers scattered over all the furniture. On closer inspection, they were pages cut from *Godey's Lady's Book*. Dozens of pages. Illustrations of every facet of fashion imaginable. There were bonnets, hairstyles, hoop skirts, stockings. And the gowns. Gorgeous drawings of the most current styles were everywhere. In the middle of it all, her sisters sat with their customer, Miss Price. All three were talking with wild animation as they debated the most minute details of the drawings.

"What is all this?" Coralee stared around in wonder. The illustrations were beautiful and a dream to examine. But why were they there?

Cat jumped up and grabbed her hands, pulling her farther into the room. "Remember Alyssa Price, the woman who bought our medicine for her father last week?" Coralee nodded, although Cat didn't wait for an answer. Excitement bubbled from her like too many soapsuds overflowing a washtub.

"I've seen her around town a few times since and we've been talking. She's getting married and she asked me and Cecilia to help plan her wedding ensemble."

Cecilia spoke from across the room, face flushed and voice hardly more than a breathy sigh. "Look at all of this, Coralee. She has the most exquisite taste."

Alyssa laughed, a light, melodic sound that perfectly fit her delicate features. "Thank you, Cecilia. How very kind." She turned to Coralee, contentment gracing every inch of her face. "Mrs. Evans, how lovely to see you again. I hope you don't mind my preparations taking over your home for a few hours."

Coralee forced a smile. "Of course not. And, please, call me Coralee. Are you getting married here? I hadn't heard of any recent engagements in town."

Alyssa shook her head, pink tinting her cheeks as she spoke of her intended. "Actually, he's from California and we'll live there on his large cattle ranch. He's just a lovely man, so patient to wait for me while I visit Papa before continuing out for the wedding. Papa doesn't feel that he's up to the long trip, so this is likely our only visit for some time. He's a dear, wanting to be sure I had the best wedding ensemble ever worn in California. He insisted I have it made here where he could see it completed."

Coralee liked this woman's spirit. She was intelligent and seemed like the sort who got what she wanted without using feminine wiles in the process. "Well, I'm glad you asked my sisters to help. Cat has a great eye for fashion and Cecilia is the best seamstress."

Alyssa agreed as she started picking through the pages again. Coralee had no talent with fabric and had always admired her sisters' natural abilities. Or maybe it had more to do with the amount of time they had spent alongside Aunt Lily while Coralee had been at the shop with Papa. Either way, Coralee couldn't come close to their skill.

As her sisters fussed over ideas for Alyssa's wedding gown, Coralee's mind wandered. Memories of her own wedding flooded her. It had been a much simpler affair than Alyssa's would be. But it had been beautiful. Alyssa's bridal excitement reminded Coralee of her own feelings in the days leading up to her wedding.

A sudden vision of Jake in wedding finery took her by surprise. Handsome and smiling, she imagined him standing next to the preacher, waiting for her to reach him. What would his expression be when he saw her walking toward him in a lovely wedding gown?

The imaginary scene evaporated as she realized that all the ladies were staring at her. Her cheeks heated. How long had she been lost in silly daydreams that would never be? She mumbled an excuse and hurried to the kitchen, her aching heart unable to take any more of the happy chatter.

Coralee dropped into a chair and leaned back, eyes closed. Jake had hurt her more than once, yet she still cared for him. So much more than she wanted to admit. She couldn't let these unrequited feelings continue. If Jake was going to shut her out of his life, she would have to protect her heart.

Jake was miserable. It hadn't even been a week, but he missed Coralee. He missed her smile and the easy way she had with the twins. He missed her quick mind. But most of all, he missed her steady friendship.

Most hours of the day, guilt gnawed at him. Coralee had to know by now that he was avoiding her. He hated that she would be hurt by that. Especially since that day a few weeks back when his parents had pointed out that he had done almost the same thing to her after she'd rejected his proposal. His heart ached with the knowledge that, to her, he had once again excluded her from his life. No explanation, no apology.

He had tried to make the best choice he could, but he couldn't get Coralee out of his mind. As he went about the farm chores, he thought of working next to her at the shop while they'd tested elements for her medicine. When he sat to eat with the twins and his parents, he saw her face glowing with gentle compassion at dinner that first night he'd had Louisa and Phillip. No matter what he did, she was never far from his thoughts.

Samuel hadn't said another word about Coralee

and Jake hadn't brought it up. But there was strained tension between them when they were together at the clinic. Jake offered to do all the visits that required riding out of town just so he didn't have to be with Samuel as much.

More and more Jake wondered what had driven the older doctor to have such a complete aversion to Coralee. It sounded like he'd had a cordial working relationship with her father. And he didn't seem to dislike her as a person. It was simply the fact of her running Holbrook's that upset the man.

Church on Sunday morning was the worst part of Jake's week. Before he even got the twins out of the wagon, a voice behind him made him cringe.

"Jake Hadley, what do you mean by hurting my sister again?"

He should have known perceptive Cat would see what was going on. And she would never let him off easy. He turned to face the fiery youngest Holbrook. "Cat, there's more to it than you know."

Cat stood close in front of him, hands planted on her hips and eyes flashing. "Then why don't you explain to me just what's going on here?"

There was no way Cat would appreciate his reasons for relenting to Samuel's demands. She had never been the type of person who felt responsibility for others. But if he couldn't explain the situation to Coralee himself, maybe Cat would accept enough of his reasoning to help her sister hurt a little less.

"I had to make an impossible choice, Cat. Samuel won't allow me to keep my position with him while helping Coralee." He ran a hand through his hair, searching for words that might make Cat see the situation he'd been put in. He gestured to the children playing in the wagon. "The twins. My parents. They all depend on me. I care about Coralee, but I can't let them down."

Cat looked at him askance. "She didn't even know you'd moved out to the farm until yesterday. She had to hear it from Mrs. Collins, that old busybody."

Jake's eyes slid closed. How much must that have hurt her? "I'm sorry. More than you know. But I don't know what else to do."

Cat's lips tightened. "I don't see how you could make that choice, Jake. You're better than that, giving in to a bitter old man's ultimatum. But I can see you feel terrible about it. As you should." She poked him sharply in the chest. "You ought to at least explain to Coralee. Dr. Jay can't control who you talk to."

With that, Cat turned on her heel and marched to the church, head high and shoulders squared. Jake leaned against the wagon, letting the warm sun wash over his face. Maybe Dr. Jay didn't have the right to determine who he could talk to, but Jake was afraid to take that chance. Too much rested on him keeping the position at the clinic. And, after all, maybe it was better for her to just think he was cruel than for her to know he cared, but still chose to hurt her.

His spirit was in turmoil as he walked Louisa and Phillip into the church. He couldn't keep his mind on the service. Coralee was so close, just a few rows ahead of where Jake sat with his parents and the children. As usual, she looked lovely. If he told her so, would that pretty blush appear on her cheeks again?

But even as the thought ran through his mind, he remembered that no matter how nice it sounded, he couldn't risk any pleasant conversations after the service. No joining the ladies for lunch or spending a quiet afternoon walking along the creek with her and the twins. Dr. Jay was sure to react with swift retribution if he felt Jake had disregarded his demands again.

Jake spent most of the service with his head bowed. For a while his thoughts ran rampant, unfocused. But eventually the tumult settled and one prayer emerged. *Lord, show me how to do the right thing for everyone I love.*

Letting all the thoughts empty from his mind, he hoped the Lord would offer him a solution. The preacher's words filtered through the emptiness. "Most of the people I talk to worry about God's will. They're afraid that they'll miss what He wants them to do."

Jake's head shot up. Wasn't that just what he'd been worrying about? He paid more attention to what the minister was saying now. "But He's already told us what we need to do." The man laid his hand on the Bible in front of him. "Love the Lord and love our neighbors."

Listening to the words while staring across the room at Coralee, realization hit him. Going along with Samuel's ultimatum wasn't helping the doctor move past whatever was causing his bitterness toward Coralee. Letting him continue to live in anger wasn't showing him love. Jake cared about the older man, so he couldn't let Samuel keep wallowing in negative feelings. He had to stand up to his mentor, even if that meant things in his own life didn't work out how he'd planned. Confidence washed over him. God would care for his family. Jake just needed to follow His lead.

He hurried the twins out before the last notes of the final hymn faded away. Waiting for his parents in the churchyard, he tried to occupy himself with greeting patients and chasing the twins. It was cowardly, but he hoped Coralee wouldn't confront him. He had to handle the situation with Samuel before he could explain to her and apologize. Again.

But Ma didn't seem to be on the same page about that. She came out of the church with Coralee at her side and walked straight to him. Shuffling his feet, Jake prayed that Coralee wouldn't confront him. Not yet.

"Jake, dear, will you get that basket from the back of the wagon for Coralee? It's some lace trim and fabric her sisters asked for. I need to run over and talk to Mrs. Collins before she leaves."

Without waiting for a response, Ma rushed away, leaving Jake and Coralee alone with the awkwardness between them. She refused to meet his eyes, just waited, biting her lower lip. Jake retrieved the basket and held it out to her. But when she reached for it, he didn't let go right away.

"I guess I need to explain, Coralee. I—"

"No, Jake. You don't need to explain yourself. I believe everything is quite clear. Now, please unhand the basket and I'll be on my way." Her voice was tight and cold.

His heart sank. She wasn't going to listen to a word he had to say.

Reluctantly he let go of the basket and watched her stalk off. He was sure that there was no way to fix his relationship with her until he stood up to Samuel and did what God was urging him to do. Only once he undid his bad decision could he show her that he knew he was wrong. He would find a way to get her to listen to him and pray that she would understand.

The rest of the day Jake felt peace growing. While he and the twins ate lunch with his parents. During the children's nap. Doing the evening chores. Nothing dislodged the certainty that he was finally doing the right thing. He would work things out with Samuel tomorrow, then he would make it up to Coralee. He hoped that she would find it in her heart to listen when he explained everything to her. That she could forgive him one more time. And from then on out, he planned to do everything in his power to keep from hurting her again.

Coralee had forgotten about the two men from Saturday evening until she saw them again as she walked to Holbrook's on Monday morning. There they were, lounging against the same building down the street, boldly watching as she and Cat opened the shop. She didn't say anything to Cat right then. As long as they stayed down the street, she didn't want to risk her impulsive sister confronting them. Later she would warn both her sisters and Aunt Lily to be careful when they were out.

She tried to convince herself that there was nothing sinister about the two strangers. It wasn't that unusual for people to sit outside businesses, watching the street and greeting neighbors. There was just something about these two men. Maybe the way their eyes followed her. It felt intentional, as if they wanted her to know they were watching.

All day, she found herself peeking out the large front windows. They were still there after a young mother left with ointment for her children's constant scratches. She caught a glimpse of them shifting around when an old miner came in for a ginger compound he'd ordered for his indigestion. And Charlie Albridge caught her peering around him while he was asking her for some of their new medicine.

"Coralee, just what is going on out there that you're so interested in?" Charlie searched the street as she flushed at being called out.

"It's nothing. Just a couple rough characters I've seen out there a few times."

Charlie snapped to attention. "Have they approached you? Threatened the store?"

"Oh, nothing like that." She waved off his concern, hoping he didn't push the issue. She didn't want to draw attention to her paranoia. But deep down her gut screamed at her to listen to the unsettled feeling their presence caused.

"If you're worried, I can walk you ladies to and from the store." His eyes strayed to Cat as he offered and Coralee suppressed a grin at his obvious desire to spend time with her sister.

"No, Charlie. We don't need you to do that. If anything happens, we'll come to you." She could only imagine the gossip if the banker started escorting them everywhere. Particularly since Jake was no longer spending so much time with her.

Charlie glanced at Cat again. "I think I must insist. I could never forgive myself if anything happened to any of you."

Shaking her head, Coralee started to protest. "Really, we'll be fine—"

Stomping toward them, Cat interrupted. "Charlie Albridge, I've told you this before. I don't need your protection." She stood shoulder-to-shoulder with Coralee. "My sisters and I are grown women, capable of getting ourselves where we need to go."

The banker raised both hands as if warding off her temper. "I'm sorry. I was only thinking of your safety with strangers lurking about. Never would I claim that you can't handle yourself, my dear Cat."

The glare that followed his comment was enough to send Charlie out the door. They heard him muttering as he left, something about a woman who wouldn't give him a chance. Coralee just shook her head at Cat's antics. Charlie would have to buck up a bit if he intended to pursue her youngest sister.

As seemed to happen more and more, her mind turned to Jake. She wished she could talk to him about the men. He wouldn't overreact and confront them. Or think that her worry was due to female hysterics. When they weren't fighting with each other, he was good at looking at a situation with objectivity. An ache sliced through her. She missed seeing him every day. And she missed the twins terribly. Their sweet little faces and adorable giggles were always in the back of her mind.

No matter how hard she tried, Coralee couldn't get her feelings under control. Every day, she thought this would be the day that she would be stronger. She wouldn't think about Jake, or miss him, or imagine his smile. But building up a wall against him was not as easy as she hoped.

Cat tapped on the counter with her fingers as she passed behind it, breaking Coralee's reverie. "You're lost in your own world today. Anything you want to talk about?"

Coralee narrowed her eyes. Cat usually didn't like talking about serious topics, especially emotional ones. There was a reason she asked the question. "I was thinking about the twins. I miss them."

Cat nodded. "To be honest, I do, too. Imagine that. Me, Catrina Holbrook, sad that there aren't two small children underfoot." After a rueful laugh at her own expense, she paused, smile fading. Her eyes darted to Coralee then away. That wasn't a good sign. Coralee braced herself for more bad news, coming through the grapevine rather than from Jake himself. "I need to be honest about something else, too. I talked to Jake yesterday."

"I see. And what did you talk about?" A sick feeling settled in Coralee's stomach at the mention of his name.

"You. And him. I overheard Mrs. Collins tell you that he'd moved out to the farm. I know that hurt your feelings. How could it not? He's such a dunce. Anyway, I was a little upset with him, so I decided to confront him, ask him why he would hurt you again."

Coralee leaned on the counter, not sure she wanted to know the answer, but unable to keep from asking. "And? What did he tell you?"

Cat's lips thinned into a tight line. "He blamed it on Dr. Jay. He said the old man made it clear Jake would lose his position if he continued to spend time with you. He didn't see any way to keep supporting the twins and his parents if that happened. I don't think that's a good excuse, but even I could see he was pretty torn up about it. I don't think he wanted to hurt you."

A small crack formed in the wall she'd been trying to build up against Jake. How impossible the situation must feel to him. It still hurt to know that he had chosen to abandon her to keep his employment. But she had a feeling that if she had been faced with the same terrible decision, she might have done the same thing.

Monday morning started far too early for Jake. He was roused from sleep before the sun came up by the door to his room creaking open ever so slowly. Cracking open one eye, he saw Louisa's little blond head peek in. Then her shoulders. Then she was standing in the doorway.

Wondering what she would do, he waited. Soon enough, she tiptoed to the bed and stood next to it. "Jake?"

He sat up and reached out to pull her into bed with him. "What's the matter, darling?"

"I sick." She nestled her head into his chest as she spoke the words. His heart nearly broke at her quiet, sad tone.

"Oh, no. You can rest right here with me for a bit and see if that helps you feel better."

It didn't take long for Louisa to doze off, curled against his chest and snoring lightly. But Jake couldn't get back to sleep. In the dimness before dawn, all he could do was wonder what life would be like when he finally found a permanent family for the children. They had grown to be such an integral part of his world in just a short amount of time. He didn't like to think about how much he would miss them when they left.

Along with his lack of experience with children, Jake had never felt a strong interest in them. He had assumed at some point in his life he would marry and have a family. He had put a lot of thought into what marriage would look like before that awful fight with Coralee. But he hadn't considered what it would be like to have children in his life. To be a father.

And now he had two sweet little ones under his

care and he felt like a parent more and more every day. But he constantly had to remind himself that they weren't his children. They deserved a home with parents who knew what they were doing, who could provide them with siblings and all the usual family dynamics.

Jake's mind flashed back to Coralee's revelation that she might never have children of her own. At first he had thought it must be devastating for her to be denied a family. But after coming to care so much for the twins—children who weren't his own—Jake hated that his initial response had been negative.

There was something wonderful about giving orphans a chance to have a loving family. It didn't matter how that family was formed, it was just as vital as one created through biology. He prayed that Louisa and Phillip would find that kind of love wherever God placed them.

He had to talk himself into going to the clinic that day. As the morning wore on, he kept hemming and hawing about getting to town, knowing that he had to confront Samuel when he got there. He spent longer than necessary making sure Louisa wasn't too sick for his mother to handle. Then he made several house calls to farms near his parents' house before heading toward town. He made a house call on First Street and stopped to have an early lunch at Lily's. But the time came when he couldn't put it off any longer. All that was left was to gather his courage and do what God was asking him to do.

He swallowed hard as he entered the clinic, palms

so slick with sweat that he had to wipe them on his pants before turning the doorknob. Relief and nerves battled inside him when he saw that Samuel was in his office. He decided it was now or never and walked straight to the office, knowing that if he stopped at his desk, he would never make himself get up.

The older man bent over his desk, scribbling in a file. "Samuel, I need to speak with you, if you have a moment?"

The doctor looked up and gestured Jake in, leaning back in the chair and stretching his fingers. "Sure, Hadley. I could use a break from catching up on all these files, anyway."

Jake took a deep breath and jumped right in. "It's about our conversation last week. About Coralee."

Samuel steepled his fingers together. "Ah, yes. Well, out with it."

"Sir, I don't feel right about the situation. Coralee has been a good friend for most of my life. I can't just abandon her because you don't like her." He licked dry lips as nerves washed over him again. "I understand if you want to end our arrangement. But I hope that you can see how impossible the situation is for me. Please give me a chance to show you that she isn't a threat to this town."

Samuel turned in his chair and stared out the window behind him. The silence stretched long enough that Jake shifted from one foot to the other, wondering if Samuel would respond at all. Finally, without looking at Jake, he answered. "It's clear that you care for the woman. Perhaps that emotion is clouding your judgment."

Jake's heart squeezed tight. Was this the end of his dreams? "I assure you, I am not acting merely on emotion. My conscience won't let me continue to hurt an innocent person just to stay comfortable here. Don't get me wrong, this position means the world to me. But my first allegiance is to God and He has made it clear that I can't treat Coralee that way."

His mentor turned the chair around so fast it was in danger of tipping over. "While I don't claim any allegiance to God, I know that faith is a powerful motivator for some. So what would God have you do, Hadley? Abandon your parents in their old age? Go back on your word to me when you took this position?"

Lowering himself into a chair, Jake leaned forward, meeting Samuel's skeptical gaze head-on. "God asks me to live for His glory. Anything more than that, He'll handle. He's told us to love others more than ourselves and that's what I'm trying to do. And it isn't all about Coralee. I care about you, too, Samuel. I can't sit back and watch you live in bitterness if I have a chance to help you heal. And I don't think I can do that if I make the choice you seem to expect me to."

Unidentifiable emotions flashed across Samuel's face as Jake waited for his verdict. The older man's voice was gruff when he finally spoke. "I appreciate the sentiment, Hadley. But there's nothing that can help me heal now. Not you and not God." He waved a hand at the door as he turned back to his paper-work. "Get back to work, Hadley."

"That's it? I still have a position here?"

"Yes. Now go. I have quite a bit to catch up on and it won't get done sitting around talking about our feelings." Jake got the sense Samuel wasn't just giving up because Jake's words had convinced him he was wrong. Something was lurking under the surface of the doctor's quick change of heart. Jake only hoped it wasn't something worse than the ultimatum he had just faced.

He left the office before the older doctor could change his mind again. The day seemed to drag on, with the prospect of visiting Coralee waiting at the end. It would be a hard conversation, but he had missed her enough that he was just happy for the chance to be near her again. At least, he hoped she would give him the chance to be near her.

The afternoon was busy, which Jake was thankful for. Several patients came in to consult with Samuel. Jake was called out to examine little Timothy Smith after he fell off a horse, thankfully just twisting an ankle. Then he rode out to his parents' farm to do a few chores and pick up the twins before heading back into town to visit Coralee.

Pulling up in front of Holbrook's, Jake was pleased to see customers entering and exiting the shop. His mother had told him they seemed to be doing more business that week and he couldn't be more proud to see that her assessment had been true.

When they entered the building, several customers stood at the counter, examining displays while they waited. Cat was at the far end of the room, discussing a remedy with a customer. Closer to the door, Coralee counted out tablets of her new medication while Mr. Collins, the mercantile owner, waited. She filled a small tin with the remedy and wrapped up the order.

Jake took the only available seat at a table and leaned back to watch her at work.

"Now, Mr. Collins, you'll need to make sure your wife takes one tablet with a cup of tea every four hours. Come back and see me tomorrow if she isn't feeling better."

The man took his package just as the twins barreled past him and around the counter to Coralee, their shouts drowning out his response. "Coree!"

Her face lit up. "If it isn't my two favorite people." She picked up each child and sat them on the counter, one on each side of her. "I think you've both grown since I last saw you. You must be, oh, ten feet tall."

The little ones giggled. Louisa leaned close to Coralee. "I sing song."

"A song? Could you sing it for me?"

Louisa nodded, her face solemn, then hummed a little tune his mother had taught her. Tender love radiated from Coralee as she listened. Jake's eyes slid shut. It was abundantly clear that Coralee loved the twins. They needed all the love they could get after losing everything they had ever known. How could he have thought the separation wouldn't hurt them as much as it hurt him and Coralee? He had been so selfish.

Longing caught him off guard when Coralee leaned forward and planted a light kiss on each child's forehead before lifting them down from the counter. It was the same kind of kiss his mother had always given him as a child. For a moment he could imagine that he was sitting there watching her with his own children, their children. And he wanted that scene to be real more than he ever thought he would. All the time he had spent with the twins had awakened a desire for a family that he hadn't expected, a desire to make Coralee his wife, adopt the twins, and give both her and the children the family they deserved.

But his own actions continued to drive Coralee away at every turn. Reality crashed back down on him. He was there to fix his terrible mistake. Or try to fix it, anyway. Nervous energy built as Cat and Coralee finished helping the last few customers and the shop emptied. It was almost closing time. Time for Jake to own up to his failures.

Chapter Nine

Coralee was sure she could have cut the tension in the air with a knife as Jake watched her from across the shop. She had no idea why he had showed up now, but she was thankful for the chance to see the twins. Their happy greetings had filled her with so much emotion, she thought it might just burst out of her.

The little ones had wiggled their way right into her heart when she wasn't looking. To her shame, she realized that she was secretly glad no family had come forward to take the children in. She scolded herself for that thought as Louisa and Phillip ran to the workroom to play. Those darling children deserved all the best and a good, loving family was the first step.

As she wrapped a glass bottle in brown paper for an older man, Coralee's eyes met Jake's. For a moment, she couldn't look away. Quickly, she busied herself with her customer, forcing the warm feelings deep down. Even if the reasons for his recent actions were as understandable as Cat had made them sound, Jake had hurt her. Again. She wasn't quite ready to let that go.

Jake's presence stirred the longing she wanted with all her heart to stamp out. When he'd left for medical school without trying to mend their relationship, she had convinced herself she'd misunderstood his intentions. It had seemed like he loved her, but he couldn't have felt the same way she had, no matter what his words seemed to imply. Not if he had been willing to leave her like that.

Now, even after years of change and growth, she couldn't allow herself to believe anything between them had changed. He claimed to want her in his life, but then he'd turned around and chosen to push her out of it without so much as a word of explanation. No matter what she longed for, the reality was clear. Jake did not care for her any more now than he had all those years ago.

Feeling his eyes on her as she helped the last few customers of the day, her throat went dry. She knew as soon as the last person left, she would have to face Jake and whatever he had come to say. Her heart pulled in two different directions. She dreaded the confrontation and the pain it could bring, but at the same time she longed to know if he would say the words she wanted to hear.

When the last customer left, Jake pushed up from his seat and crossed to the counter. "I'm thrilled to see so many people in the shop, Coralee. You've accomplished what you set out to do. And your father would have been proud."

She couldn't help but smile at that. "Thank you, Jake. I'm just relieved that Papa's idea was as sound as he hoped and that people appreciate it. It would have been devastating to lose everything he'd worked so hard for."

Jake nodded and they both looked away, awkwardness settling between them. Coralee wondered if he would ever just say what he had come to say. She could tell there was something on his mind.

Before either of them could break the silence, Cat shooed the twins out of the workroom, where she was trying to clean up for the day. Phillip ran straight to Coralee and she swung him up high in the air before wrapping her arms around him. "Well, little man. It's about time for us to lock up the shop. Want to help me?"

With more gravity than she usually saw from him, Phillip nodded. He ran ahead of her to the back door and she showed him how to fit the key in the lock and turn it to secure the door. Then she stood him on a chair pulled up to the counter and let him wipe down the large scale while Cat set Louisa to sweeping the floor.

In no time, they were heading out the front door. Cat hurried on ahead, claiming she was already late for an appointment. Coralee was fairly certain her sister just wanted to give them some time alone. Even as she shook her head at her sister's antics, she glanced down the street. A burst of unease tightened her chest. There they were: two strange men with their eyes on her, focused even through the steady stream of people out enjoying the warm evening. Trying not to stare back at them, she turned and found Jake following the direction of her gaze. Heat burned her neck. A few days ago she would have spilled her fears about the men to him. But now she just wanted to get home without any incidents. She tried to keep her eyes straight ahead rather than straying back to the strangers.

They stopped at Jake's wagon, tension hanging between them as the twins climbed into the back. "Coralee, I was thinking maybe…you would agree to have dinner with me tonight?"

That was the last thing she'd expected him to say. Glancing up in surprise, she caught a cringe on his face. If he was that unhappy about having dinner with her, why had he asked in the first place? Her chin lifted, lips pursed. "I don't think that's necessary. If you'll just take me home, you can be on your way."

"Wait, Coralee." His voice implored her but she did her best to ignore it. "I need to talk to you. It's high time we get all our differences out in the open."

Her heart lurched. She wasn't sure that sounded like an apology was forthcoming. Still refusing to meet his eyes, her mind raced to come up with an excuse. Her gaze strayed down the street again, meeting the blatant smirk of one of the two strangers. Distracted by the men, she jumped when Jake's fingertips brushed her chin and he turned her face to his.

"Please. Just let me give you a ride home and consider giving me a chance to explain."

Against her better judgment, Coralee's heart melted a little. She nodded and let Jake help her up onto the wagon seat. She still wasn't sure it was a good idea to have dinner with him, but maybe she would at least hear him out. Her gaze again turned to the street behind them. And, just as she'd feared, the two men still hadn't stopped watching her.

Jake held the reins still and faced her. "Coralee, you keep looking behind us and you seem worried. Is something going on?"

She hesitated, twisting a bit of hair that had come loose from under her bonnet. His face was rigid with concern. He wasn't going to let it go until she told him what was going on. She decided it wouldn't hurt to mention the two men. Most likely the entire thing was her imagination running wild, anyway. "I'm sure it's nothing. There are a couple of men back there that have been watching the shop for the last few days. There must be a reasonable explanation as to why they're there. They probably aren't even really watching me. I'm just a little jumpy."

Jake swiveled on the hard seat to see for himself. Coralee refused to turn again. She knew exactly what he would see. "Have they approached you? Spoken to you?" Jake's voice sounded tight and hard as he turned back to her and Coralee prayed that he wouldn't do something silly like jump out of the wagon and confront the men.

"No, nothing like that. They just stand there. It

seems to me that they're watching the shop. But I can't come up with any reason why they would do that."

He didn't respond right away and Coralee worried that he would do something reckless. But his expression turned thoughtful. "Did Mr. Johnson say he would have anyone checking in? They don't look like the sort to be working with the Association, but maybe he sent them."

Coralee shook her head. "No, he said a proctor would arrive to administer the examination if I sent in the paperwork. But nothing else."

Jake urged the horse into action, heading toward home. "Well, I'm fairly certain the Association wouldn't hire men like that, anyway. I'm trying to come up with a reasonable, innocent explanation. We'll keep an eye on them. If something happens at the shop, anything that bothers you or seems unusual, tell me right away. And I'll try to stop by often during the day to make sure they stay in line."

Coralee looked away, unable to answer. No matter how hard she tried to convince herself Jake's words meant nothing more than worry for a friend, her too eager heart warmed at his obvious concern and the thought of seeing him more.

All the way to Coralee's house, Jake kicked himself for not just apologizing at the shop. Coralee had been so happy to see the twins and, to be honest, he was dreading the conversation. So he'd put it off. But the evening wasn't going to last forever. If she would listen, he would have to explain himself when they got to her house.

Cecilia met them at the door when they arrived. "Aunt Lily asked me to send you over to the café, Coralee. It's slow tonight, so she's working on some new recipes and wanted taste-testers."

Coralee turned to him, looking ready to dismiss him. But before she could, Cecilia spoke again, eyes wide with feigned innocence and voice syrupy sweet. "Why don't you go, too, Jake? Aunt Lily would love more opinions. I'll keep the twins and get them some supper here. Then you two can enjoy a meal in peace."

Jake caught the quelling look Coralee sent her sister and jumped in to answer before she could refuse the offer. He wasn't going to miss this chance to make his apology. "Thanks, Cecilia. That would be nice. Coralee?" He held out his arm to her, glad when she didn't protest. She simply threaded her arm through his and let him lead her to Lily's.

As Cecilia had said, the restaurant was almost deserted. Jake picked a table near the large front window and held Coralee's chair before taking his seat. Scanning the room, he tried to find the words he needed to say. He rubbed damp palms on his trousers. This was harder than he'd imagined it would be. All the explanations he wanted to give her sounded flimsy. The last thing he wanted to do was upset her more by making her think he was creating excuses for his behavior.

His gaze settled on her. Even just sitting there,

dressed in a plain work dress with her hair mussed from a busy day, she was beautiful. He couldn't take his eyes off her as she watched the street. Coralee must have felt him staring. She turned to meet his eyes as he started to speak. "Do you remember when we came here that first time after I got back to town?"

She tilted her head to one side. "So much has happened since then, hasn't it?" Her blue eyes stayed locked on his, taking Jake's breath away. He became aware of familiar emotions welling up between them, almost palpable. A warning echoed through his mind as warmth grew in his heart. As much as he wanted her in his life, he also wanted their connection to stay limited to friendship. But those endless blue eyes drew him in, made him wish there could be so much more between them. He was almost relieved when Lily walked up, breaking the moment.

"I'm glad to see you made it, Coralee, my dear. And you brought along our Jake, too." She hugged each of them then rattled off a list of recipes she had prepared. Jake chose a stew that sounded rather interesting and Coralee asked for the roast. Lily headed to the kitchen, promising the food would be out in no time.

Sure enough, a girl he didn't recognize brought their food just a few minutes later. Jake snuck peeks at Coralee between bites, admiring her all over again as she watched the few other patrons. Jake had to admit that in spite of his best efforts, he couldn't help noticing her. She was smart, independent, capable and, to top it all off, beautiful. Any man would pay attention to a woman like that. His heart squeezed hard at the idea that at some point, a man would pay attention. Then she would likely remarry and build a life. Without him.

"How is the stew?" It was Coralee who finally broke the silence, much to Jake's relief. His thoughts were going in a direction he didn't much like.

"Delicious. Want a taste?" Jake had no idea why he'd asked that. As soon as the words left his mouth, he cringed at how intimate they sounded. But she didn't seem to notice, just nodded, eyes on his bowl.

He filled his spoon and reached it across the table, holding his hand underneath so the liquid wouldn't spill on the clean tablecloth.

Coralee took the bite he offered, closing her eyes as the taste hit her tongue. "You're right. That is delicious. Thank you for sharing."

Jake couldn't find any words for a moment. His heart raced and he fought to keep his breath coming evenly. Searching for a distraction, his eyes fell on her empty plate. "How was yours? The combination of spices Lily used sounded quite different from the roast Ma makes."

"It was different, but in a good way. I enjoyed it. But then, I've always enjoyed adventurous food. Growing up with Lily's constant kitchen experiments, I guess I had to." Coralee's eyes finally regained the happy sparkle he was used to seeing as she shared memories of growing up with her aunt's cooking.

They laughed and reminisced about Lily's past culinary trials until the waitress returned and cleared their plates. A heavy silence settled between them. Jake knew it was now or never. He had to confess his mistakes, even if it hurt her again. "Coralee, I think you're aware that there are some things I need to say."

Her lips had barely parted to reply when a pretty blond woman appeared at their table. She had a hand pressed to her side and was gasping for breath, as if she'd run the length of Spring Hill. Jake's medical training kicked in and put him on alert. Something was wrong.

"Oh, Coralee, there you are. Cecilia told me you'd be here."

Coralee jumped up and took the woman by the arms. "Alyssa, what's wrong? Is it your father?"

"His headache is so bad this time that he won't eat and he nearly fell when he tried to get out of bed. He just lays there moaning. I didn't know if I should give him a higher dose of your medicine, so I came to find you. What should I do?"

Jake stood, ready to jump into action. Both women looked at him. A sudden thought halted the words on his tongue. He couldn't charge ahead without thinking of Coralee. "Miss, I'm Dr. Hadley. If it's all right with Coralee, could we visit your father? If we can examine him, Coralee can decide how much of the medication he needs." He looked to Coralee, thrilled when she consented with eyes shining. Maybe he had finally done something right.

"Oh, yes. Thank you, Doctor. I'm Alyssa Price." He tipped his hat as they followed her out of the café and down First Street to a small, neat house. Inside, she led them straight to a darkened bedroom, where her father lay in bed, tossing fitfully. Covered with a heavy quilt even on the warm evening, all they could see of Mr. Price was white hair sticking out every which way. Alyssa woke her father with a gentle voice and light shake.

"Papa, I found Mrs. Evans and she brought Dr. Hadley along. They're going to check you over and decide how much of the medicine you need."

Jake examined the older man while Coralee asked him questions about his condition. "Mr. Price, how often do you have headaches?"

His answer was barely audible through clenched teeth. "At least once a week."

"How much pain would you say you're in right now?"

"More than any other time in my life."

Mr. Price's eyes were bloodshot. Jake had the man watch his finger move back and forth, checking to see if his eyes tracked well.

Coralee made notes in a small, bound book that she'd borrowed from Alyssa. "And where do you feel the most pain?"

He pointed to a spot on his head and Jake stepped back to let Coralee take a look before he examined the spot. A bit warm, but not swollen. Painful to even the lightest touch.

"And any dizziness?"

Jake was pleased that Coralee thought to ask the question. She had a quick mind, just one of the traits that made her a wonderful apothecary.

Mr. Price started to nod then raised a hand to his head with a moan. Jake met Coralee's eyes and he saw her add a note to her list about increased pain upon movement. While Coralee finished her notes, Jake checked the man's pulse and the rate of his breathing. Then they excused themselves and stepped out of the room to confer.

"Mr. Price seems fine physically, except for the pain and dizziness. Any symptoms I saw are likely related to the headache. What do you suggest, Coralee?" Jake watched as she paced the hallway, fascinated by the play of emotions on her face as she thought through Mr. Price's condition. After several minutes she stopped pacing and looked up.

"From what I've learned about the medication from patients, there haven't been any notable side effects. So I feel it's safe to increase his dose. Alyssa said they're out and I don't have any in my case at home, so I'll run back to the shop to measure out what he needs."

"I'll let them know we'll be right back."

"No, Jake. You stay here in case Mr. Price's condition changes. Alyssa is distraught. I hate to think that he might worsen while they're here waiting on us. I can get there and back just fine on my own."

Jake took hold of her shoulders. "I don't like the idea of you going out there alone. Not with those men loitering by the shop."

Coralee's lips pressed into a tight line. "I'm not a damsel in distress, Jake. I'm sure I've blown the situation out of proportion and those men won't even be around so late in the evening. I'll be fine."

She spun on her heel and marched out of the small house, leaving Jake wavering. He wanted to follow her, but he didn't want to disregard her request and upset her again. He took a step toward the door then stopped. Heaviness settled in his stomach. He couldn't destroy the tentative peace between them by acting like he didn't trust her. With a deep breath, he forced the unsettled feeling away and went back to the bedroom to sit with Mr. Price until Coralee returned. And he had to believe that she would return, safe and sound.

The blood thrummed in Coralee's veins as she hurried through town toward Holbrook's. As soon as she stepped out of Mr. Price's house into the darkness, she knew it would have been wiser to have Jake accompany her. But she had survived on her own too long to start depending on a man again. Jake had just started to treat her as an equal, a capable person in her own right. It would be terrible if a little silly fear diminished his respect for her.

Trying to focus on something besides the tightness in her chest, she let her mind turn to the dinner they had shared. The emotions that had been stirred up by that intimate time together scared her. She wanted Jake and the twins in her life, but she wasn't sure she could handle anything more than being his friend. Losing Alan had left her inconsolable for too long. Her mind screamed that taking that risk again was too perilous. But her stubborn heart refused to listen to that logic and kept feeling things she hadn't felt since before Alan had gotten sick.

Pushing her shoulders back, Coralee walked with as much confidence as she could manage. Doing this alone would help her prove to herself that she didn't need Jake. She could have him in her life without relying on him too heavily. Without opening her heart up to more sorrow than it could handle.

Relief flooded her when she turned onto the street the shop was on and saw that it was completely deserted. No strangers stood in the shadows across from the shop. Whatever reason the men had for being there, they were gone now. Feeling lighter and much more confident, she reached the shop door and turned her key in the lock.

As the door swung shut behind her, Coralee paused. It must have been her nerves, but she thought she heard a sound like feet shuffling in the back of the shop. After waiting several moments, she didn't hear anything else. Shaking it off as her imagination running wild, she took several tentative steps, hands outstretched as she tried to find her way in the dark.

This time, when the shuffling sound came, she was certain she'd heard it. She froze, breath coming in shallow gasps that she tried to keep quiet with little success. Her eyes swung back and forth, but she didn't see anything in the dark shop. Ever so slowly, she backed toward the door.

With an abrupt crash, a shadowy shape started moving behind the counter. She fought for air, gasping and frozen in place again. The figure ran through the back of the shop. It felt like an eternity before her feet finally moved. She stepped back, hitting the door with her elbow as she fumbled for the knob without taking her eyes off the intruder. But before she could get it open and run, the dark shape disappeared out the back door, leaving it swinging open to the night.

The sound of her pounding heart filled Coralee's ears. Every instinct told her to get out of there. But she had to see what had happened, see if there was anything stolen or damaged. With great effort, she forced her weak legs to step forward rather than turn and flee from the shop. She took slow steps into the room, eyes scanning the back for more moving shadows.

When she reached the counter, another sensation caught her attention. A whiff of something familiar yet out of place mingled with the usual smell of herbs and soap. A slight popping sound. It hit her in a rush. Smoke. Now she heard the recognizable crackling sound coming from her workroom. She lunged behind the counter. Reaching the open door, her worst fear was confirmed. Holbrook's was on fire.

Coralee turned and raced to the front entrance, hands shaking so hard that she could hardly grip the doorknob. When she finally managed to pull it open, she took off racing toward the Price house. The only thought she could register was that Jake would know what to do. She had to get to Jake.

She was almost there when she heard the church bell start to ring. Of course. She should have sounded the alarm first to alert the town to fire. At least someone else had noticed and sent out the warning. She kept running and clambered into the small house, unable to control the racket she was making. Jake emerged from Mr. Price's bedroom just as she reached the hallway, Alyssa standing behind him with mouth agape.

As soon as Coralee caught sight of Jake standing there with worry creasing his face, she broke apart. Falling into his arms, she sobbed, unable to stop long enough to answer his panicked questions. Every ounce of fear and anguish poured out of her. Finally, Jake pushed her back and grabbed her by the arms, shaking her lightly.

"Please talk to me. Are you all right? You have to tell me what's happened."

His terrified voice snapped her out of the weeping. "It's the shop." The words stuck in her throat as it swelled. "Fire." She'd just managed to croak the word out. As soon as it left her lips, Jake sprang into action. He took Coralee's hand and they ran back toward Holbrook's. When they got close, they started to see people gathering. The whole town was drawn to the scene by the sound of the church bell ringing the alarm and the men who were shouting out warnings.

Coralee's heart pounded from more than just all the running. She dreaded rounding the corner where the shop would come into view. How much damage would the fire have done by now?

Smoke was everywhere as they ran closer, stirred up by a strong wind blowing in from the south. Several men were organizing the onlookers into two lines and passing out leather buckets. Jake looked at her in frustration, voice raised so he could be heard over the noise of the fire and the gathering crowd. "Where's the fire company? Is this our only means of fighting the blaze?"

Coralee shrugged. "The town grew so fast, no one has taken the time to get fire equipment. This is the best we can do. I'm going to join the bucket return line."

Jake grabbed her hand before she turned away. "Be careful, Coralee." Intensity burned in his eyes, just as bright as the flames that now licked the roof of Holbrook's. Her breath caught and all she could do was nod as he released her hand and they moved off to find places in line.

Coralee joined the women and younger boys in a line that passed empty buckets back to the nearest well to be refilled. The full buckets were then moved down a line of older boys and men to the blaze. Anyone who wasn't in the lines got drafted to clear furniture and items of value out of the buildings to the north. They tried to save what they could from the businesses that were in danger of catching fire from the flying sparks.

The work was dirty and exhausting. Coralee's arms ached, even though she was only passing empty buckets. Soot and sparks flew everywhere, singeing her clothes and hair and covering her in a fine, black dust. Fear and worry formed a heavy rock in the pit of her stomach. She couldn't slow her racing thoughts enough to pray even a single word.

Spurred on by the wind, the blaze crossed a gap next to Holbrook's and moved down the row of closely packed businesses. Shouts rose, warning those clearing out valuables in the next few buildings. Efforts to empty the buildings further down the fire's path intensified. If they couldn't save the structures, at least they could save some belongings.

The town's residents worked into the night. But it wasn't until the flames reached a wide break in the row of buildings that the fire could be controlled. The crews moved to the gap and stamped out every spark that tried to ignite on the ground. Finally the flames were put out. Overcome by emotion, Coralee didn't even want to count how many businesses had burned to the ground.

Those who didn't have reason to stay trudged home to clean up and rest. Others remained to sift through what they could, sorting out rescued items and taking inventory of the damage. All around, people speculated on what had caused the fire to start. They bemoaned the dry summer that had made it so easy for the blaze to spread.

Coralee could only sit on the ground in front of Holbrook's, now reduced to a smoldering pile of ash and melted glass.

Through the numbness of loss and exhaustion, she

waited for the reality of her failure to come crashing down on her. She had pulled Papa's shop through losing customers and a tarnished reputation, only to see it physically destroyed right before her eyes. There was nothing left. None of Papa's notes. None of the remedies he had worked so hard to bring to their town. His entire legacy had just gone up in flames.

Fire shot up all around Coralee. She tried to scream for help, but no sound would come out. Standing in the middle of Holbrook's, the flames were licking the floor close by her feet and blocking her from the doors. Shadowy faces leered at her from the other side of the blaze. As she scrambled to find a way out, sharp voices cut through the crackling, creaking sounds of the fire. A shout nearby brought her out of sleep with a jerk. It had only been a nightmare.

But what was the shouting about? Awareness started to return and she realized she was not snug in her bed at home. Why was she outside on the ground? The terrifying night came back in a rush as she climbed to her feet, every inch of her body sore and stiff. The man in the shop. The horrible fire. She remembered sitting in the rubble and waiting for the usual flood of guilt over her failure, but it never came. She must have fallen asleep. Pushing to her feet, she did her best not to look at the destruction she knew was behind her.

"Here's Coralee! She's alive!" Cat was the one doing the shouting that had woken her up. Her youngest sister ran over and grabbed her in a hug so tight she started to see stars. Pushing back from Cat, Coralee sucked in a deep breath.

"Oh, Coralee, we were all so worried about you." Cecilia and Aunt Lily hurried to join them as Cat spoke in a rush. "We heard the fire bell and tried to help, but there was nothing anyone could do. It spread so fast. And then when morning came and we realized you weren't home, we had to come out searching for you."

Cecilia chimed in, sniffling as she tried to hold back sobs. "I'm just so glad you're safe." The four women embraced, tears flowing as they rejoiced and mourned at the same time. Seeing her sisters' faces as they surveyed the wreckage, sadness washed over Coralee. She realized for the first time that even though they didn't love working in the shop, Papa's business had meant just as much to them as it had to her. They had lost their father's legacy, just as she had. If their pain felt anything like the hole that had been ripped open in her heart, she wished desperately that she had a way to heal it for them.

Practical Cat was the first to pull away. "What happened, Coralee? We've heard that it started here in the shop, but how?"

Coralee finally turned and stared at the ruins of Holbrook's. Her stomach dropped, hard as a rock as she told the story. "Alyssa's father had a severe headache and they needed more of our medication right away. I didn't have my travel case so I came here to get some. When I entered the shop, there was a man running out the back and I smelled the smoke. It started in the workroom, although I couldn't see what caused it. I ran to get…" Her voice trailed off as the world started to spin around her. "Jake. He came with me, but I didn't see him again after we joined in fighting the fire. Where is he?" She glanced frantically at her family.

Aunt Lily rested a calming hand on her arm. "He breathed in too much smoke and collapsed. They took him out to the farm until Dr. Jay could examine him. I took the twins out to Beth as soon as we heard, but Dr. Jay hadn't arrived, yet. We don't know any more than that."

Coralee grasped her sisters' hands to keep from falling. *Not Jake, too. Lord, haven't I lost enough? Alan. Papa. The shop. And now Jake? It's too much.*

"Do you want me to saddle the horse for you? There isn't much we can do here, so you may as well go sit with Jake."

Cat's suggestion caused a chill to wash over Coralee. She looked at the circle of well-meaning faces and it felt like the very sky was closing in on her. She started backing away. "No. I… I need some time. I'm sorry." She turned and ran as the tears started to fall again.

When she reached the creek, Coralee checked behind her, relieved that no one had followed. She realized she had blindly run to the same spot where she and Jake had come with the twins weeks before, the day she'd discovered the ingredient for Papa's medicine. She dropped to her knees underneath the willow tree Jake had cut bark from, staring out at the narrow band of water as it rippled softly.

The turmoil in her heart strangled any appreciation she might have felt for the peaceful landscape. The shop was gone. Papa's dream—her dream—up in smoke. And Jake. The ache in her chest spread. Jake was hurt and no one knew if he would recover. If his throat or lungs had been scalded too much by the hot smoke, he might not survive.

She leaned forward, forcing her body to pull in air so she wouldn't faint. How had this happened again? She had tried so hard to keep from relying on another man after losing Alan and Papa. She couldn't withstand another loss. The shop was bad enough. But she had come to care for Jake again, to rely on his friendship, and maybe to hope for more than that. And now he was being ripped from her life, just like the other men she had cared for.

Her spine straightened with purpose as the panic subsided. She wasn't going to let this happen without doing something. Maybe she couldn't help Jake, but she could go back and be there for her sisters. Standing, Coralee looked down at her rumpled, soot-covered clothing. Since she was already a mess, she might as well help the others dig through what was left. Until she figured out what to do without Holbrook's, she would keep putting one foot in front of the other, doing whatever was right in front of her.

When she walked down Second Street, stepping around piles of items that had been pulled from the path of the fire, her sisters and aunt all stopped working. They stood in the ruins of her hopes and dreams, waiting for her to respond. She stopped in the middle of the street, wondering if she had the strength to go on.

Cecilia stepped close, eyes full of concern. "Are you all right? We didn't mean to upset you. You seemed so worried about Jake that we thought you'd want to see for yourself how he's doing. We weren't trying to push you."

Coralee blanched at the mention of his name but forced herself to stay in control. "I understand and I'm fine. We need to see if there's anything that can be saved. Each of us can take a corner and we'll meet in the middle." She saw the concerned looks the other women were exchanging, but she chose to ignore them. Some good, hard work would make everything look better. Taking a deep breath, she stepped into the rubble, refusing to meet anyone's eyes. "Let's salvage what we can of Papa's dream."

But the work wasn't as easy as that. Every recognizable item she pulled out of the ashes made tears well up in her eyes. There was next to nothing that they could save. And to top it all off, Aunt Lily refused to stop hinting that Coralee should go see Jake.

When the others stopped for lunch, she decided enough was enough. The thought of food turned her stomach anyway, so she would go to the Hadley farm. Just to keep Aunt Lily from making any more pointed remarks.

The ride out to the Hadley farm gave Coralee too much time to worry. But at the same time she almost wished the ride took longer, just to put off the pain of seeing Jake hurt. Relief and fear warred within her as the house came into view. What would she find when she got there? Why had she agreed to come?

She almost turned around and rode right back to town when her heeled boots hit the floorboards of the porch. The panic was returning. It would be too much like when Alan was ill. All the hours she had spent at his bedside flooded her mind. Hours of watching him waste away, unable to do anything for him. Her breath was coming in gasps when Beth opened the door.

"Oh, my dear. I'm glad to see you're all right." The older woman pulled Coralee into a hug, holding tight. She sank into the embrace as it calmed her spirit. But she wasn't here for comfort. Pulling away, she scanned Beth's face for any sign of Jake's condition. She looked worried but not grieved.

"I heard Jake was injured last night. How is he, Beth?"

One corner of her mouth lifted in a sad half smile. "He hasn't woken up yet. Dr. Jay was here soon after they brought Jake in. Said he couldn't tell yet how much damage there is. He's returning soon to see if we can wake Jake up." She rested a hand on Coralee's shoulder. "You can go up and look in on him."

Coralee swallowed hard as her throat went dry. This was silly. She had been at dozens of bedsides since losing Alan. Why was this so different?

Because you love him.

Her hands shook. No. She wasn't going to think

like that. Jake was her friend. Squaring her shoulders, she forced the thought away and marched up the stairs, determined to prove her own mind wrong. Beth went ahead of her and opened the door quietly, peeking in, then gesturing Coralee to the doorway. With a deep breath, she looked into Jake's bedroom.

Her eyes scanned the room before settling on the bed. She had been there several times when they were younger and the room looked much the same as she remembered. A few childhood mementos and family photographs. A lamp on the table by his bed. Stacks of books. Her heart lifted the tiniest bit when she saw several of the twins' toys in one corner.

But Jake's still form finally drew her attention. He was too pale. Her eyes snapped shut, squeezing so tightly that she saw stars behind her eyelids. Pulling in another deep breath, she followed Beth to the bedside. With a will of its own, her hand reached out and brushed his where it rested on the quilt. A memory flashed in her mind of holding Alan's hand in his final moments. The air sucked out of the room. She had to go. Barely waving to Beth, she rushed from the room and left the Hadley house as fast as she could.

Chapter Ten

Jake woke to searing pain in his throat, disoriented. The events of the night before came back to him in pieces. Coralee insisting on going to Holbrook's alone. The paralyzing fear when she'd stumbled into the Price home crying. Fighting the fire for what felt like an eternity. But no matter how hard he tried, after the hours spent passing buckets in the line, he didn't remember anything.

He was in his own bed at the farm but wasn't sure how he'd gotten there. He took inventory of his body as he lay still. The painful swelling in his throat and the pounding headache must mean he had succumbed to smoke while at the scene of the fire.

A quiet conversation outside the open door drew his attention. "Doc, how will we know if he's going to recover?" Ma's voice was hushed, but Jake could still hear the strain of worry in her tone.

Samuel's low voice answered her. "We'll have to watch him closely for several days. He may seem fine now but worsen later. We just won't know how severe his injuries are until some time has passed."

The doctor appeared in the doorway. "Ah, our patient is awake." Samuel set his bag on the end of the bed and opened it, digging for the tools he needed as Ma followed him into the room.

"Jake, my dear, how do you feel?" His mother perched on the edge of a chair that was pulled up next to his bed, twisting the corner of her apron in her fingers.

But Samuel stepped in. "Don't try to talk, Hadley." The older doctor explained the situation as he checked Jake's vitals. "You collapsed while fighting the fire last night. I believe you have some damage to your throat from the smoke. My recommendation is rest and no speaking for several days. I was just explaining to your mother that it will take at least that long for the full extent of your injuries to become clear."

Samuel finished his examination and busied himself with putting his tools back in his bag. "You know how this can go. We're watching for infection or delayed symptoms. If anything starts to feel worse, let someone know right away. I've told your mother what to watch for."

Jake nodded, but Samuel didn't look his way again before hurrying from the room. Jake turned and examined his mother, noting her red-rimmed, bloodshot eyes. She was still twisting the corner of her apron in her fingers. He reached his arms out for her, nearly breaking apart himself when she fell into his embrace and burst out in tears. His condition must be serious for his strong ma to be this distraught.

"Oh, Jake. I'm sorry for acting so emotional. Dr. Jay couldn't tell us for sure that you would survive the night. We've been so worried."

Jake couldn't reassure her with words, so he tried to communicate his understanding by squeezing her hand tight. She stood and helped him get a drink from the glass on his bedside table. He winced as the water raked down his throat and she sniffed back more tears. But she just tucked him into bed and kissed his forehead like she always had when he was a child. He was asleep before she left the room.

Nightmares haunted Jake's fitful sleep. He kept hearing the crackling flames as they consumed Holbrook's. He dreamed he could see Coralee through the smoke, but when he tried to reach for her, the fire shot up between them. When it died back down, she was gone. But there were his parents and the twins, standing in the shadow of a building as the fire licked at the walls. Jake could see that it was going to collapse on them and he tried to warn them. But he couldn't move, couldn't scream a warning.

He woke with a jerk, just as the wall started to fall on his family. There were no flames, just his room, darkened with the falling dusk. Letting his pounding head fall back onto the pillow, he focused on the image of Coralee from his nightmare. Was she all right? Fear made his breath come faster, in painful spurts. What if she was injured, too? What if she needed him?

The worst part was knowing that he had put off apologizing to her, saying the words she needed to hear. And now he may never get the chance to tell her how wrong he'd been. She deserved so much more than he had given her. He prayed that if he got the chance to apologize to her, he could do it right. That somehow he could show her he understood all the pain he had caused her in the past and convince her that he wanted more than anything to make up for it.

His impulse was to jump right out of that bed and find her, no matter the state of his health. The nightmare had stirred up all the feelings he had wanted to ignore for weeks. He could no longer deny that he loved Coralee. He wasn't sure when he had let that happen again, but he had. And now it might be too late to do anything about it.

Ma peeked into the room, fear on her face. He wondered what kind of noises he had made in his sleep to bring her to his bedside so quickly. As she got him a drink and rearranged his blankets, Jake tried to pantomime to her. It took several frustrating tries at communicating before she jumped up and found paper and a pencil on his desk. Relieved, Jake wrote out his questions.

How is Coralee? And how bad was the fire?

Ma smiled tiredly. "I don't believe there were any other injuries. Coralee stopped by this morning. She was…rather upset when she saw you. As for the shop, well, it's gone. And the rest of the buildings to the north of it. Some property was recovered, but we're all just thankful no lives were lost."

Yet.

The word remained unspoken, but Jake knew it was in Ma's mind. He felt like he would recover. He imagined he could feel his body healing. But effects from breathing in smoke like this could be tricky. Samuel was right: it would be several days before they knew for sure if Jake was out of danger.

Ma patted his hand and left the room. Jake lay still in bed as his thoughts raced. If he took a turn for the worse, what would happen to his parents? And the twins? Ma couldn't raise them for long, not with Pa's injury and the farm to handle. He worried about Coralee. She must be devastated after losing the shop. Was anyone there to comfort her? Jake's hands clenched into fists. He hated that he was stuck there in bed, doing nothing while Coralee suffered.

He closed his eyes, deliberately taking slow breaths in an effort to relax. Getting upset about things he couldn't control would only hinder the healing process. For several minutes Jake let all his frustrated, helpless thoughts spin into prayers. He couldn't handle anything on his own right now, but he was learning that God could handle everything better than he ever could.

Rustling in the hall drew his attention and he watched as two little blond heads peeked around the door frame. With a grin, he gestured Louisa and Phillip to his side. They ran straight to him and clambered up onto the bed on either side of him. But then they just sat and stared. Jake's eyes slid closed. These precious children hadn't seen their parents ill, but they'd known they had lost something important. The many tears they had shed in the first few weeks he'd had them were evidence of that. And now the person they had come to rely on most was hurt. Ignoring the pain in his arms, Jake pulled their small bodies close.

Looking into their trusting, love-filled faces, realization hit him with sudden intensity. He wanted to keep them with him forever. In that moment Jake knew that he couldn't give Louisa and Phillip up to anyone else. He loved them. They were a family now and he couldn't force them to give that up again. He squeezed the children—his children—closer still.

Even as he basked in the knowledge that he didn't have to watch the twins leave his care, Jake knew that there was one more thing he had to do to make their family complete. The minute his health returned he would confess his mistakes and his love to Coralee. And this time he wouldn't give her reason to doubt any of his intentions.

After leaving the Hadley farm, Coralee rode the horse straight back to where the shop used to stand. The street was deserted. Most of the wreckage of the other buildings had been sorted through and deemed unsalvageable. But Coralee couldn't seem to stop digging in the ashes.

As the afternoon shadows lengthened, she knew it was over. Nothing was going to be saved. She started to wipe her hands on her skirt until she looked down and saw how ruined it was with stains. A bath and her soft bed sounded wonderful. How long had it been since she'd eaten? But somehow she couldn't bring herself to leave the site and just go home.

Even as she stood there debating what to do next, Aunt Lily came marching down the street with a basket. "I thought you could use a bite to eat." She turned all the way around, examining the devastation along Second Street. With a deep, sad sigh, she plopped down on the remains of the raised boardwalk in front of the shop.

After a moment of hesitation Coralee joined her aunt. She might as well eat before deciding what to do next. They unloaded the basket in silence before Aunt Lily offered a prayer over their meal.

"We're thankful for Your provision for us, Father. And for protecting Coralee and our neighbors from the fire. Bless those who have to rebuild now, especially my dear niece. I know You have the best plans for her. Help her see where to go from here. Amen."

The prayer stirred Coralee's heart. She watched Aunt Lily as the older woman started in on her meal, trying to put her finger on what had caught her attention. When her aunt finally noticed Coralee's gaze, her eyebrows rose in question. "What'd I say, my dear?"

"It's just…how can you be so certain? About God, I mean." She gestured to the destruction behind them. "I want to believe this is all for a good reason, but I just can't see it."

"Ah, my girl." Aunt Lily put down her sandwich and took Coralee's hand in her own wrinkled one. "We all have worries in life. Maybe they're not always as big as what you've had to endure, but each of us has to learn to trust God somehow. I can't carry it all by myself. I need the good Lord to lean on and people I love around me to help shoulder the load. Not one of us can live life all alone."

Coralee focused on her untouched sandwich. "I don't think I'm strong enough to risk losing someone else."

"There's always a risk in letting people into your life. Did I ever tell you about my first love?" Coralee pulled back in surprise and Aunt Lily chuckled. "Yes, it's true. Your old aunt did fancy a young man at one time. He was so dashing. And he was in love with my dearest friend, although I didn't know it. I only found out when they eloped."

Coralee's heart dropped at the pain her aunt must have endured. "How did you get through it?"

"Well, I had Mama and Papa to lean on. And your papa, who threatened to run off that young man if he ever showed his face in town again. But for years I shut my heart away, determined that I wouldn't let anyone hurt me like that again. And I missed out on more than one opportunity to find love. I regret that today and I think you will, too, if you don't let yourself take the chance." Aunt Lily fell silent as she finished her sandwich.

Coralee ate in tiny bites, letting her aunt's words sink into her heart. Before she finished, Aunt Lily stood, brushing off her skirt and straightening her bonnet. "I've got to get back to the café. I'll see you later, my dear. Remember, your family loves you and so does God. He'll always be there for you."

Sitting in the quiet, unexpected peace came over her. She started to speak a hushed prayer, one she hadn't been able to articulate before that moment. "I don't know why the shop burned down, or why Jake was hurt. I don't know why Papa and Alan were taken from me. But You said that You work out everything for our good and I think I'm finally ready to believe that."

As the whispered words faded away, Coralee realized that Aunt Lily had hit on the core of her problem. The idea of letting Jake in scared her. It was a huge risk to her heart. But she was starting to see that if she didn't, the lifetime of regret would be worse. She had loved Alan deeply. Even the pain of losing him and living without him was worth it for her memories of the years they had been together. If she had a second chance at that kind of love, why was she sitting here in the ruins of her past? Jake's condition might get worse. Or maybe he would still want to keep her out of his life. But at least she would know that she had been there when he needed her.

First thing the next morning, she saddled the horse and rode to the Hadley farm again. There was a little less fear this time, but not by much. The only thing that kept her pointed in the direction of the farm was Aunt Lily's words about regret from the day before, echoing in her mind over and over.

This time, Jake's father heard her knock and opened the door. "Well, Coralee. We're mighty glad you're safe."

"Thank you, Ezra." She cleared her throat, hoping to get the words out around the lump that had formed without choking. "I came to see how Jake's doing."

"He woke up late yesterday. His throat is pretty sore and he tells us everything from his stomach to his head hurts. Doc said he looks good, considering what his body has been through. But it will be a few days until we know for sure if he'll get better or worse."

Coralee slumped against the door post, tears gathering in her eyes. He might be fine, or they could still lose him. But for now, he was alive. She brushed away the tears, determined not to give in to the fear. Silent prayers poured through her mind, the only thing she could think to do with the emotion that threatened to overwhelm her.

Ezra led her inside and pointed to the stairs. "I suppose you ought to go see Jake. The boy can't talk yet, but he'll be mighty glad to see you. Been asking about you since he woke up."

Coralee nodded even as she blushed at the thought of Jake worrying about her. She took the stairs and headed down the hall to the bedroom at the back. The door was open. She peeked in to see sunlight streaming through the window, slanting across the quilt-covered bed where Jake was sleeping. Coralee paused in the doorway, not wanting to wake him if he needed rest. But just as she was about to tiptoe away, his eyes fluttered open and turned to her. A slow smile broke out on his face. It felt as if everything in the world shifted back into the right place.

He gestured for her to sit in the chair by his bed. As soon as she did, he reached for the paper and pencil lying next to him, wrote and turned the paper to face her. Even as she scanned the short sentence, she felt his hand grasp hers and squeeze gently.

How are you?

"I'm fine. Not quite sure what to do with myself, but I'm not hurt." She couldn't resist resting her free hand on his cheek. His eyes slid shut at the contact then opened again so he could scribble another sentence.

What happened the night the fire started?

"When I went to the shop to get the medicine for Mr. Price, someone was there. I just saw a shadow running out the back door. Then I smelled the fire. It started in my workroom, but I don't know what caused it." She paused as a wave of sorrow hit her. "The shop is gone. And five more businesses."

Jake nodded, his eyes holding hers with an intensity that made her heart race. She turned away, focusing on the sounds filtering through the open window. The twins were shouting and laughing as they played in the yard with Jake's father. Smooth-

ing back wayward tendrils of hair, Coralee snuck a
glance at Jake and found he was still staring at her.

The children's happy shouts, the sunlight shining
in the window, the gentle breeze ruffling her hair.
It all faded away. Coralee was only aware of sinking in the warmth that emanated from Jake's eyes.
Flustered, she tore her eyes away and stood so suddenly her chair almost tipped over.

"I... I hope you'll start to feel better soon. I need
to go." She had barely choked the words out when his
hand grabbed hers, holding her in place. He shook
his head. The message was clear: don't run away.

She knew the impulse to leave was an attempt to
avoid her new reality. If she stopped long enough,
she would have to admit that her feelings for Jake
were deeper than she wanted them to be. She would
have to face the fact that even if Jake fully recovered,
anything could happen in the future that would take
him away from her. She had never seen Jake so pale
and weak, lying there in bed. He was always steady,
so certain. But now, even the certainty of Jake's presence was gone. Nothing was secure.

Not even Papa's shop, his legacy to her. Her livelihood, the only thing she had accomplished on her
own, devoured by the flames. It would take her years
to recreate the kind of stock her father had gathered
before he died. And that was if she could even find
the money for a new building. All the money she had
left from Alan and Papa had gone into running the
shop for those last few hard months. They had only

just started to bounce back with the new medicine bringing customers in.

It all threatened to overwhelm her. Her world was completely shattered. How could she ever recover any semblance of security? Her eyes turned to meet Jake's. With the hand that still held hers, he pulled her closer. She sat on the edge of the bed, so close to him. Too close. He released her hand and wrote again.

I'm sorry about the shop. I know how important it was to you. But God has His hand on
you. He kept you safe for a reason. You don't
have to be afraid to face the uncertainty. You
aren't alone.

It was the second time in as many days that someone she cared about had told her that. God has a plan.
You're not alone. She bit her lip, searching Jake's
eyes. Could that be all there was to it? Could she
just decide to trust God and risk leaning on Jake? It
seemed too simple.

Jake's pulse raced with Coralee's closeness. Seeing her walk into his room, unharmed by the fire,
his heart felt lighter than air. If only he could get out
of this bed, he would have held her the moment he
laid eyes on her. Instead he could only lie there and
watch her heart break.

He shifted, frustrated by his new limitations. He
wanted to be there for her. Taking a deep breath,

he tried to push himself up in bed. Never mind the pain in his head and throat or the nausea that washed over him when he moved. He could ignore it all long enough to get to her.

But before he could even sit all the way up, dizziness made him slump back against the headboard. Her sharp gasp brought his eyes to her face. Leaning over, she helped him settle back onto the pillow. Then she rearranged the covers twice before finally meeting his gaze. He had never been surer of anything in his life. Now was the time to act.

He captured her hand again, watching the emotions play across her face as she resisted the urge to run. Airy warmth rushed into his chest. She was confronting her fears. For him. He reached up with his free hand and cupped her cheek, running the pad of his thumb over her soft skin. His hand slid around the back of her neck and he gently pulled her closer.

The moment their lips touched would be forever etched in his memory. The kiss was everything he could have hoped. Her lips were soft and warm on his. She tensed for a moment but relaxed into his embrace as he moved his lips on hers. Jake knew he should pull away, but he couldn't make any effort to do so. He was sinking further into the swirling warmth when the sound of a polite cough came from the doorway, finally breaking the kiss.

Coralee jumped away, flustered and flushed. As she retreated to sit in the chair by his bed, Samuel stepped into the room with eyebrows arched. Jake refused to be apologetic for a moment that he could never regret. He gestured for his mentor to enter the room.

"Mrs. Evans, I'm glad you're here. There are some things we need to discuss." Samuel lowered himself into a chair as Coralee's eyes met Jake's, confusion all over her face. Jake shrugged. He had no idea what Samuel had to say that would involve them both. But as he watched the older man struggle for words, he could see a sense of brokenness in Samuel that had never been there before. Whatever the man wanted to get off his chest, it was important.

"The events surrounding the fire were my fault."

Jake stared at Samuel, mouth falling open in shock.

Coralee voiced the words he couldn't force out around the pain and swelling. "Dr. Jay, we've had more than our share of differences in the past few years, that's true. But I saw a figure in my shop when the fire started and I'm certain it was not you."

Samuel shook his head, eyes glued to his hands as they fidgeted in his lap. "I didn't start the blaze, but it is my responsibility, nonetheless. I hired two men to watch you, Mrs. Evans. I hoped they would see something I could use to discredit you. As soon as I met them, I was uncomfortable with the arrangement. But I went through with it anyway."

He met their confused gazes head-on as the confession poured from his lips. "I want to be clear that I didn't ask them to go into your shop. In fact, I gave them specific instructions that they were only to watch and report back to me. They weren't supposed to do anything else. But they took it upon themselves to break into your shop and search through your things, hoping to find something to give me. One of them came and confessed before they left town. They were just leaving the shop when you arrived, Mrs. Evans. The sound of the door opening startled one of them and he knocked over a lantern, which started the fire."

Coralee sucked in a breath. "And where are these men now? Why didn't you stop them from leaving?"

"I am getting along in years, you know. There was no way I could physically stop them." He hung his head. "I'm humiliated to admit that I've been the biggest sort of coward. I felt so responsible that I didn't go to the sheriff when they left, afraid I would be arrested for my part in the affair. And then I came here, cared for Jake, acted like I was shocked by the events of that night when all along I was afraid to confess my involvement. I can't tell you how sorry I am."

"I don't understand, Dr. Jay. Why do you dislike me so much? Why have you done everything in your power to ruin my business?"

Samuel heaved a sad sigh at her imploring words. "That's a very long story."

Coralee leaned back in the chair and crossed her arms, eyes shooting sparks. "We have time. I think I have a right to know what's caused my life and family so much harm."

"Yes, I suppose you do. It may surprise you to know that I was married, once, years ago. She was the loveliest woman I've ever seen. Gentle and kind.

We came west with some of the first settlers. It was rough in those days, but she was a strong woman and doctors were needed badly. So we worked hard and carved out a life for ourselves. When the time came for her to deliver our first child, she insisted that the area midwife attend her. She didn't want me to feel that I had to stay with her if an emergency arose."

He looked up at them, sadness etched in every line of his face. "The woman that arrived had vastly overrated her own skills. And, sure enough, before the baby was born a neighbor needed my services for an emergency. By the time I returned and realized the midwife didn't know what she was doing, it was too late. My darling wife and baby were both lost."

Samuel stood and paced the room as words continued to pour out, his voice hoarse with emotion. "I've seen it too many times. Charlatans inflating their abilities to make money off unsuspecting patients. Risking the lives of the people I vowed to heal." He turned to face them with stooped shoulders.

Jake couldn't believe how different this man looked from the overconfident doctor he had worked with.

"When Mrs. Evans took over the apothecary business, all I could see was a woman who came out of nowhere. She was uncertified and, I assumed, unqualified." He stepped closer to where Coralee was listening to his story with parted lips and sympathetic eyes. "Dr. Hadley tried to tell me that you are more than capable of treating the people of Spring

Hill. But my pride stood in the way of admitting that he could be right. Until now. Seeing the horrible results of that pride, I imagine I may have been wrong about you. I'm just sorry I let it all get so out of hand before I realized that."

Looking older and more tired than Jake could ever have imagined, Samuel knelt in front of Coralee and took her hand in both of his. "Mrs. Evans, I hope you can one day forgive me for all I've done. I hurt you because I couldn't let go of my own bitterness and grief. And I regret that more than I can express."

"Oh, Dr. Jay. I had no idea what you've gone through. I know a thing or two about losing someone you love. That kind of pain can cause us to react in ways we aren't proud of." She peeked at Jake over Samuel's head and her full lips lifted in a slight smile. "Of course, I forgive you. I hope you can also forgive me for reacting with anger, rather than trying to understand what drove you to such lengths."

Samuel patted her hand with one slow, deliberate nod.

He stood and turned to Jake. "I'm pleased to say that I do believe you'll make a full recovery, Dr. Hadley. If you give yourself time to heal. The last item I need to cover is the state of my practice in the wake of my deplorable actions. I left some paperwork with your mother, along with instructions for sending it to my solicitor in St. Louis. When you sign those papers, my practice is yours. I know you'll do the position more justice than I have."

Coralee jumped from her chair as the older doctor turned to leave. "But what will you do?"

Samuel placed his hat over disheveled white hair. "My sister in St. Louis is doing poorly. I spent more time tending to her on my most recent trip than I did at the hospital. So I plan to go live with her and look after her needs. If I know my sister, she'll keep me plenty busy."

He paused in the doorway, meeting Jake's eyes. "Dr. Hadley, I suggest you grab the happiness that's right in front of you. Don't let the past weigh down your future like I let mine." He bent his head meaningfully in Coralee's direction and it was all Jake could do not to laugh. It was hard to believe his staunch, practical mentor was playing a little matchmaker.

Then Samuel was gone. Jake and Coralee both stared at the empty doorway, processing all that had just happened. Jake's heart ached for Samuel and the burden the older man had carried on his own for so long. Seeing such a proud man broken down made Jake realize that he could end up the same way if he didn't make things right with Coralee.

After a day filled with so many emotional revelations, Coralee had a good night of deep, dreamless sleep. She woke to find her sisters and Aunt Lily gathered at home, a rare event for a weekday. The four women sat in their favorite seats to eat breakfast while Coralee caught them up on the events of the last few days.

"I can't believe that old grump was married. She must have been some woman to put up with him," Cat grumbled while she nibbled a slice of bread spread with butter.

"What happens now, Coralee? Dr. Jay can't think people will take this lightly." Cecilia, ever concerned about others, sipped her tea with a furrowed brow.

"Dr. Jay is moving to St. Louis to care for his sister. And Jake has the paperwork to make the practice his. He finally gets to see his dream fulfilled." Coralee tried to sound happy but it was clear from the looks on the faces around her that she wasn't succeeding.

"It sounds like a happy ending, but you don't look too pleased, my girl."

Coralee avoided Aunt Lily's eyes. "Yes, it's a happy ending for Jake. And maybe for Dr. Jay. But I don't know what to do next. The shop is gone and there's no money to rebuild it." She could hear the contrary tone in her own voice, but didn't bother to try to hide it. She had forgiven Dr. Jay, but that didn't mean it would be pleasant to live with the consequences of his actions.

Cat's eyebrows shot up. "I've never known you to fuss about things like this, Coralee. Why don't you admit what's really upsetting you?"

"And what would that be, Cat?" Coralee's shoulders tensed. Who was Cat to talk about fessing up? She never shared her feelings about anything.

"You know very well. I've seen the way you blush when Jake Hadley's around."

As Cat spoke, Coralee almost wanted to wipe the smug look off her sister's face. But if she was honest, she was tired of avoiding her feelings all the time. It was making her cranky. "You're right, Cat."

Her youngest sister started to argue then stopped short. "Wait, did you just admit I'm right?"

Aunt Lily chuckled. "It's about time someone around here displayed some honesty. Coralee, dear, what are you saying, exactly?"

"Cat's right. I care for Jake. I thought he cared for me, too, but he chose to shut me out of his life. He almost died the night of the fire. Shouldn't that be enough to make him admit any feelings he might have for me?" Jake's kiss flashed in her mind, bringing heat to her cheeks. But she wasn't about to mention it to her family. It was hard to believe that one kiss meant anything when he hadn't made any promises to go with it. Her heart skipped a beat as she relived the moment his lips touched hers. Could it possibly mean what she hoped, after all?

She looked up to see an understanding smile on Aunt Lily's wrinkled face. "Men do things in their own time. Give him a chance to admit he can't live without you. He's probably already realized that and is trying to find the perfect way to say it."

Cecilia nodded emphatically, a dreamy look on her face. "He can't talk, after all. I'll bet he's waiting until his throat heals and then he'll tell you everything you've been waiting to hear."

Coralee didn't want to ask the question, but it

snuck out anyway. "But what if he pushes me out of his life again?"

"You have to decide if you can trust him, even if it seems like he's excluding you. It takes time to change and grow. It takes practice. He'll forget, sometimes, and try to do things alone. But if you're still standing there next to him, he'll realize he messed up and fix it."

Coralee stared at her aunt, understanding for the first time what had gone wrong all those years ago. When Jake had left her out of his decision to go to St. Louis, she hadn't trusted that he was thinking about her dreams, too. Without knowing his feelings, she had been too afraid to trust him. So she'd walked away without giving him a chance to realize his mistake or to fix it. If she had stayed with him, given him time to explain his intentions instead of running, would the situation have played out differently? She had thought he loved her. Would that have turned out to be true if she'd given him the chance to tell her?

The women started to stir from their seats, each setting out to their own activities for the day. Coralee headed to the Hadley farm, having promised to spend some time with the twins to give Ezra and Beth a break. But when she arrived, she was surprised to see several empty buggies waiting near the house. Had Beth forgotten to tell her about a ladies' society meeting?

There was no one in sight, so Coralee let herself in the kitchen door. She would just peek in on whatever meeting was happening and get Beth's attention, let the older woman know she was there. Inside the neat parlor, Coralee's eyes fell on Jake first. A jolt of excitement raced up her spine. He was sitting up in a chair and looking much improved from yesterday. Her gaze traveled the room, taking in the mayor, Charlie, Beth and several prominent Spring Hill businessmen. This was no ladies' society meeting.

Charlie was speaking to the group in a tone that was unusually serious for him. "Dr. Hadley and I have had our differences in the past. But I must agree with everything he's written in the proposal for this meeting. Spring Hill is growing in leaps and bounds. This fire was devastating, but if we don't plan ahead, next time could be worse. Loss of property is one thing. Loss of life is another. So I will support his suggestion to raise funds for fire equipment and the training of a brigade, both with my time and finances. I hope that each of you gentlemen will choose do the same."

As the room filled with conversation about the proposal, Coralee stepped back into the kitchen, leaning against the wall next to the open door. Jake had put together this meeting to start a campaign raising money for a proper fire brigade?

Her heart filled with emotions too big for words. His gesture of concern and love for their town brought clarity to the confusion that had plagued her since his return. Jake showed his affection in quiet, practical ways. Maybe he wasn't good at remembering to involve her in his decisions. She hadn't exactly done that, either. Wasn't that something they could work through together if she would give him the chance?

Coralee peered around the doorway into the parlor again. Jake was scribbling on his paper, writing out answers to questions as the men in the room talked. In spite of how frustrating it must be to write out every word, his eyes were shining and he held his chin high. She could see he was pleased to be able to do something to help the town he loved.

Memories flitted through her mind of all the times he'd gone out of his way to help her. Especially recently, when he had given up time in the clinic—his own dream—to help with her medication. And the way he had taken in the twins, changing his life around to accommodate the needs of children who weren't even his own. Even now, not fully recovered from his injuries, he was working to make others safer. Maybe he didn't say it the way she expected, but it was so clear now that Jake cared about her. His everyday actions showed it.

Leaning against the wall in the Hadleys' kitchen with the hum of voices filtering through the doorway, Coralee realized that she had failed. All the time she had spent trying to protect her heart from pain and risk had been wasted. She was in love with Jake. And it was fine. More than fine. She couldn't stop the smile that broke out on her face. Yes, she could lose him at any moment. He could—and probably would—hurt her again someday. He was only human, after all. He might not even want her in his life anymore.

But the truth Aunt Lily had been trying to tell her for months was finally sinking in. She had the choice to give in to her fears or to stand for what she wanted in spite of them. And it was time for her to stand. She had already lived through one of the things she had been most afraid of when she lost Papa's shop. It was a nightmare, but she had survived. And she would do the same if Jake didn't love her. She knew now that the possibility of spending her life loving him far outweighed the risk to her heart.

Chapter Eleven

Jake leaned back in the chair, trying to gather his strength to head upstairs and lay down for a rest. His guests had just left with a flurry of handshakes and pleased discussion. He was getting ready to push up from the seat when movement at the kitchen door caught his attention. Just the sight of Coralee standing there in a flattering, flowered dress with her dark hair curling around her face gave him a burst of energy.

She had left right on the heels of Samuel's visit the day before and Jake worried all night that his kiss had scared her off. But here she was, looking for all the world like she was happy to see him. She crossed the room and stood near him, blue eyes sparkling.

"Jake, you're downstairs. That's a wonderful sign. You must be feeling quite a bit better."

He started to grab his paper to write out a response but she stayed his hand with a touch. From her spot across the room, his mother cleared her throat, causing a pretty flush to creep up Coralee's cheeks.

"I'm sorry we weren't able to greet you when you got here. Jake, here, had a wonderful idea to raise money for fire equipment and a brigade. The ladies' society will put on several events now that the town leaders have given their approval for the plan."

Coralee turned back to him, warmth in her gaze. "And it was all your idea?"

He shrugged. Her approval was gratifying but he had to admit that someone would have done it eventually. He had just started the process before anyone else.

She leaned over and gave him a brief hug. Too brief for his liking. As she pulled away, little footsteps echoed from the kitchen. They turned and watched Louisa and Phillip skipping in, Pa following close behind. The older man lowered himself into a chair with some effort. "Whew. Those two sure have more than their share of energy. I'm beat."

The children noticed Coralee and ran to greet her. "Coree!" Louisa gave Coralee's legs a quick squeeze then climbed up in Jake's lap, leaning her head back against his chest.

Phillip happily started emptying his pockets, showing off every treasure to the adults in the room. "Little rocks. And grass."

"Those are so nice, Phillip."

The boy looked up at her with big eyes. "Coree, I miss you."

"Oh, darling. I missed you, too."

Jake's heart ached as he watched her envelop the boy in a tight embrace. How could he ever have thought separating himself and the children from Coralee was a good idea? The twins had lost so much in their short lives. Jake found that all he wanted now was to give them back anything he could. If they wanted time with Coralee, he would see that they got it, no matter what.

Jake set Louisa down and pushed up from his chair, still feeling a bit sore. He offered his arm to Coralee, raising his eyebrows in question. His heart lifted when she took his arm without hesitation. With the twins following along, he led Coralee through the kitchen and out the back door.

Taking the children's hands, he and Coralee strolled around the yard. They walked through the barn, pausing at every stall, where Coralee talked with the twins about the animals. Jake's heart swelled when he heard how well Louisa was saying animal names and sounds. The children were growing so quickly and seemed to be thriving. He and the twins had come a long way since those first few uncertain days.

It was easy to see, as he stood watching the children interact with Coralee, just how she would fit into their new little family. For the first time since returning to Spring Hill, Jake let himself imagine what life would be like with Coralee. The idea of sharing a home with her, raising the twins together and spending their days together, was appealing. But maybe that wasn't what she wanted. Was her heart still tied to Alan? Would she want to rebuild Holbrook's and run it again, alone? He knew this time he needed to ask for her opinion.

By the time they returned to the porch, Jake lowered himself into a chair, frustrated to find that he needed a rest. In theory, he knew that the healing would take time. But the reality of simple things taking longer was hard to swallow. Coralee must have noticed his eyes drooping. She led the twins near the porch and showed them how to draw in the dirt with small sticks. Then she joined him and settled into her own rocking chair.

"Are you terribly tired?"

He shook his head and indicated with his fingers that it was only a little. He didn't want her to fuss over him when all he needed was a rest. Pulling out his paper, he wrote a question and turned the page so she could read it.

What do you plan to do about the shop?

Her gaze slid away from him and a small sigh escaped her lips. "I don't know, Jake. The shop has been my life since…well, since Alan died. Without it, I don't have much of a purpose."

Jake scribbled his response, wishing he could just tell her how wrong that was.

Holbrook's didn't define who you are. It was important to you, but not the whole purpose of your life. We don't have any idea what God may have in store, but there's a reason for what happened to the shop. You can trust that He'll lead you in the right direction.

As she read, her mouth hung open then snapped closed. She bit her lip. "Do you think so? For so long, I've felt like the shop was God's only purpose for me. That's all I had left. No husband, no children, no Papa."

I know God's purpose for you is bigger than that. You may not see it right now, but I know it will be wonderful.

Once she had read it, Jake took the paper and slid it back in his pocket. He stood and pulled her up, wrapping his arms around her. She rested her head on his shoulder. He could have stood there holding her forever, but he felt a tug on his trouser leg and turned to see Louisa. Coralee pulled away and grinned as Phillip ran up, too.

"Thank you for helping me realize the truth. Everything you said is just what I needed to hear. I'm going to make it a point to pray for direction and see where God leads. Now, I'll play with the children and you rest up. This town needs you healthy, Dr. Hadley."

Over the next week Jake felt better all the time. He still tried to rest his voice now and then, but the swelling and pain were completely gone. By the time the first event to raise money for the fire equipment rolled around, he was more than ready to escape the farm for a few hours.

The amount of work the women from the ladies' society had done in just a few days was incredible. Early that morning, Jake had left the twins with his parents and headed to the café to check on their progress. The yard behind the building had been transformed into an elegant location for an afternoon tea. Tables had been moved from the café and were set with a variety of linens and pretty china gathered from the women's own homes. The trees along the bank of the creek were decorated with ribbon streamers as a backdrop to a small platform where the announcements would take place.

The women shooed Jake away almost as soon as he got there, so he left them to finish and went to the clinic. It was the first time he'd been back since the fire and Samuel's confession. He had a hard time believing it was all his now. The path had been much more convoluted than he had ever imagined, but the dreams Jake had held close for years were finally clicking into place. God had been faithful to him.

As the time for the tea approached, Jake finished up his work in the clinic. He had moved most of the furniture out of the waiting room and cleared the walls. Just a few more preparations and the clinic was ready for a special surprise he had planned for Coralee when the afternoon tea was over. Once he was pleased with his efforts, Jake locked the clinic and started his walk down the street to the café.

It wasn't that far to the event, but he found that people wanted to stop and talk with him every few feet. Everyone had heard that the only injury from the fire was the new doctor. And many had heard that he was now the town's only doctor, although they didn't know the circumstances behind Samuel's departure. Naturally, anyone who recognized him wanted to ask about his health and when he would be returning to the practice.

But as time ticked away and Jake wasn't able to make any progress in getting to the café he started to get frustrated. This day was too important to be stuck chatting with every neighbor he passed. He didn't want to be late and miss being by Coralee's side.

He managed to slip away from a quick chat with James and Martha Smith and offer a brief wave as he passed Mrs. Hardy from the boardinghouse. Finally he made it to the yard behind the café. Charlie was just taking the stage to start the event when Jake slid into a seat next to Coralee. Her beaming smile was worth the trouble it had taken to get there on time.

The crowd hushed when Charlie raised his hands and started speaking. "Ladies and gentlemen, thank you all for coming today. We're gathered for a cause that is important to all of us in the wake of our recent tragedy. The funds gathered from this and several other events will go toward purchasing fire equipment and training a fire brigade to protect our fine town from future fires."

The gathered guests clapped with enthusiasm.

Someone in the back whistled, sharp and loud, causing a ripple of laughter to pass through the crowd. Charlie gestured for silence again. "One more thing before I give the stage over to the fine proprietress of Lily's Café. I think we all need to give a big thank you to the man who organized this campaign. Our new doctor, Jake Hadley."

Applause broke out across the yard again. Coralee tugged at Jake's arm, encouraging him to stand. Cringing, he rose halfway from his seat and responded with a quick wave and what he hoped was a smile and not a grimace. He had never been more relieved than he was when Charlie went on to introduce Lily and the guests turned away from him. But his embarrassment evaporated when Coralee intertwined her arm through his. His skin heated at the contact. Maybe she would be more willing to forgive him than he thought.

Lily took Charlie's place on the stage and Jake's heart beat faster. He couldn't wait to see Coralee's face during this announcement, a special surprise he had planned just for her. "My brother, William Holbrook, was a man who loved this town. He worked hard until the day he died to build up Holbrook's Apothecary so the people in Spring Hill would have access to the medicine we need. Losing that shop to the fire is a terrible loss for all of us."

Jake heard a sniffle and saw Coralee wiping wetness from her cheeks. He reached over and squeezed her hand, glad to see her smile at him through the tears as Lily continued. "William would have been proud of our town as we come together to protect ourselves for the future. I'm proud to announce that, because of his contributions to Spring Hill, our new fire equipment will be dedicated in his honor."

More applause followed the statement for long moments before fading out. The guests started visiting with each other as Lily left the stage. Coralee was crying and hugging her sisters. They all looked proud of their father and they had every right to be. When Lily and Charlie arrived and took their seats at the table, Coralee leaned close to Jake's ear and spoke in a low voice, for him alone. "Thank you, Jake. I have a feeling that was your idea."

Her voice was soft and eyes glowing. He couldn't help resting his arm along her chair, pressed against her back. It was as close as he could come to holding her in such a public place. Jake had trouble containing his impatience through the rest of the tea. There was soft music in the background, dainty finger foods that weren't very filling and, of course, plenty of tea. Several women from the ladies' society recited poems and the children from Cecilia's school sang a song.

It seemed to take all day, but finally the program was over and guests started leaving. As they stood from the table, Jake cupped Coralee's elbow and spoke quietly, sweat breaking out on his forehead. It was time. "I have something to show you at the clinic. Feel like a little walk?"

She took his arm and they walked down First Street, in the direction of the clinic. Jake's heart felt ready to burst with pride. Just the thought that this kind, intelligent, beautiful woman chose to walk at his side was enough to bring Jake to his knees in thankfulness. But he had some business with her before they reached the clinic.

"Coralee, I owe you a terrific apology. Before the fire, I behaved in the worst possible way. I let my fear get the best of me and hurt you in the process. When Samuel returned from St. Louis, he was mad as a hornet because I was helping you. He threatened my position in his practice. I was wrong to even consider that choosing to hurt you was the right response. But I was worried about my parents and I didn't know what would happen to the twins if I had to leave town to practice medicine."

Her face tilted up to look at him. "Jake, it's all right. I understand the pressure you were facing."

He lightly stroked her hand where it rested on his arm. "No, I need you to know that I realize how wrong I was. I couldn't stand to let my family down. But in trying to protect them, I ended up hurting you. And, Coralee, that's just as bad. Not having you in my life for those few days was terrible and I never want that to happen again."

They came to a stop in front of the clinic as a pretty flush worked its way up her cheeks. "Thank you, Jake. I recognize the fear that drove your choices. I lived with that fear for years, ever since Alan's death. So I forgive you, for all of it."

He couldn't contain the giant grin that stretched across his face. "You don't know how happy that makes me. Now, get ready, because I have a surprise that I think you're going to love."

Jake stepped back to open the clinic door for her. Coralee hesitated on the threshold and his muscles tensed. How would she respond to what she saw inside?

"Jake, what is all this?"

Before the tea, Jake had pushed his old desk into the middle of the empty room. On it, he had unrolled several large pages, the corners secured with tools. From his spot behind Coralee, he rested his hands on her waist and urged her closer. "Why don't you take a look?"

He watched her eyes roam over the building plans. She took in the outline of the clinic building, with the new addition off one side of the waiting room. He looked over her shoulder as she flipped to the next page: a drawing of a wall of shelves with counter space underneath, similar to what had been in Holbrook's. She spun around, wide blue eyes searching his face.

"I'll ask again. What is this, Jake?"

He bounced on his toes, excitement and nerves clashing inside. "I hope you aren't upset that I had these drawn up without asking you first. But I wanted you to see it before you decided. It occurred to me that the perfect place for an apothecary to operate is right in the doctor's office. The patients won't have to go across town for what they need, and we can consult together on the best course of treatment."

His excitement started to win the internal battle as he explained the plan to Coralee. She blinked a few times, lips pursed as she studied the plans again. "You want me to have a shop right here? In your office?"

He laughed, taking her by the hand and pulling her to the wall, gesturing as he explained. "Yes. We'll open up this wall right here." Leaving her in the middle of the room, he jogged to the other side. "I'll have another examination room built in this part of the waiting room, but we'll share the rest. We can put up whatever kind of partitions we find necessary, but it will all be accessible from this spot." He returned to stand near her, his whole body coiled tight as he waited for her reaction.

"Oh, Jake. That's so kind and thoughtful. But I can't just let you spend that kind of money. And what would people say about us working in the same building all day?" Even as she protested, he saw her eyes exploring the spots he'd pointed out. He knew she was envisioning the changes he had come up with.

But there was hesitation in her eyes when she turned to him. Fear washed over him, but Jake forced it away. Now was the time. He was ready to lay out his love for her to see, ready to risk rejection again. The chance of winning her heart was worth it. And this time, he was going to be perfectly clear about all of his intentions. Even if she said no in the end, he was going to do this right. Gathering every ounce of his courage and love, Jake reached for her.

* * *

As Coralee stared at the wall, seeing the plans Jake had made in her mind's eye, she was ready to decline his generous offer. It was almost the perfect arrangement, but she couldn't agree to it. She had no idea how Jake felt about their relationship now, but she knew how she felt. She loved him. His selflessness, his generosity, his loving way with the twins. She loved every bit of it. Even his tendency to do things on his own, while it frustrated her, was part of who he was, and she would gladly live with it.

But she wasn't sure she could stand the pain of working across the building from him every day if he didn't return the feelings she could no longer deny. She turned to face him, heart heavy, mouth opening to explain that she couldn't accept what he was offering.

It stopped her in her tracks when he took her in his arms. "I've thought through all your arguments. I want to do this as partners, not just in business, but in life. I love you, Coralee. I always have, even before I left for school. I know I've made mistakes in the past. Letting you walk away all those years ago without telling you how I felt is something I regret every day. I hope you can forgive me and accept this. All of it." His voice lowered as he held her gaze, sincerity written on every inch of his face. "I'm going to be clear this time. I love you. I want to spend my life with you. I want you to help me make every decision from here on out. Will you marry me?"

Was this real? After everything that had happened

between them over the years, they had the chance to be in love with each other again? Her eyes scanned his face as she searched for words. His lips parted as he sucked in a breath and she realized how long she'd left him standing there with the question unanswered. Her heart screamed to say yes but—

No, there wasn't a single reason to do anything but accept. She rested her head on his chest. "Yes, Jake. I love you and I will marry you."

He squeezed her tight enough that her feet lifted off the ground. Then he leaned in and lowered his lips to hers. The sweet kiss held all the promises she wanted to make, all the things she had hoped for, but didn't dare believe could be hers.

Jake broke the kiss but then came back for another. And another. When he finally pulled away and released her from his arms, they were both flushed and breathless. Leaning against the edge of the desk, Jake's shining eyes held the same longing she felt.

"There's one more thing I wanted to discuss. I never thought much about what it would be like to have children. But since I've been caring for the twins, I've come to realize how important and wonderful a family of my own could be."

Coralee's breath caught in her throat. He had just proposed. Was he going to tell her now that he was upset that she couldn't have children? Had he just remembered and decided to take back his declaration? The urge to run almost took over. But Coralee refused to give in to it. She was a different woman now. She would choose to trust Jake and hear him out instead of fleeing from what scared her.

He took both her hands in his, thumbs caressing her skin. "I think you know how much I've come to love the twins. And I'm pretty sure you love them, too." She nodded emphatically and his smile grew. "What do you think about adopting them? Making the four of us a family?"

Without warning, tears filled her eyes as relief made her knees weak. He wasn't going to take back his sweet words. He was offering the chance for all her dreams to come true. She started sniffling. Jake crossed the room and took her in his arms again, looking worried. She laughed unsteadily. "You must think I'm so silly. One of the happiest moments in life and here I am, blubbering like a baby."

He shook his head. "I don't think you're silly. But I'm not sure why you're crying, either."

"For so long, I've lived with hurt and loss and fear. Now, all my dreams are falling into place, right in front of my eyes. You, a new shop and the children I've longed for. Most couples have time to get used to the idea, but as soon as we marry, we'll have a full-fledged family."

He tilted his head. "It's a big idea to get used to. But is it what you want?"

Joy surged through her. His declaration of love and proposal were wonderful. But more than anything, that little question showed evidence that he had changed. He cared about what she wanted and he was making a point to seek her opinion rather than assuming she would go along with his plans. She wandered around the waiting room, pausing here and there, envisioning the changes he had planned for the space and the changes on the horizon for their lives. Finally she turned back to him with a grin. "Yes. I want you. I want the twins. I want the shop here by your clinic. All of it. For the rest of my life."

Jake let out a whoop of joy and ran to her, swinging her around in his arms before holding her close again. He lowered his head toward her lips, whispering just before they touched, "And I want it all, too."

It was several moments before either of them could speak. Coralee pulled away first. "I think, since we have the twins to consider, maybe we shouldn't have a long engagement."

With mock sincerity and sparkling eyes, Jake nodded. "Oh, yes, for the sake of the children, we should move things along."

She playfully swatted his arm. "I meant it. I have everything we need to set up a home. We don't need to spend time arranging a trousseau. And my sisters can whip up a dress in no time."

Jake pointed out the large front window. "Along with this building, Samuel passed on the parcel of land on the north side, closest to the creek. He said he intended to build a house on it, but it didn't seem important after a while." He turned back to her. "I know the whole town would help, so we could put up a house in no time."

The only answer she could manage around the lump in her throat was a happy smile. All the dreams she hadn't dared to hope for over the last two years were in her grasp. Awareness of God's goodness washed over her. Anything she said would be inadequate, so she just snuggled back into Jake's arms, right where she wanted to be forever.

Epilogue

It was a beautiful September morning but Coralee hardly even noticed. She paced the floor of Jake's bedroom at the Hadley farm, peeking through the light cotton curtains when she crossed to the window. The road outside the house was empty, just as it had been every other time she'd looked in the last hour.

"You won't get him here any faster by fretting." Aunt Lily's voice was full of barely restrained amusement as she entered the bedroom.

"I know. But he's late. Cat said Charlie's been teasing about Jake getting cold feet and hopping on a steamboat instead of coming back. I mean, of course, he wouldn't do that, but I'm worried that something happened to him."

Aunt Lily didn't try to contain her laughter this time, letting out a full-blown chortle. "My dear girl, you aren't the first bride to worry that things won't go well on her wedding day. And you won't be the last. He'll be here as soon as he can. There's not much that could have happened to him between town and here."

Coralee plopped down into a chair, pale gray skirts pooling around her. The satin gown was a sight to behold. It had wide sleeves in the latest style and a beautiful, pleated bodice that had taken Cecilia too many evenings to sew. The fitted waist was finished with a thin belt, tied in a bow with tails that cascaded down the back of the voluminous skirts.

In spite of her arguments that the creation was too much for a widow's second wedding, Cecilia and Cat had insisted that it was their gift to her. She still couldn't believe her sisters had accomplished the making of such an elaborate gown in just a few weeks. They had finished the ensemble with a coronet of fresh flowers tucked into her intricately braided and pinned hair. Coralee had to admit, she did look stunning.

But now, it all seemed like too much when she was faced with the question of whether Jake would even attend their nuptials. He had only gone to town to get their marriage license. He should have been back long ago.

Just when she was about to tell Aunt Lily to get her out of the beautiful gown so she could go find him, a shout from below made her rush to the window. There was Jake, riding up in a hurry. He swung off the horse and dashed into the house, out of their sight.

Aunt Lily laughed. "Didn't I tell you he'd be here?

That man is far too in love to let anything keep him from his wedding."

Coralee was smoothing her gown and checking her hair one last time when Cat stuck her head in the doorway. "Ready, Coralee? Your groom's waiting."

With a deep breath, Coralee squared her shoulders. It was finally time for her and Jake to join their lives together forever. Now that she knew he was there, the nerves calmed and all she felt was happiness and a longing to be at his side.

Strains of music floated from the first floor as Coralee followed her aunt and sisters down the stairs. They passed under an arch of flowers built around the parlor doorway and then she was face-to-face with Jake. Her first love, the man she had always dreamed of pledging her life to but almost missed.

Her groom met her at the door and tucked her hand into the crook of his elbow. She scanned his handsome face, taking in every familiar detail. "Jake, was there a problem getting the license? We expected you earlier."

He patted her hand and smiled, eyes alight with excitement. "No problem, just an errand I needed to see to. But I want to tell you about it along with everyone else."

Tilting her head, Coralee watched him for a moment. Jake started to step forward but she pulled on his arm, holding him back. "There's one more thing I wanted to say before we go in."

Turning to face her, Jake gave her his full attention. Coralee took a deep breath. "For too long, I let fear drive my decisions. I think we both did. But I don't want to live that way anymore. You encouraged me to take a chance on applying to the Association and I can see now that you were right. Since I'll have a shop again, thanks to you, I'm going to take the examination. And I'm confident that I'll become the first female member, just like you said."

Jake's strong arms slid around her as he pulled her close. "Coralee, I'll support you no matter what. But I'm so proud of you for taking this chance, for overcoming your fear."

With one last look into each other's eyes, they turned and walked through the crowd of friends and family that had gathered until they came to a stop in front of the minister. Cecilia urged the twins to run up and stand with them, Louisa next to Coralee and Phillip next to Jake.

Charlie leaned into the aisle and teased Jake from where he stood by Cat. "Finally got over the cold feet, I see." Scattered chuckles accompanied his words.

Jake never took his eyes off Coralee. "Actually, I had a little extra business at the county office that held me up."

Coralee cocked her head, ready to find out what had been so important that he had risked being late to their wedding. Jake reached into his jacket and pulled a sheaf of folded papers from a pocket. "I had a few extra papers drawn up. Official documents to record our adoption of Louisa and Phillip."

Happy gasps and murmurs spread through the

room. But Coralee and Jake couldn't take their eyes off each other as past, present and future collided into one moment of happiness. Hand in hand, with the twins at their side, they turned to the minister. They were finally ready to commit their lives to each other and to the children they loved as their own.

* * * * *

Dear Reader,

I'm so honored that you chose to read my first book! Writing this story was a giant leap of faith for me. But God led me through every step of it and I pray it will bless you.

My inspiration for this story started with Coralee. I imagined her as a woman with a driving mission and research revealed the perfect project: an alternative to the addictive, dangerous pain medications common at the time. Later in the 1800s, that willow bark extract would be used to create aspirin.

The twins would have to be my favorite part. The way those kids make Jake and Coralee grow and change is so true to my life. It doesn't hurt that I modeled them after my own mischievous, energetic two-year-old!

I would love to connect with you! You can find me on Facebook at www.facebook.com/molliecampbellauthor and on Twitter as @MollieACampbell.

Blessings,
Mollie Campbell

MONTANA COWBOY'S BABY
Big Sky Country • by Linda Ford

Cowboy Conner Marshall doesn't know the first thing about fatherhood, but he's determined to do right by the abandoned baby left on his doorstep. As the doctor's daughter, Kate Baker, helps him care for the sick baby, they forge a bond that has him wondering if Kate and baby Ellie belong on his ranch forever!

THE ENGAGEMENT CHARADE
Smoky Mountain Matches • by Karen Kirst

In order to protect his pregnant, widowed employee, Ellie Jameson, from her controlling in-laws, Alexander Copeland pretends to be her fiancé. But can this temporary engagement help them heal old wounds...and fall in love?

THE RENEGADE'S REDEMPTION
by Stacy Henrie

With nowhere else to go, injured Tex Beckett turns to his ex, Ravena Reid, who allows him to stay on her farm under one condition: he must help her with the orphans she's taking care of. But what will she do if she finds out he's an outlaw?

LONE STAR BRIDE
by Jolene Navarro

When Sofia De Zavala's father discovers she dressed as a boy to go on a cattle drive and prove she can run the ranch, he forces her to marry trail boss Jackson McCreed to save her reputation. Now she must convince Jackson their union can become a loving partnership.

SPECIAL EXCERPT FROM

Love Inspired **HISTORICAL**

Cowboy Conner Marshall doesn't know the first thing about fatherhood, but he's determined to do right by the abandoned baby left on his doorstep. As the doctor's daughter, Kate Baker, helps him care for the sick baby, they forge a bond that has him wondering if Kate and baby Ellie belong on his ranch forever!

Read on for a sneak preview of
MONTANA COWBOY'S BABY *by* **Linda Ford,**
available July 2017 from Love Inspired Historical!

"Did anything you tried last night get Ellie's attention?" Kate asked Conner.

"She seemed to like to hear me sing." Heat swept over his chest at how foolish he felt admitting it.

"Well, then, I suggest you sing to her."

"You're bossy. Did you know that?" It was his turn to chuckle as pink blossomed in her cheeks.

She gave a little toss of her head. "I'm simply speaking with authority. You did ask me to stay and help. I assumed you wanted my medical assistance."

No mistaking the challenge in her voice.

"Your medical assistance, yes, of course." He humbled his voice and did his best to look contrite.

"You sing to her and I'll try to get more sugar water into her."

He cleared his throat. "'Sleep, my love, and peace attend thee. All through the night; Guardian angels God will lend thee, All through the night.'"

Ellie blinked and brought her gaze to him.

"Excellent," Kate whispered and leaned over Conner's arm to ease the syringe between Ellie's lips. The baby swallowed three times and then her eyes closed.

"Sleep is good, too," Kate murmured, leaning back. "I think she likes your voice."

He stopped himself from meeting Kate's eyes. Warmth filled them and he allowed himself a little glow of victory. "Thelma hated my singing." He hadn't meant to say that. Certainly not aloud.

Kate's eyes cooled considerably. "You're referring to Ellie's mother?"

"That's right." No need to say more.

"Do you mind me asking where she is?"

"'Fraid I can't answer that."

She waited.

"I don't know. I haven't seen her in over a year."

"I see."

Only it was obvious she didn't. But he wasn't going to explain. Not until he figured out what Thelma was up to.

Kate pushed to her feet.

"How long before we wake her to feed her again?" he asked.

"Fifteen minutes. You hold her and rest. I don't suppose you got much sleep last night."

There she went being bossy and authoritative again. Not that he truly minded. It was nice to know someone cared how tired he was and also knew how to deal with Ellie.

Don't miss
MONTANA COWBOY'S BABY by Linda Ford,
available July 2017 wherever
Love Inspired® Historical books and ebooks are sold.

www.LoveInspired.com

SPECIAL EXCERPT FROM

*Nell Stoltzfus falls for the new local veterinarian in town,
James Pierce. But their love is forbidden since he's
English and she's Amish. If Nell follows her heart,
will love conquer all?*

Read on for a sneak preview of
A SECRET AMISH LOVE by *Rebecca Kertz*,
available July 2017 from Love Inspired!

"You said your *bruder* was called out on an emergency,"
Nell said. "What does he do?"

"He's a veterinarian. He's recently opened a clinic here
in Happiness."

The strange sensation settled over Nell. Despite the
difference in their last names, could James be Maggie's
brother? "What's his name?" she asked.

"James Pierce." Maggie smiled. "He owns Pierce
Veterinary Clinic. Have you heard of him?"

"*Ja.* In fact, 'twas your *bruder* who treated my dog,
Jonas."

"Then you've met him!" Maggie looked delighted. "Is he
a *gut* veterinarian?"

Startled by this new knowledge, Nell could only nod
at first. "He was wonderful with Jonas. He's a kind and
compassionate man." She studied Maggie and recognized
the family resemblance. "How is he a Pierce and you a
Troyer?"

"I am a Pierce." Maggie grinned. "Abigail is, too. But
we don't go by the Pierce name. Adam is our stepfather,

LIEXP0617

and he is our *dat* now." Maggie's eyes filled with sadness. "I was too young to care, but James had a hard time with it. He loved Dad, and he'd wanted to be a veterinarian like him since he was ten. He became more determined to follow in Dad's footsteps."

Nell felt her heart break for James, who must have suffered after his father's death. "You chose the Amish life, but James chose a different path."

"And he's doing well," Maggie said. "My family is thrilled that he set up his practice in Happiness."

Later that afternoon, James arrived to spend time with his family.

She recognized his car immediately as he drove into the barnyard. James stood a moment, searching for family members. Nell couldn't move as he crossed the yard to where tables and bench seats had been set up. Soon, James headed to the gathering of young people, including his sisters Maggie and Abigail.

Nell found it heartwarming to see that his siblings regarded him with the same depth of love and affection. James spoke briefly to Maggie, clearly delighted that he'd handled his emergency then decided to come. She heard the siblings teasing and the ensuing laughter. Maggie said something to James as she gestured in Nell's direction.

James saw her, and Nell froze. Her heart started to beat hard when he broke away from the group to approach her.

Don't miss
A SECRET AMISH LOVE
by Rebecca Kertz, available July 2017 wherever
Love Inspired® books and ebooks are sold.

www.LoveInspired.com

Love Inspired

Love the Love Inspired book you just read?

Your opinion matters.

Review this book on your favorite book site, review site, blog or your own social media properties and share your opinion with other readers!